TEMPTED by the NANNY

T.K. LEIGH WRITING AS
TRACY LEIGH

TEMPTED BY THE NANNY

Published by Carpe Per Diem Publishing, Inc

Cover Design: Cat Head Media, Inc.

Cover assets © 2026

Illustrated stock used under license from Qamber Designs

For a full list of all of Tracy's books, including recommended reading order, please visit her website:

www.tracyleighbooks.com

Books and reading order for her spicy billionaire romance alter ego, T.K. Leigh, can be found here:

www.tkleighauthor.com

For exclusive sales and excerpts,
sign up for Tracy Leigh's VIP list!

https://www.tracyleighbooks.com/subscribe

Or scan the code below

Some of the author's books may contain content that could be triggering for sensitive readers. For a full list of content warnings for each book and/or series, please visit her website.

https://geni.us/TKLContentWarnings

For the readers who believe life is better when you say yes to things that scare you.

ONE

Hayden

The pancake flips out of the pan, hits the stovetop, and folds in on itself like a four-year-old attempting to do yoga.

Great. Just what I need today.

Jeremiah giggles from his high chair as if this is a performance designed specifically for his entertainment. Oatmeal is drying on the floor from his earlier launch attempt, a feat that would have earned NASA funding if it hadn't landed on the cabinets.

Presley, my seven-year-old, sits at the table quietly sketching. The stack of pancakes in front of her is darker than intended. Not burnt, technically. More like aggressively toasted.

She hasn't touched them.

She hasn't touched much food lately.

And she hasn't spoken a single word since the accident.

In a few weeks, it will be one year since our lives were forever altered.

I thought I'd have my shit together by now.

Instead, it still feels like I'm on a merry-go-round that spins faster and faster with every passing day.

Cora made this look so easy. She never burned Presley's pancakes. Hell, she'd make her pancakes while holding Jemmy because he was teething.

The memory causes a lump to form in my throat, but I push it down, kneeling by the high chair, scrubbing oatmeal off the hardwood like a man who definitely has his life together.

I'm a doctor, for crying out loud. Prior to moving back home, I'd worked in one of the busiest emergency rooms in the country. I thrived on the chaos. Loved the challenge of never knowing what would roll through those doors. Gunshot wounds. Stabbings. Car wrecks.

I never expected my own family to come through those doors, too.

"Good morning!" the sound of Dylan's voice pulls me out of my thoughts.

My sister blows into the kitchen like a caffeinated cartoon character, all smiles and energy. Jemmy immediately starts clapping. Presley actually cracks a smile.

It's a tiny one, but I'll take it.

"Dee Dee!" Jeremiah exclaims.

Dylan kisses the top of his head and ruffles his dark hair. Then she moves to Presley, wrapping her in a long hug.

I pretend I'm not watching too closely.

Pretend it doesn't bother me that my sister seems to have a stronger connection to my daughter than I do.

Dylan picks up one of the pancakes on Presley's plate and squints at it. "What the hell do you call this?"

"Breakfast," I respond with a shrug, cleaning up the last of the oatmeal and discarding the paper towels in the trash.

She takes a bite, then makes a fake gagging sound. "You're the only person I know who can screw up pancakes."

"They're not screwed up."

"I wouldn't serve these even to my worst enemy." She pushes me out of the way and starts digging through my cabinets, pulling out ingredients like she lives here.

Which she basically does.

When I moved back from Chicago after losing Cora, Dylan and Mom became my village. Babysitters. Emotional support system. My kids' favorite people.

My lifeline, if I'm being honest.

While my job at the family medical practice isn't as demanding as working at a busy metropolitan hospital, I'm still floundering.

Still trying to figure out how to be everything my kids need now that their mom is gone.

Still scared I'm screwing everything up.

"Where's Grace?" Dylan asks as she whisks together pancake batter from scratch. No box. No instructions.

I'm not surprised. She *is* the professional. It's part of the reason I find myself in this predicament.

While my sister happily dropped everything to help me in the aftermath of Cora's death, it's been almost a year. She put her own dreams on hold for me. It's time for her to finally pursue her dreams, even if it's made things difficult for me.

"Didn't work out," I respond.

"That's…what? Your fourth nanny in two months?" She pours batter onto the griddle with ease.

"Fifth," I correct.

"And why did this one leave?" She smooths a tendril of blonde hair behind her ear.

I glance at Presley, who's back to sketching, focused and far away.

"I see," Dylan says without me having to explain.

Presley can be a lot.

Despite every single nanny I've hired having great qualifications, none have been all that understanding when it comes to Presley's refusal to speak.

Granted, I also get frustrated at times, but there's a reason for it. The last words she ever spoke were to her mother. Speaking would mean admitting she's gone.

I still struggle with admitting it myself.

"Who's watching them today?" Dylan asks.

"Abbey's taking Jemmy. I'll drop Presley at school first."

Over the past year, my village has grown quite a bit, thanks to each of my brothers falling in love and settling down. Between Haley, Abbey, and Genevieve, as well as my mom and brothers, I'm usually able to find someone to watch them.

But I hate the instability.

I thought hiring a nanny would give them some sort of routine and might help Presley finally speak, as her therapist suggested.

But not a single nanny I've hired has been a good fit.

"What are your plans for hiring a replacement?" she asks as she heats up a fresh pot of oatmeal for Jemmy.

"I'm not sure. I can see if Jeannie or Robert have another recommendation."

"Because their recommendations have worked so far," she snorts, her disdain for my in-laws apparent.

They're not bad people, but Dylan tends to blame them for why I left emergency medicine.

It was Robert's dream that Cora would eventually return to Sycamore Falls and take over the medical practice that's been in his family since this town was settled in the 1800s. Moving back here and taking her place was the least I could do, considering it's my fault she's gone.

I'm a doctor trained in emergency medicine. I've saved countless lives.

But when it really mattered, I couldn't even save my own wife.

"Jeannie's been a teacher in the school system here since I was a kid," I remind her. "And Robert's been running the medical practice for just as long. They know everyone. Plus, they're the kids' grandparents."

Dylan opens the cupboard and grabs the bag of chocolate chips. I part my lips to tell her Presley doesn't need chocolate chips on her pancakes, but at this point, I'll agree to smother her breakfast with chocolate syrup and whipped cream if she'll eat it.

"With horrible taste in childcare." After carefully adding the chocolate chips to the pancake, she flips it, then gives the oatmeal a stir. "You don't need someone who checks all the boxes on paper. You need someone who clicks with them. Someone like…" She trails off.

But I know what she was about to say.

"Someone like Cora," I finish, my throat tightening around her name.

You'd think after a year it wouldn't hurt as much.

"The nannies you've hired are the complete opposite of her. In fact, they're like you."

I cross my arms in front of my chest. "What's that supposed to mean?"

"Just that you can be a bit…stiff. And boring."

"I'm not boring."

"You fold your boxer briefs. And your closet is color-coded."

"It's not that bad. And why were you going through my underwear drawer anyway?"

"Because I used to do your laundry."

She turns off the burners, then places Presley's pancake on a plate, making a face out of strawberries and blueberries. After cutting up a banana, she adds the slices along with some brown sugar to Jeremiah's oatmeal before setting their fresh meals in front of them.

To my surprise, both kids start eating. Presley even helps Jeremiah so he doesn't make as big of a mess as he usually does.

"Are you sure you don't want to come back and watch them?" I joke. "I'll pay you this time."

"You know I love you and them… But no." She

gives me a sympathetic smile, then inhales a sharp breath.

"What is it?" I look from her to my kids, worried something is wrong.

"I might know someone who can help. Someone infinitely better than the people you've been hiring."

"Who?"

"Her name's Rowan. She just started volunteering at the animal shelter. She mentioned she used to nanny and is between jobs right now."

"I'm not just hiring some…stranger off the street to watch my kids. You've known this person, what? A few weeks?"

She shrugs. "She has good energy."

"I'm not hiring a nanny based on good energy. I've known everyone I've hired. Or Robert or Jeannie did."

"And how have your carefully vetted, well-connected nannies worked out so far?" she counters.

"I'm not letting a stranger watch my kids."

"Remember what Presley's therapist said. She needs stability. This past year has been anything but stable. This revolving door of caregivers isn't doing you any favors. Or her."

I push out a sigh, knowing she's right. Presley does need some stability. We all do. But it's not that easy.

"They've had a shit year, Hayden," Dylan says, placing her hand on my arm. "They deserve someone a bit more fun than Grace Henderson, whose idea of a fun activity for Presley was math flashcards. And Rowan is definitely fun."

"Math's an important skill."

"She's seven. Do you want her to develop an intense hatred for math at such a young age? Because that's what Grace was doing. And she never sat on the floor to play with Jemmy. None of them did. They were all older. They need someone fun. Young. Full of life."

I steal a glance at my kids, both of them nearly finished with their breakfast.

No thanks to me.

Maybe Dylan is right. Maybe they need some fun in their lives. Because whatever I've been doing obviously hasn't been working.

"Fine." I shift my attention back to my sister. "Talk to her and see if she's interested. But I need to meet her before you just offer her the job."

She beams. "You'll love her."

"It doesn't matter if I do." I gesture toward my kids. "All that matters is if they do."

"They will. I can feel it."

"We'll see about that."

TWO

Rowan

It's amazing how seemingly insignificant choices can drastically change the trajectory of your life.

Take, for instance, my current predicament of attempting to wrangle a seventy-five pound rambunctious Labrador Retriever down Main Street of an adorable small town I stumbled on a few weeks ago.

I came here because I heard the diner had the best pie around.

And if there's one thing I'll never say no to, it's pie. All flavors. Apple. Pumpkin. Cherry. Chocolate. Peanut Butter.

If it has the word "pie" attached to it, I'm eating it.

Except for Shepherd's Pie. In my opinion, that dish has no business calling itself a pie.

But that's a story for another day.

This love affair with pie isn't born from a relentless

sweet tooth, although I've never been one to turn down something filled with sugar.

Instead, it's because there was a time when I didn't think I'd ever get to taste pie again. Or a cake on my birthday. Or my favorite deep-dish Chicago pizza. Or a New England lobster roll. Or a Maryland crab cake.

Now that I have a second chance, I'm doing all those things. Trying to experience everything life has to offer. Saying yes to any and every new adventure that comes my way.

I know better than anyone it can all be taken away tomorrow.

This drive to say yes is how I ended up staying in this small town instead of just stopping by for a piece of pie.

Because after that piece of pie, I decided to walk off some of the sugar before continuing on my way, which led me to striking up a conversation with a woman around my age walking a dog.

Who told me the local shelter was looking for volunteers to help walk the dogs waiting to be adopted.

I had no choice but to say yes.

Although, as Bark Twain practically pulls me down Main Street, I can't help but question whether it was a good idea.

"Slow down, Bark Twain," I huff, trying to pull on his leash to reel him in. But there are too many smells and sights for him.

It's obvious he's happy to be out of that kennel. I can't blame him. I feel the same sense of exhilaration every time I visit a new city. New town. Have a new experience.

"I get that this is exciting, but I need to take it easy."

To my surprise, he actually listens to me. I nearly trip over the yellow lab as he slows to a complete stop.

"Huh. Maybe I'm, like, the dog whisperer or something," I muse.

But it only takes a matter of seconds for me to realize I'm no dog whisperer. Instead, what had him come to a stop wasn't my plea or hold on his leash.

It was his nemesis.

The squirrel.

The second I see the tiny creature a block away, I try to tighten my grip on the leash.

But it's no use.

He's already on the attack.

The leash slices through my palm as he rockets forward. One moment I'm in control. The next, the leash is airborne.

"Bark Twain! Heel!" I shout, sprinting after him. "It's a squirrel! Not a jar of peanut butter!"

The world blurs into storefronts and early-morning diner scents. I dodge a chalkboard sign advertising Tuesday Bingo at the senior center. Thankfully, there are enough obstacles between Bark Twain and the squirrel that I'm able to catch up to him and snag his collar.

"Got you," I say, feeling victorious.

And that's when I slam into what feels like a brick wall.

Except it's not a wall.

It's a body.

My gaze travels up a broad chest straining beneath a dark suit, to dark eyes sharp enough to cut glass and along a jawline scruffy enough to inspire questionable thoughts I absolutely do not have time for this morning.

And then I reach his mouth.

Correction.

I reach his scowl.

If there were a competition for biggest scowl, this one would win. Hands down.

Which is why my stomach shouldn't be fluttering and my heart shouldn't be skipping a proverbial beat.

Not a real beat.

That would be concerning.

"Oh, my god, I'm so sorry!" I push myself upright as I attempt to keep Bark Twain's leash firmly in my grasp.

Thankfully, the squirrel realized he was being targeted and scaled a tree.

"If you can't control your dog," the man grumbles, flinging spilled coffee from his hands, "maybe you shouldn't have one."

I blink. Once. Twice. Taken aback by just how rude he is, even after I apologized. But I refuse to let it get to me. Life's too short to walk around angry.

Maybe Mr. Grump in a Suit needs to realize that.

"I'll get you another coffee," I offer, smiling wide. "My treat."

"Don't bother." He sidesteps me like the sight of me disgusts him.

Granted, I haven't showered yet today. My dark hair is a bit disheveled in the messy bun piled on top of my head. I'm not wearing any makeup, but I'm not a big fan of it anyway. I'm still dressed in pajama pants with tacos all over them and a sweatshirt that says "undiagnosed but something is definitely wrong". I discreetly sniff myself to make sure I put on deodorant, and I'm happy to report I did.

"I'm already late," he says with an air of importance as he stalks off, shoulders tight, scowl deepening.

I watch as he hurries down the sidewalk, everyone seeming to stay out of his way. The lights on a dark Porsche Cayenne blink as he approaches, and he slides into the driver's seat.

Of course he drives a freaking Porsche. In a town where the local diner still serves pie on mismatched plates.

I crouch down and meet Bark Twain's dark, apologetic eyes. He looks so sad. No doubt Mr. Grump in a Suit's energy oozed onto this sweet dog who doesn't know any better.

But Mr. Grump does.

"It's okay," I assure Bark Twain as I scratch behind his ears. "I'm not mad. I could never be mad at you. This is why dogs are infinitely better than humans."

I glance at the Porsche as Mr. Grump in a Suit drives away.

I half expect him to speed. He doesn't. In fact, he drives very carefully.

But as he passes me, his eyes find mine, and he treats me to a glare to end all glares.

Which I return with a bright smile, refusing to allow his negative energy to impact my day.

Once he rolls past me, I turn my attention to Bark

Twain. "Especially that human," I mutter under my breath.

The dog leans further into my touch, and I give him a few more head scratches before pulling myself up to my full height.

"Come on. Let's go get you a pup cup."

That's all it takes for Bark Twain to dance in circles, the run-in with Mr. Grump in a Suit long forgotten.

THREE

Hayden

I walk into Sycamore Falls Family Medicine with the same energy most people reserve for stepping on a Lego barefoot.

The waiting room is packed. Flu season is already hitting us, and I have a feeling this one will be a doozy.

Margaret looks up from the reception desk, treating me to the same congenial smile I remember from whenever I managed to injure myself during my childhood.

"Morning, Doc," she says.

"Morning."

She tilts her head. "Rough start?"

I think back to the war zone formerly known as my kitchen. "You can say that."

She hums knowingly before returning to her computer, the click of the keyboard cutting over the TV in the waiting room playing some home improvement show.

I head down the corridor. The walls are lined with portraits of every physician who's ever practiced here, going all the way back to the 1800s. A timeline of medical history in a small town.

Then there's Cora.

Her portrait hangs right outside my office door.

She never worked here. Hell, she didn't even want to work here. Her specialty was pediatrics.

But her father hung it anyway out of pride. Grief. Legacy.

Or maybe he just wanted me to have a daily reminder that she should still be here.

That it's my fault she's gone.

I slip into my office and close the door behind me. The silence is welcome. No toddler tantrums. No burned pancakes. No stains.

Except for the one currently on my shirt.

I peel off my suit jacket, loosen my tie, and unbutton the stained shirt. I swap it for the clean one hanging in the closet. I'd much rather be in scrubs, but Robert insists the community needs a doctor who looks like they have their life together.

Spoiler alert: I do *not* have my life together.

I knot the tie, shrug into my white coat, and brace myself for a day full of sick people coughing on me as well as those insisting they have cancer or something equally as bad because of an article they read on the internet.

Just as I'm about to reach for the knob on my office door, it swings open.

No knock.

No warning.

No sense of personal boundaries.

"There you are," Robert says.

He glances at the clock, but doesn't comment. Weaponized silence is his specialty.

"Had a bit of a slow start this morning," I explain.

"Would that have anything to do with firing Grace?" He arches a single brow.

"She didn't click with the kids."

"Both of them?" He crosses his arms in front of his chest, his stomach seeming to protrude even more.

I know what he's getting at. He thinks Presley is the problem.

He keeps telling me she just needs structure. A consequence for not speaking, instead of the patience, care, and compassion I've shown her.

"Yes," I say through gritted teeth. "Both of them. Jeremiah needs someone who'll get on the floor and be a dragon or dinosaur. Presley needs someone who won't look at her like there's something wrong with her."

He gives me a look. He doesn't have to say the words for me to know what he's thinking.

That there *is* something wrong with her.

At least in his eyes.

Do I wish she'd finally talk again? Of course. I'd give anything to hear her sweet voice and her bright laughter.

But she's suffered a traumatic event at a young age.

Like her therapist has told me. She just needs reassurance she's loved and safe.

That's what I've spent the past year trying to do. Showing her she's loved. And keeping her safe.

"Who's watching them today?" Robert asks.

"Abbey."

"Where?" he scoffs. "The brewery?"

The disgust is subtle but familiar.

"She hasn't worked there in months," I retort, keeping my voice even. "She works for a clean water initiative now. Writes grants from home. But she was more than happy to use personal time to spend the day with Jemmy."

I leave out the part where Abbey plans on bringing both Jeremiah and Presley to the brewery after she picks her up from school to play on the playground my brother, Jude, installed a few years ago by the outdoor patio.

"I'll have Jeannie find you a new nanny," Robert declares. "And this time, don't fire them. There are only so many people to choose from." He starts to turn from my office.

"That won't be necessary," I say, stopping him. "Dylan has someone in mind."

He faces me once more. "Are you sure your sister's the right person? I'm not sure she knows what those kids need."

I push down my irritation with his obvious disdain for my sister.

Hell, for most people.

"She took care of them for the better part of the

year. Sacrificed her own dreams to step up when no one else would." I give him a pointed look.

As much as Robert likes to have a say in who watches his grandkids, he's not exactly involved in their lives. He doesn't take them fishing or to the park or on a bike ride. Not like my family does.

From the second I returned to Sycamore Falls after losing Cora, my mom, brothers, and sister have done everything they can to pitch in. I can't say the same for Robert and Jeannie.

"And who is this person?" Robert inquires. "What are her qualifications?"

"I don't know yet. I haven't met her. She volunteers at the shelter with Dylan."

His face pinches. "You're letting a stranger watch your children?"

I don't even bother softening my glare. Granted, I voiced the same concern to Dylan less than an hour ago. But hearing Robert say it grates on my nerves.

"They're my kids. I'll decide who takes care of them. And if Dylan thinks she might be a good fit, I'd like to give her a chance. If we're done here, I have patients to see." I move past him.

"Have you chosen the readings?"

His question stops me, and I glance over my shoulder. "Readings?"

"For the memorial."

Right.

It's not enough that I'm still mourning the loss of the love of my life even nearly a year later.

Robert seems to feel the need to remind me she's gone every chance he gets.

From the portrait right outside my office.

To the monthly church services said in her memory.

To weekly vigils at her gravesite.

And now this… A memorial on the anniversary of her death.

It's the absolute last thing I want to sit through.

It's not that I want to forget Cora. I'll never do that. Never stop loving her.

But I'm not sure how much more of this I can take. And every time I join Robert and Jeannie at church or at Cora's gravesite, I can't help but feel their disapproval.

As if I'm not mourning her enough.

As if I don't miss her enough when every damn minute of every damn day I'm reminded that a giant piece of my heart is gone.

"I'll get them to you this week," I tell Robert through the ache in my throat.

Then I head down the hall, the heaviness on my chest growing more suffocating with every step.

FOUR

Rowan

I pull up to the end of a quiet cul-de-sac and immediately feel like my van doesn't belong here. It looks like the kind of neighborhood I imagined for myself in my old life.

Manicured lawns. Identical mailboxes. Wide driveways. The kind of community where packages are probably safe being left unattended.

I check the address on my phone.

Then the house.

Then the address again.

This is the place.

I turn off my van and sit for a second with my eyes closed, sending out positive vibes and gratitude to the universe.

Despite the somewhat rough start to my day, I've

remained positive. Didn't let Mr. Grump in a Suit turn me into someone negative or angry. And the universe rewarded me when, just minutes after I dropped off Bark Twain at the shelter, my phone pinged with a text from another volunteer asking if I was interested in a potential nanny job.

While nannying has never been a lifelong dream, my mantra kicked in before I could question it.

Say yes.

So that's what I did.

I glance at the time. Two minutes early. Apparently punctuality is the one habit I've maintained from my old life, along with my ability to parallel park and an unhealthy fondness for pens in every color possible. And journals. And just office supplies in general.

I hop out of the van and head up the driveway, the crisp late autumn air chilly against my skin.

I climb onto the front porch and am about to ring the doorbell when I hear a wail, high-pitched and furious.

Definitely a toddler.

Then a man's voice comes through. "Jemmy, you need to eat. No. Don't throw that. What did I just say?"

It sounds like this guy has his hands full. It's probably not the best time for a job interview, and I consider retreating.

Then again, chaos is part of being a nanny. If anything, this feels like a live audition.

I take a breath and ring the doorbell.

The tantrum continues uninterrupted.

I wait.

And wait.

And wait.

I start to wonder if the doorbell was swallowed by the noise when the door finally swings open.

And my breath catches.

Because my potential boss is none other than Mr. Grump in a Suit.

Except he's no longer wearing a suit.

He's in gray sweatpants and a faded Northwestern t-shirt that looks like it's been washed a thousand times. The fabric stretches across a broad chest, the sleeves clinging to his biceps in a way that feels extremely inconvenient.

And I thought he was sex on a stick in that suit.

Before he opened his mouth, of course.

But that has nothing on him in gray sweatpants.

Gray. Fucking. Sweatpants.

I've died and gone to gray sweatpants heaven.

For half a second, I forget how to breathe. How to think. How to speak.

Then he opens his mouth.

"Can I help you?" he barks out.

"I'm Dylan's friend, Rowan. She mentioned you're looking for a nanny and said to stop by at six."

"Absolutely not," he says flatly. "If you couldn't control your dog earlier, there's no way in hell I'm trusting you with my kids." He starts to close the door.

I almost let him.

I don't exactly need this job.

I could hop back in my van and follow my nose until I find my next destination.

But my hand shoots out and catches the door, as if some bigger force is at play, not allowing me to retreat.

His eyes snap to mine, startled.

"I'm not one to judge, but it sounds like you're having a rough time," I say, the words tumbling out before I can overthink them.

"It's fine. He's just tired. And hungry. I burned his grilled cheese. Again."

I don't break eye contact. "Let me help. I'm already here. You might as well get something out of it."

He parts his lips and I can practically hear the refusal about to slip free.

That's when the smoke alarm goes off.

"Shit," he mutters. "The grilled cheese."

He spins around and bolts inside, leaving the door open.

I hesitate for a second before I cross the threshold, toeing off my sneakers.

The house is big. Open floor plan. Tall ceilings. Neutral walls and floors.

But it feels…overwhelmed.

Tiny socks abandoned mid-stride. Sneakers kicked off without ceremony. Toys everywhere — blocks, Barbies, plastic dinosaurs, a rogue crayon crushed into the rug.

The farther I walk, the more it feels like life happens here faster than anyone can keep up.

Then I reach the kitchen.

Smoke billows from a pan on the stove. The smell of burnt bread hangs thick in the air. Mr. Gray Sweatpants (upgraded from Mr. Grump in a Suit) is standing on a chair, arms raised, desperately trying to silence the smoke detector.

At the table a few feet away, a little boy with a full head of dark hair sits in a high chair, his face and shirt covered in ketchup, his wails almost as loud as the smoke detector.

Beside him, a girl of maybe six or seven sits with her head bowed, hands pressed over her ears, making herself small.

Finally, the alarm stops.

Seconds later, the boy's cries taper off and silence settles in the room. It almost feels louder.

Mr. Gray Sweatpants steps down from the chair and drags a hand over his face. He looks exhausted, like even sleeping for days on end wouldn't be able to fix it.

"As you can see," he says quietly, "now's not a good time."

Something in his voice cracks my chest open.

This man isn't grumpy. He's drowning, in desperate need of a lifesaver.

So that's what I'll be, even if just for tonight.

I move toward the stove and grab the pan, dumping the contents into the trash can, where there are at least three previous grilled cheese casualties, each one progressively darker.

"Why don't you go clean up the little one," I suggest. "By the time you're done, I'll have un-charred grilled cheese ready."

"You don't have to. I can—"

"Handle it yourself?" I arch a brow.

I try not to sound judgmental. We're all on different

paths, on different parts of our journey. He's obviously floundering, but is too proud to admit it. As if accepting help makes him "less than".

I know that feeling all too well.

"I thought I'd have it together by now."

The words are barely audible.

But I hear them.

"Go," I say softly. "I'll keep an eye on…" I glance toward the petite brunette sitting at the table, her wide eyes seemingly glued on me. I get the feeling she's a little shy, considering she hasn't uttered a single word while the little boy hasn't stopped babbling.

"That's Presley," Mr. Gray Sweatpants says, nodding toward the girl. "And the ketchup disaster is Jeremiah. Jemmy."

I approach the table with a smile. "Nice to meet you, Jemmy." Then I look to the little girl. "Presley. That's a great name. My name's Rowan."

She doesn't respond. Instead, she averts her gaze.

"She doesn't talk," Mr. Gray Sweatpants explains. "Hasn't in almost a year."

Something shifts in my chest, and it takes everything in me not to cry. No wonder she cowers in her own body. No doubt everyone looks at her with pity. But I won't.

I know how it feels to have everyone whisper about you behind your back because of something out of your control.

"That's okay," I say brightly. "Talking's overrated anyway. There are tons of other ways to communicate." My eyes flick to her sketchpad. "Like drawing."

She perks up, lifting her gaze to mine.

"Did you know people used drawings to communicate before written language even existed?"

Her posture softens a little, and I count it as a win. Anything to make her feel relaxed. Like she matters.

"I told you," I say over my shoulder to Mr. Gray Sweatpants, who's looking at me like I've grown three heads. "I've got this. Go clean Jemmy."

He stares at me for several protracted seconds, and I expect for him to reiterate his argument that he doesn't need me.

Instead, he steps toward the high chair and lifts Jemmy out of it.

"Come on, bud. Let's get you cleaned up." He presses a kiss to the little boy's head, ketchup and all, and something warm flickers in my chest.

Gray sweatpants. Tight shirt. And good with kids?

My ovaries are officially on overdrive right now, but I do my best to keep my libido in check. After all, this man could soon be my boss.

I went into this interview not caring one way or another if it worked out, trusting the universe would make it happen if it was meant to be.

But now I'm praying it works out. I can't quite explain it. I feel this pull inside me, telling me this is where I need to be right now. And not for these kids or Mr. Gray Sweatpants.

But for myself.

"Thank you, Rowan," Mr. Gray Sweatpants says, pulling me out of my thoughts.

"Of course…" I trail off, furrowing my brows. "You never told me your name."

His lips lift in a tiny smile. "Hayden."

"Hayden," I repeat quietly.

He holds my gaze for a beat longer than necessary.

Then he leaves the kitchen.

FIVE

Hayden

Water sloshes over the side of the tub as Jemmy sinks another ship with his toy dinosaur, but I barely notice it. Instead, my thoughts seem focused on one thing and one thing only.

Rowan.

Can I hire her as my kids' nanny? She's so different from the last few nannies they've had. Maybe that's a good thing.

She's the first person who didn't look at Presley with sympathy or pity after learning she doesn't talk. Maybe it's because everyone else I've hired already knew our tragic story. Knew about our loss.

But Rowan just rolled with Presley not talking like I told her she prefers grape juice over apple. No gasp. No sorrowful eyes. No whispered *poor baby* energy.

Just acceptance. Casual. Uncomplicated.

Maybe that's what she needs.

What we *all* need.

"Easy, buddy," I say, attempting to get a firm grip on Jemmy's head so I can wash the ketchup out of his hair. "This is a bath. Not a water park."

He picks up his toy dinosaur and roars.

"Point taken."

He returns his attention to the tub filled with toys, and I take advantage of his momentary distraction and lather shampoo into his hair.

"What do you think of Rowan?" I ask as I rinse the suds away. "Would you want her to play with you during the day?"

He looks at me. "Dino?"

I laugh. "Yeah, bud. I'm pretty sure she'd have no problem playing dinosaur with you. Or building race-tracks. Or playing giant in the forest."

His eyes brighten, as if I just promised him a pet T-Rex.

"Does that mean you think I should hire her?"

"Yes," he declares.

Then he picks up his dinosaur and dive-bombs it into the tub, another tsunami of water splashing over the ledge.

By the time I carry a now-dry version of Jemmy downstairs, the house feels different. Cleaner. Brighter. Like someone turned the contrast up.

The smell of burnt cheese and bread that had permeated the kitchen twenty minutes ago is gone. In its place is something clean and lemony. The clutter that once covered every surface has vanished. And there's music playing in the background. For a second, I feel like I've fallen down the rabbit hole and am in a different world.

Until my eyes land on the kitchen table. Rowan sits beside Presley, both of them taking turns making doodles and sketches in Presley's pad. Even better, Presley's plate has essentially been wiped clean, only a few crumbs remaining.

But that's not what stops me in my tracks.

It's Presley's smile.

I don't think she ever smiled around the other nannies.

Hell, I don't think she's smiled much this past year. She hasn't had much to smile about.

But it warms my heart to see it again.

Jeremiah wiggles, his tiny arms extended toward Rowan. "Play dino."

Rowan snaps her head up, her eyes locking with mine. And for the first time, I really look at her. Her dark hair falls in soft waves to her mid-back. She wears a pair of light jeans and her socks have tacos all over them. She's wearing a t-shirt that says "it's a good day to read a book." I squint slightly, noticing what looks like part of a tattoo snaking along her collarbone. It makes me wonder what the rest of her tattoo looks like… And where it goes.

Which is the last thing I should be thinking about,

considering I may very well hire her as my kids' nanny. But there's no denying it.

Rowan is beautiful.

And probably more than ten years younger than me.

"Are you ready for your grilled cheese, Jemmy?" She scoots back from her chair and heads toward the stove, as if she's lived here for months.

"I can do it."

She gives me a pointed stare. "The evidence suggests otherwise." She puts a small pat of butter on the pan. "Apparently, culinary skills don't run in the family."

I put Jemmy back in his high-chair, along with some crayons and his coloring book, then head toward the stove.

"I'm normally not this bad," I say, leaning against the counter. "While Dylan is definitely the chef in the family, our mom taught all of us how to cook. It's just…" I blow out a long breath. "It's been a day. Hell. A year."

Why am I telling her this?

I never share this kind of thing with anyone, my family included. But there's something about her that makes the truth slip out easier than intended. Like she gets it. Like she won't make it weird.

I felt that way around Cora, too.

We'd grown close when I took my father to his doctor appointments after he'd been diagnosed with ALS. Cora worked at the sandwich shop next to my father's neurologist's office where I'd often wait. She always kept me company between customers. She didn't ask how I was coping with my father essentially receiving a death sentence. Instead, she spoke to me without that look of pity I got from everyone else in town.

Just like Rowan.

"Would you like a sandwich, too?" she asks, cutting through my thoughts. "Or something else? I may not be as good as your sister, but I quite enjoy cooking."

"You don't have to. Dylan dropped off some lasagna for me this morning. I'll reheat it once I get these two to bed."

"Okay." She shifts her attention back to the pan, lifting the sandwich to check the color, a silence falling between us.

Despite Jemmy's incessant babbling and singing as he colors, the quiet feels heavy.

"Listen," I begin at the same time as Rowan says, "I'm not—"

We both stop short.

"You go first," I tell her.

She nods, checking the grilled cheese and flipping it. "I just wanted to say I'm usually better at controlling the dogs I walk. Bark Twain hasn't—"

"Bark Twain?" I ask, confused.

She looks at me. "The dog I was walking."

I arch a brow, folding my arms in front of my chest. "The dog's name is Bark Twain?"

She grins, and her smile does something to me.

Something I can't quite explain.

"I'm quite proud of that one. I was there when he was brought in so I got to name him, along with a few others."

"And what did you name them?"

This has absolutely nothing to do with her ability to take care of my kids, but it's like some other force is at play, encouraging me to engage with this woman when I've spent the past year distancing myself from everyone.

"Bilbo Waggins is one, naturally."

I chuckle. "Naturally."

"There's also Sherlock Bones and Winnie the Pooch."

"I'm catching a theme here."

"I love books," she explains somewhat sheepishly. "Oh, and there's also Dogberry. He's named after—"

"The constable from *Much Ado About Nothing*."

She gives a low whistle. "I'm impressed."

"What can I say? I have a knack for remembering useless information."

She holds my gaze for a beat, then quickly looks away, checking on the grilled cheese once more.

"Since they're stuck in the shelter, they spend most of their days in a cramped space. So when Bark Twain got the chance to stretch his legs, he was like, *freedom!*" she explains, doing her best impression of Mel Gibson in *Braveheart*. Then she scrunches her nose. "Maybe I should have named him William Woof-lace instead."

I chuckle again, this time even louder than before.

Presley looks up from her sketchpad, her eyes finding mine. I can feel her confusion from across the room. She hasn't heard me laugh like this in ages.

"It's not your fault. Or Bark Twain's," I say, glancing back at Rowan. "I had a rough morning around here.

That spilled coffee sort of tipped me over the edge. I was an ass and you didn't deserve that, so I'm sorry."

"Apology accepted."

She turns off the burner and places the sandwich on a cutting board. Grabbing a pizza slicer I didn't even know I owned, she cuts the grilled cheese into bite-size pieces before depositing them in front of Jemmy.

"I'll just clean up and be on my way," she says, heading to the sink.

"No need. You've already cleaned up quite a bit." More than any of my other nannies ever did, but I don't tell her that. "I can take it from here."

"Of course." She heads toward the table and grabs her hoodie, sliding it on. "It was great hanging out with you, Presley." She makes a fist and extends her arm toward my daughter.

To my surprise, Presley mirrors her movements and gives her a fist bump. Then Rowan heads toward Jemmy and tousles his hair.

"No more ketchup disasters, okay?"

"K."

She gives me one last smile, then walks out of the kitchen, the sound of her footfalls growing softer with each retreating step.

I look back at my kids, both of whom are staring at me. I don't even have to ask to know what they're thinking.

Because I'm thinking the same thing.

That I'd be an absolute idiot if I don't give Rowan a chance.

"Keep an eye on your brother," I instruct Presley. "And keep the ketchup away from him."

Presley nods, her lips quirking up into another slight smile.

I head out of the kitchen, spotting Rowan as she's sliding her sneakers back on.

"Rowan?"

She straightens, meeting my eyes.

"Maybe we can…give it a try."

"Give what a try?"

"The nanny job. On a trial basis. If you're still interested after what you walked in on tonight. There may be more nights like this and you'll need to be able to handle it yourself. I love my kids, but they can be…a lot."

"If you're trying to scare me off, you'll have to try harder. I've never been one to shy away from a challenge."

"Those two can *definitely* be a challenge. Did Dylan tell you any of the details?"

"Not really, other than that you have two kids."

"I work at the medical practice here in town."

"Dylan did mention you were a doctor."

"There are some nights and weekends I'll be on phone duty, meaning if someone calls our non-emergency line, I'll need to field those. I can't do that while wrangling the kids. Which is why I'd really like a live-in nanny this time around. You won't be on the clock twenty-four seven. And there's an in-law apartment, so it's not like we'll be sharing a living space. I need someone here and available to step in. Is any of that a problem?"

"It'll be nice to live somewhere that's not on wheels."

I furrow my brows. "Not on wheels?"

"I've been living out of my van," she says proudly, as if it's the most normal thing in the world.

"Your…van?" I ask, questioning whether this is the right decision yet again.

I need someone dependable. Maybe I'm being quick to judge, but someone who's living out of her damn car doesn't exactly sound dependable.

"It's a converted van with a bed and a little kitchen," she explains. "That way my home is with me wherever I go. But it will definitely be nice not having to shower at a truck stop or campground. And to have a real toilet again."

"So you're living out of your van," I say, still trying to wrap my head around this.

"I am." She beams. "It's actually kind of freeing to not be tied down. To go wherever I want, whenever I want. To not be stuck in one place."

"And how long were you planning on staying here in town?"

She shrugs. "Until I find a reason to leave, I suppose."

"I see." I study her, my skepticism about whether this is a good decision increasing the more I learn about her unconventional living situation.

"It probably sounds like I'm a flake, but I'm not. I'm extremely responsible. I just…" She trails off, briefly looking past me before returning her eyes to mine. "I went through something about a year ago that made me re-evaluate what's important in life. I realized it's not the high-paying job or the expensive car or the luxurious apartment. I was done letting life pass me by and saying no to new experiences because of work or bills or other responsibilities. I wanted to say yes to everything. To experience life. So I quit my job, moved all my stuff into storage, and bought a van so I could finally *live*."

I run a hand over my face, blowing out a long breath. Rowan is probably the last kind of person I'd normally hire to watch my kids. But this isn't about me. It's about them. In less than an hour, she did what my previous nannies couldn't do in weeks.

"Okay. We'll give it a try. Can you start tomorrow?"

"Of course. What time?"

"Seven. In the morning," I clarify.

I half expect her to flinch at the early hour.

She doesn't.

"Seven it is. See you then."

SIX

Rowan

I pull my van in front of Hayden's house and stare at it for a beat longer than necessary before killing the engine.

Unlike last night, the cul-de-sac is a beehive of activity, even before seven in the morning.

A woman power-walks with a golden retriever wearing a bandana. A guy in workout clothes stretches before jogging down the street. Two houses down, a man slips out of the front door and into his truck with the name of a construction company on it, obviously on his way to work.

And then there's me.

My van is definitely out of place among all the manicured lawns and curated perfection.

But I don't care.

Let them stare. If I worried what strangers thought about me, I never would have traded my office for a van in the first place. I would have been stuck watching my life slip by until I retired.

No thank you.

Slinging my bag over my shoulder, I jump out of the van and make my way up the driveway. Unlike last night, Hayden's house is quiet as I approach.

No smoke alarm screaming for mercy.

No toddler wails rattling the windows.

No frustrated shouts.

Just…calm.

I lift my hand to ring the doorbell, but the door opens before I have a chance.

Hayden appears in pajama pants and a plain white T-shirt, his dark hair rumpled from sleep.

For a moment, I forget how to speak.

Somehow, he looks even sexier than he did in the gray sweatpants. Less guarded. Less armored. More…human.

"Jemmy's still sleeping," he explains quietly, stepping aside to allow me to enter. "Didn't want the doorbell to wake him."

"What time does he start to stir?" I whisper back, following him into the kitchen after sliding off my sneakers.

"Usually between seven and seven-thirty. So anytime now."

"And Presley?"

"She likes to get up early on school days to draw

before breakfast. She's pretty good at entertaining herself, though."

As if summoned by her name, Presley pads into the kitchen, carrying a sketchpad. Her eyes light up when she sees me.

"Morning, Presley," I say softly.

She smiles in greeting.

"What would you like for breakfast?" I ask. "I can make anything you want. Pancakes?"

She nods enthusiastically.

"Plain?" I offer.

She scowls.

"Okay. Definitely not plain. Blueberry?"

She scrunches her nose in disgust.

"Chocolate chip?"

Her expression brightens.

"Chocolate chip pancakes it is," I declare.

"Why don't I show you where you'll be staying before you get started?" Hayden interjects before shifting his attention toward Presley. "Five more minutes, okay?"

She nods and slides into her chair, already flipping open her sketchpad.

He gives me a quick tour of the bedrooms, playroom, and living spaces before leading me down a hallway off the living room that's secluded from the rest of the house.

"This is your space," he states, leading me into a small living area with a couch and two chairs.

It's a little drab and boring, but nothing a few accent

pillows and art pieces can't fix. Even better, there's a kitchenette. To most it would seem small, but for someone who's used to cooking on a hot plate, this is like heaven.

And there's a separate bedroom with a queen-sized bed that doesn't need to be folded into a bench seat every day.

"If there's anything you need, just let me know," he offers.

"I've been living in a van for months. This is like a five-star hotel."

"Right," he says, like he's still trying to wrap his head around my unusual living arrangement. "What made—"

The sound of Jemmy's babbling from the baby monitor in his hand cuts him off.

Hayden glances down at it. Jemmy is sitting up in his crib, flipping through a book as he babbles, as if he's reading to himself.

I pick up a few words, like moon and brush.

"I'll grab him." Hayden spins on his heels and stalks down the hallway.

I catch up to him, almost having to jog, and reach him as he's about to head up the stairs, taking the monitor from him. "I can take care of it, then make breakfast for him and Presley."

"I don't mind. I—"

"I'm here to lighten your load. So go get ready for your day."

He hesitates. "He's still in diapers."

"I noticed."

"Do you know how to change a diaper? I guess I should have asked last night, but I was a bit…frazzled."

"It's been a few years since I've had to, but unless they've changed the design in that time, I'm all set."

"Are you sure? I—"

"Go. Shower. Otherwise, you'll be late and take it out on yet another unsuspecting dog walker."

He exhales, half-laughing. "I'm sorry about—"

"Go," I repeat, pushing past him and moving toward Jemmy's room, opening the door before he can stop me.

The instant I appear, Jemmy beams.

"Dino!" he exclaims as he stands in his crib.

"Is that today's agenda?" I lift him and carry him toward the changing table, setting him on the pad. "Dinosaurs all day?"

He roars.

"Excellent," I say solemnly. "I accept these terms."

I open the top drawer and find rows of perfectly arranged diapers. The sections are even labeled "day" and "night".

I grab one and put it to the side before unzipping Jemmy's pajamas. As I remove the diaper and wipe his bottom, I notice Hayden lingering in the doorway.

"I've got this," I tell him.

He nods, watching for another second, then finally leaves.

"I'm guessing Daddy has control issues," I whisper to Jemmy.

He roars again.

"Exactly."

By the time Hayden comes back downstairs, now dressed in a suit, both kids are eating, Jemmy some oatmeal and Presley pancakes with a side of fruit.

"Wow," he says, stopping short in the doorway.

"What? Didn't think I could handle breakfast?"

"They can be a lot."

"Kids feed off the energy in the room," I tell him. "If you're calm, they're calm. If you're tense, they feel it."

He studies me like I just handed him a missing puzzle piece. Then he places a stack of papers in front of me.

"What's this? An onboarding manual?" I joke, although that's exactly what it looks like.

"Just important things I'd like you to be aware of as far as the kids are concerned. Most of the time, you'll only be with Jemmy since Presley's in school. I drop her off on my way in and either my brother, Beckham, or sister-in-law, Haley, will drop her off after school. Some- times my mom if they're busy."

"I don't mind picking her up."

Hayden shakes his head. "It's during Jemmy's nap time. Plus we have a system worked out. I drop off and they pick up, since their daughter goes to the same school."

"Well, if you ever need me to do drop off, I can."

"We'll see how things go first before adding to your responsibilities."

I have to fight the urge to roll my eyes. Yup. Definitely a man with control issues. This extensive manual of his kid's schedule, permitted snacks, and dozens of emergency phone numbers proves it.

"Jemmy gets a snack at around ten, then lunch at noon. He takes one nap a day. I'd like him to be asleep by two at the latest, so after lunch I'd prefer only calm play. No dinosaurs or army men."

"Should I teach him to meditate?"

"Meditate?" He scrunches his brows. "He's only…" He pushes out a breath. "That was a joke, wasn't it?"

I give him a reassuring smile. "Relax. I know how to take care of kids."

"This nap is important. If he's too wound up, he'll fight it. Then he'll be exhausted and will fall asleep too early and will wake up at three or four in the morning, so—"

I cut him off with a hand to his forearm. The second I touch him, he darts his eyes toward my hand. He's practically a stranger, but I can't ignore the subtle buzzing beneath my palm.

The slight flutter in my heart.

"I've got it." I slowly remove my hand. "Now what would you like for breakfast?"

He straightens, obviously taken aback by my question. "Your job is to take care of my kids. Not me."

"Trust me. This is part of it. By taking this task off your plate, it allows you to spend some time with them." I point to a chair at the table in the breakfast nook. "Now sit."

At first, he doesn't move, as if wanting to argue with me. But it's an argument he won't win. I won't let him.

It's obvious this man's been running on empty for quite a while. It makes me curious about his story. What happened to the mother of his kids? Did she walk out on them? Or is it something worse?

I sense it's the latter.

I walk over to a bowl on the counter and grab an avocado, feeling it for ripeness. "How does some avocado toast sound?"

"Better than what I'd make for myself."

"I'm guessing that's usually nothing?" I ask as I slice into the avocado and take out the pit.

"Unless Dylan stops by in the morning. She makes sure I eat. Mom, too. It's not that I can't cook. I can, despite what you witnessed last night. But lately I'm just…"

"It's okay. I quite enjoy cooking. It's…therapeutic. And after having to cook on a hot plate and in a space no bigger than a closet, it's nice to be in a regular kitchen. And yours is beautiful."

"Well, feel free to use it anytime you want."

I look up to find him studying me with intensity. As if I'm a puzzle he's desperately trying to put together. "Thank you."

"Of course."

I slice the avocado and a tomato. Once the toast pops, I arrange the slices on top before sprinkling on some feta cheese.

"Thank you," he says quietly as I place his breakfast in front of him, his eyes locking with mine. "I mean it."

"You're welcome." I hold his gaze for a beat, then head back toward the island to tidy up.

As I wipe down the counters, I watch him with his kids. He seems awkward and unsure. Almost like he doesn't know how to talk to or be around them. As if he's not used to spending time with them like this.

When was the last time he was able to just enjoy his kids instead of rushing to feed, bathe, and get them ready for bed? Probably a while.

Hopefully, by my being here, he'll finally have a chance to spend some quality time with his kids and get to know them.

And for them to get to know him, too.

———

"If anything comes up, be sure to call me," Hayden instructs after breakfast as I follow him and Presley toward the front door while still keeping an eye on Jemmy, who's currently building a castle out of blocks in the living room. "If I don't answer, call the front desk number. I also left that in the instructions. Tell them who you are and someone will come get me. But if it's an emergency, call 911 first."

"Really?" I feign surprise mixed with confusion. "Is that what I should do?"

I can sense his frustration with me, but he needs to relax.

"Jemmy likes to get into trouble."

"He's just exploring his world." I look back at Jemmy as he holds a block in front of his eyes, examining it with the intensity of an archeologist who has just uncovered a hidden artifact from centuries ago.

"You still need to keep a close eye on him. He likes to put Barbie shoes up his nose. And everything goes in his mouth, so you have to be careful to make sure he doesn't choke on anything." His eyes widen. "Wait. You know first aid, right? What to do if he's choking? You could probably manage to keep toys out of his mouth, but he sometimes chokes on his food. Maybe I—"

"Relax," I say, touching his arm again.

And again, that same sizzle of awareness courses through me from the contact.

I slowly withdraw my hand. "I'm certified in first aid and CPR. I've got this."

He glances between me and Jemmy, uncertain. I can sense how difficult this is for him.

Normally, I wouldn't waste my time working for someone who questioned my ability to perform the tasks I'm more than capable of. I experienced enough of that in my old life, and I vowed never to make myself small for anyone else ever again.

But this feels…different.

As crazy as it sounds, maybe there's a reason the universe dropped this opportunity in my lap when I was moments away from leaving this small town in search of my next adventure.

"Go," I tell Hayden. "You have my number. Call and check in anytime you need."

He hesitates before pushing out a long breath. "I'll be home around six. And Presley will be dropped off a little after three."

"I've got it," I say for what feels like the hundredth time this morning.

But it's obvious he questions whether that's true.

Finally, he ushers Presley out of the house, closing the door behind him.

It doesn't escape my notice he never gave Jemmy a hug or kiss goodbye.

SEVEN

Hayden

I'm on time for work.

Not sprinting through the front door while trying to shove a piece of cold toast into my mouth. Not fielding a call from the school because I forgot to pack Presley's lunch. Not already exhausted before my day even begins.

I have to admit, I didn't exactly have high expectations for Rowan.

Sure, she handled herself well last night. Better than I did, honestly.

Between the burned grilled cheese, Jemmy's ketchup disaster, and the smoke detector going off, I was barely holding it together.

Not Rowan, though.

She swept in like a modern-day Mary Poppins and put my house together.

A very attractive, tattooed Mary Poppins.

I figured it was a fluke.

A one-time thing.

But she was just as calm this morning. She didn't wait for me to tell her what to do. She stepped right in.

Like she's been doing this forever.

Like she's been part of our little family for longer than a few hours.

And she didn't just make sure the kids ate.

She made sure *I* ate.

I can't remember the last time I actually ate with my kids. While my mom has the entire family over for dinner once a month, that doesn't really count. She cooks, my siblings fill the house with noise, and the kids run wild.

But this morning, it was just Presley, Jemmy, and me. Like life was before Cora died.

No wonder it felt strange. Like I didn't know how to spend time with my own kids unless I was telling them what to do.

It makes me feel like a shitty father.

I try to shake it off as I walk into the clinic, waving a quick good morning to Margaret before heading toward my office, the heaviness increasing when I pass Cora's portrait.

After shrugging into my coat, I slide on my glasses and flip through the short stack of patient messages I need to return. Within seconds, Robert steps inside.

As usual, his gaze flicks to the clock.

But instead of the smug look I'm used to, his brows lift slightly. Almost…surprised.

"Is there something you need, Robert?" I ask, pretending to be focused on the messages.

He clears his throat. "I wanted to let you know I took the liberty of hiring a nanny for you."

I clench my jaw. Of course he did, even though I told him Dylan knew someone who might be a good fit.

"She's available for the hours you need. Her name's Dana. She teaches Sunday school. If you actually attended church, your kids would already know her."

I don't miss the condescension in his tone. He's made his opinion on my lack of church attendance well known. And I've made my own opinion on organized religion equally clear. He has his beliefs. I have mine. I respect his.

I wish he'd respect mine.

"I appreciate it," I begin in as even a tone as possible, "but I've already hired someone."

His eyes narrow. "Who?"

"Dylan's friend."

"The dog walker?" he sneers.

I remove my glasses, sliding them into the pocket of my coat. "Her name is Rowan, and the kids seem to like her. Even Presley."

His mouth tightens. "Dana has decades of experience with kids. How much experience can a dog walker possibly have?"

"Certainly not decades, but she's great with the kids. That's all that matters to me. That, and she's already made my life easier. She has no problem cleaning. Doing laundry. Things the nannies you hired refused to do. While she may not have the same amount of so-called experience, she has a natural talent for making my kids feel comfortable."

He studies me, clearly unconvinced. Then again, I could tell him Rowan once nannied for the British Royal Family and he'd find something lacking about her.

All because he didn't make the decision to hire her.

"I appreciate all your help in finding the last few nannies. If it doesn't work out, I'll talk to Dana. But so far, Rowan's been more than great."

I step past him before he can argue, that familiar sensation creeping in as I walk toward the nurse's station. Even though I'm an adult, Robert still has a way of making me feel like I'm constantly falling short. Like I'm not good enough.

I shouldn't care what he thinks. I try to tell myself I don't.

But he's Cora's father.

I think a part of me will always want his approval.

Will always try to please him.

Will always try to prove that I *am* good enough.

And he'll probably always make me feel like I'm inadequate.

My phone vibrates in my pocket, and I retrieve it. When I see Rowan's name flash on the screen, my stomach drops, panic overtaking me.

I open the message, already bracing for disaster.

ROWAN:

Thought you might like proof of life to ease your mind.

Below it is a picture of Jemmy holding up today's newspaper like a hostage.

I can't stop the laugh that escapes my throat. It feels foreign to laugh again after all this time.

ME:

Hope he's not giving you too much trouble.

ROWAN:

Never.

"That's something I haven't seen in a while," a voice cuts through.

I snap my head up, clicking off the screen as one of the nurses approaches.

"What's that?" I ask Nancy.

"You. Smiling. Did you meet someone?" she asks in a hushed voice, knowing all too well how Robert would react.

After all, Nancy is Cora's best friend.

Was Cora's best friend.

I open my mouth, trying to formulate a response.

I *did* meet someone.

And she is absolutely the reason I'm smiling.

But it's not like that.

Except my brain immediately reminds me of the way I kept stealing a glance her way as she made breakfast this morning.

The black leggings.

The t-shirt that rode up when she reached for the cabinets.

The tattoo of a thorny vine snaking out from under her shirt and along her collarbone.

I shouldn't be wondering what the rest of it looks like.

But I am.

I'm also wondering what other tattoos she might have.

And where.

"With what time?" I respond with a nervous laugh, worried if anyone might see through me it's Nancy. "And I'm not interested in meeting anyone."

She raises an eyebrow. "So you plan to play the grieving widower forever?"

I exhale slowly, shaking my head.

It's not the first time I've had this conversation.

At first, no one brought it up. The wound was still open, the pain too raw.

But over the past few months, people have started to mention it, especially as we near the one-year mark.

"Do you really think that's what Cora would have wanted for you?" she adds gently. "And her kids?"

"I just…" I blow out another long breath as I run a hand through my hair. "I'm not ready."

"We're never ready. But that doesn't mean we should close down and stop living. *You* shouldn't stop living, Hayden."

I search my brain for something to say, insist I'm happy. But I can't seem to say the words. Instead, I grab my phone and show her the picture of Jemmy.

"The nanny sent proof of life. That's what I was smiling at. He looks like a miniature hostage."

She laughs softly, a twinkle of nostalgia forming in her eye. "He looks so much like her."

"He does."

We stare at the screen for a beat longer than necessary. Then I clear my throat and return my phone to my pocket. "What do we have today?"

"Mr. Alba's in room two."

I arch a brow. "Again?"

"He's convinced the twitch in his left eyelid is brain cancer," she says cheerfully, handing me a tablet.

"Of course it is," I mutter under my breath.

While I would never assume to know more about a person's body than they do, ever since Mr. Alba's wife passed away earlier in the year, he's been to this clinic at least once a week, sometimes more.

I get the feeling he's just lonely, so he makes up some excuse to come here.

I head down the hallway toward the exam rooms, pulling up Mr. Alba's file on my tablet. As I'm about to knock on the door, my phone buzzes again.

A ridiculous spark of anticipation rushes through me, and I quickly open Rowan's message.

It's another picture. But this time, it's a selfie of her and Jemmy, roaring at the camera like dinosaurs.

ROWAN:

Jemmy says ROAR!

My chest tightens. Jemmy looks happy. Really happy. And Rowan looks so alive. Like joy is her default setting.

I wonder what it would be like to go through life that

way. To find joy in even the small things. I trace my gaze over her face. From her bright blue eyes. To her button nose. To her high cheekbones with a hint of pink. To her full lips.

I quickly shake my head, pocketing my phone.

Rowan's my nanny.

My *employee*.

I'm older. A single dad still grieving my wife's death.

Or maybe that's the excuse I've been hiding behind for too long now.

Either way, as I see patient after patient, Rowan's smile lingers in the back of my mind.

And for the first time in a while, I don't hate how it makes me feel.

EIGHT

Rowan

Music fills the kitchen, low but steady. I genuinely don't understand how anyone cooks without music. It's like trying to shower in silence. Technically possible, but deeply unsettling.

Presley stands on a stool by the island, her dark hair pulled back in a ponytail, sleeves pushed up. Jemmy sits in his high chair, reading a book to one of his dinosaurs.

The house smells like garlic and basil.

In other words... Heaven.

I might be overstepping. Technically, I was hired to help with the kids, not cook dinner. But after learning Hayden usually doesn't sit down to eat with them, I couldn't help myself.

I know what it's like to have parents who can't be bothered to eat dinner with you.

I don't want that for these kids.

Plus, I've been itching to cook something real.

Not that there's anything wrong with grilled cheese. I love a good grilled cheese. But there's something deeply satisfying about breading chicken, simmering sauce, and making a mess you can justify because it ends in a delicious meal.

To my surprise, Presley wanted to help.

She'd probably learn more from Dylan, considering she went to culinary school, but I've always loved cooking. There's something grounding about it. Predictable. Safe.

Presley seems to feel that way, too.

"Now we bread the chicken," I say, pointing to the bowls lined up on the counter. "Flour first, then egg, then breadcrumbs. Want me to show you?"

She nods, her eyes focused.

I pick up a piece of raw chicken and coat it in flour, tapping off the excess before dipping it into the egg mixture, then pressing it into the breadcrumbs.

"Want to try?"

I wasn't sure I'd find anything that would pull her away from her sketchpad, but the second I asked her to help, something shifted. Like she's used to being overlooked because she's quiet.

Quiet doesn't mean incapable.

Presley carefully sets the chicken into the flour, coating every inch with determination. But when she transfers it to the egg, it slips off the fork, egg splashing everywhere, including my hair and shirt.

Presley freezes, shoulders tensing, her eyes darting away like she's bracing for impact.

I laugh and gently squeeze her arm. "It's okay. You don't want to know how many times I've done that."

She looks up at me, relieved, then smiles before moving the chicken to the final bowl and pressing it into the breadcrumbs like I showed her.

She sets the fully coated chicken on the plate beside mine and looks at me expectantly.

"Great job! Want to do another one?"

This time, she doesn't hesitate. She reaches for another piece of chicken and starts the process all over again.

While she works, I fill a pot with water and set it on the stove, turning on the burner. By the time I'm done, Presley is finishing her last piece of chicken and adding it to the plate.

"You did amazing. These look better than when I do it."

She beams, pride physically oozing from her.

The sound of the front door closing echoes through the house, and we both look toward the doorway.

A few seconds later, Hayden appears, stopping short as he takes in the kitchen.

My first thought is the mess — flour on the counter, remnants of garlic on the cutting board, splashes from the sauce on the stove.

"I promise I'll clean everything once dinner's in the oven," I assure him, hoping he won't use this as a reason to fire me.

It's a strange thought, considering being a nanny or

holding down any sort of long-term job was the last thing I wanted twenty-four hours ago.

I still can't say this is a long-term thing, but I'd like to stay here more than a day.

"It's fine. I just…" He trails off, looking between Presley and Jemmy. "Usually by this point, the nannies I hired would be on the couch and the kids would be glued to the TV."

"I'm not like most nannies."

"I'm beginning to realize that." His tone is low and soft as his gaze drifts over me. Not in a way that feels inappropriate, but enough to send a small thrill through me, awareness prickling my skin.

I look away, needing to focus on something other than the way my body responds to his presence. Especially when he looks at me like this.

"I hope you like chicken parmigiana." I set a sauté pan on the stove and ignite a burner. "I figured it was a safe bet. I mean, who doesn't like chicken parm?"

"You don't have to cook for me. Just the kids."

"I can do both. That way you can all eat together. Plus Presley likes it." I gesture to the plate of breaded chicken. "She did all of those."

He looks at her. "Is that right?"

She gives a slight shrug, averting her gaze.

"You did great," I tell her. "Own it."

She perks up, a smile curving on her lips.

After adding a bit of oil to the pan, I turn back to Hayden. "Why don't you go get comfortable? This should be done in about thirty minutes. I wanted it ready when you got home, but my timing's still a work in progress."

"It's okay," he says quickly. "And…thanks."

"Of course."

He lingers for a moment longer, like he wants to say something else. Then he turns and heads out of the kitchen.

NINE

Hayden

The house feels different.

It's cleaner, for one. The floor is clutter-free. Shoes are lined up instead of scattered like leaves. There's no vague sense of chaos humming under the surface. No half-finished mess waiting for me to deal with the second I step inside.

None of the nannies Robert suggested ever cleaned like this. They'd tidy up after whatever disaster the kids created while they were on duty, but that was it. If there were shoes and socks scattered on the floor when they got here in the morning, they'd still be here when I arrived home. They never looked ahead. Never went beyond the bare minimum.

Sometimes they didn't even do that.

And they definitely didn't cook for me.

Not that I expected or asked them to. But it's

surprising how good it feels not to walk through the door already bracing myself.

With the last few nannies, I barely had a chance to set my keys down before they were heading out, leaving me to jump straight into dad mode.

Not Rowan.

Even after a day full of keeping Jemmy entertained, she's giving me time to myself.

I slip into my bedroom and take a quick shower, letting the hot water pour over me, rinsing the antiseptic smell of the office off my skin. I stand under the stream, eyes closed, enjoying the quiet.

But the longer I remain here, the guiltier I feel, so I finish quickly and dry off, pulling on jeans and a t-shirt before heading back downstairs.

Rowan's voice carries through the living room before I even reach the kitchen.

"Now you can put some sauce on each piece of chicken."

She's obviously giving Presley instructions.

When I walked into the house earlier, I was shocked to see Presley helping Rowan. To see her willingly doing anything other than sitting quietly with her sketchpad is extremely rare. But Rowan seems to have coaxed her out of her shell.

I slow my steps and linger in the doorway of the kitchen so I can watch them without interrupting.

Presley stands by the island, spooning sauce over breaded chicken with careful precision. Rowan lingers beside her, relaxed, present, like she has nowhere else to be.

My daughter looks happier. Lighter. More at ease than she has in a long time.

Maybe because Rowan doesn't talk to her like she's fragile. Or broken. Or like there's something wrong with her.

She talks to her like she's a regular kid.

"Next up is mozzarella," Rowan instructs. "You could use shredded, but I like the fresh stuff." She leans in conspiratorially. "Mostly because I can eat it while I work."

She pops a slice into her mouth.

Presley grins and follows suit.

Rowan looks up, catching sight of me. She gives me a small smile that shouldn't have any effect on me. But a strange warmth fills me.

Then she turns back to Presley, who carefully arranges the cheese over the chicken. When she finishes, there's one slice left.

Presley snatches it and shoves it into her mouth, her eyes bright with triumph.

"Hey!" Rowan gasps. "You beat me to it." She winks, lifting a cheese grater I didn't even know I owned. "Last step. Parmesan. Because there's no such thing as too much cheese."

She picks up a block of cheese and rubs it against the grater. Once there's a large pile of cheese, they sprinkle it over the chicken together.

"Thank you for your help," she says warmly after sliding the casserole dish into the oven. "Now we wait for the cheese to get all melty and gooey."

Presley beams as she heads toward the table. Then

she changes course and walks straight to me. Before I can process what's happening, she wraps her arms around my waist.

I stiffen out of instinct.

I can't remember the last time Presley hugged me like this. Or anyone, really. After Cora died, everything shifted. She closed down. Shut out the world. We both did.

Pushing out a breath, I pull her closer, my arms tightening around her. The contact feels grounding. Real. A reminder of what's important.

When she pulls away, she skips to the table, acting as if hugging me is the most normal thing in the world when it's been months since she's initiated this kind of contact with anyone.

I push off the wall and join Rowan by the island. She checks the spaghetti, then opens the fridge and pulls out romaine, tomatoes, and a cucumber.

"So," I begin, grabbing the lettuce and a knife. "Things go okay today?"

"We had a great day," she replies, slicing tomatoes. "Jemmy taught me how to roar like a dinosaur. And I taught him some yoga poses."

"Yoga?" I glance at Jemmy. "He's not even two."

"It helped him burn energy and wind down before his nap. Plus, you're never too young to check in with your body." She looks at Jemmy. "Tell Daddy what you learned."

"Down dog!" Jemmy announces proudly.

"That's right."

I smile despite myself. "Good job, buddy. You'll have to show me."

Jemmy slams his hands on the tray and kicks his legs straight out, attempting the pose from his high chair.

"Maybe later."

"K, Dada."

I put the romaine into a colander and bring it to the sink, rinsing it. "I have to admit," I begin as I place the lettuce into the salad bowl. "I'm impressed."

Rowan arches a brow. "Were your expectations so low that you'd be surprised to learn I managed to keep your kids alive?"

"No." I laugh nervously. "Maybe. I just…"

"Like I said this morning… Kids feed off your energy. If you're tense, they're tense. If you're relaxed, they relax too. Now why don't *you* go relax with your kids while I finish up?"

"I can help clean." I reach for the bowls from the breading station.

But before I can bring them over to the sink, she wraps her hand around my forearm.

The contact sends heat skittering along my skin, sharp and unexpected. Every nerve seems to zero in on that one point of contact, like my body's been waiting for it.

It's not the first time it's happened either. Every single time she's touched me, my body reacts this way.

But this time, it's even more pronounced.

Because this time, there's no barrier. It's skin against skin.

It's probably because it's been so long since I've felt anyone touch me.

Since Cora.

And even then, it never felt like this. Like something inside me is waking up, confused and unwelcome and very much alive.

"The only thing you need to do," Rowan says softly, "is spend time with your kids."

"Okay," I respond because it's the only thing I can manage right now, all my focus on the place where her skin meets mine.

"Okay," she echoes, then lets go.

It takes my legs a second to remember how to move. Then I join my kids at the table in the breakfast nook, looking between Jemmy and Presley. I search my brain for something to say, but I draw a blank. These are my kids, for crying out loud. They have my DNA running through them. It shouldn't be this hard.

And what makes it worse is that Rowan doesn't seem to have this problem, even though she was a stranger to them yesterday. Yet she connects with them effortlessly while I feel like I'm fumbling through my own life.

"How was school?" I ask Presley, unsure what else to say.

She shrugs, her way of showing indifference.

She's indifferent about most everything these days.

"Are you excited about your field trip next week?"

She grabs her notepad, writes something, and slides it toward me.

Do I have to go?

At least her handwriting has improved since she stopped talking.

Her therapist suggested teaching her sign language. I considered it. Even signed her up for classes. But Robert talked me out of it. Said it would only encourage her to remain silent.

I didn't argue. I didn't argue about much back then, too numb from grief. Now I'm not so sure it was the right call. If Cora were here, I'm pretty sure she'd tell her father to mind his own business and would do what's in Presley's best interests.

Rowan returns with plates, placing one in front of Presley and me. Presley's chicken is cut into neat pieces, and she has carrots instead of salad. Jemmy has bite-sized portions, too, and to my surprise, he digs in immediately.

"If you don't need anything else, I'm going to head to my room," Rowan states. "Everything's cleaned. You just need to load the dishwasher."

"Why don't you eat with us?" I suggest.

She lifts a container. "I packed mine to go. This is your family time."

She kisses Jemmy's head. "Thanks for playing with me today, bud." Then she moves toward Presley, giving her a squeeze. "Want to help me cook again tomorrow?"

Presley nods eagerly, her entire expression lighting up, a stark contrast from moments ago when I attempted to strike up a conversation.

"You got it," Rowan replies, then looks my way. "Good night, boss."

"Good night," I say as she turns and makes her way toward the in-law apartment.

When the sound of her footsteps fades and my kids turn their attention back to me, I know we're all thinking the same thing.

That the kitchen already seems empty without her.

TEN

Rowan

I close my door softly behind me and lean against it for half a second, allowing the quiet to wash over me.

Thank god I unpacked during Jemmy's nap, because if I had to do it right now, I might actually cry. I'm exhausted in that deep, bone-heavy way that only comes from spending an entire day with a small human who constantly needs you.

But it's a good kind of tired.

I head into my temporary bedroom and change into a pair sleep shorts and a t-shirt that's seen better days, then grab my container of chicken parm and spaghetti before collapsing onto the couch. The cushions sink under my weight, and I hunch over the coffee table as I eat, but I don't care. I can't even think about sitting at a table right now.

It's been one day. One.

And I'm already counting down to the weekend. Not because I don't want to be here. But because I want a full day where I don't have to move.

Still, as tired as I am, my heart feels full.

Jemmy is pure magic. Big imagination. Boundless energy. The kind of kid who makes the world feel brighter just by being in it.

And Presley is such a sweet girl. Quiet. Observant. Attuned to everything and everyone.

In the few hours we spent together today, I saw her walls lower a fraction. Enough to let me in.

I consider that a win.

After I finish eating, I rinse out the container, brush my teeth, and crawl into bed, sighing against the mattress. I haven't been in bed this early in years, but I don't care.

I flip on the TV and scroll until I land on a show I've seen a dozen times. Comfort background noise. Something familiar.

I've just settled in when my phone lights up with a video call, Emily's name flashing on the screen.

I groan softly, not wanting to talk to anyone right now, my best friend included. But I don't want to worry her. So I sit up and accept the call.

"Hey, Em."

She frowns immediately. "What happened? Where are you? That doesn't look like your van. Are you okay?"

"I'm fine. I promise."

She scrunches her nose. "Then where are you?"

"At the in-law apartment of the family I'm nannying for."

Her hazel eyes widen. "What? How did that happen? When we talked yesterday morning, you were literally planning your next adventure."

"Maybe I found it. I had this opportunity and—"

"You said yes." She sighs knowingly.

"I had to."

"I know." She smooths a wayward strand of blonde hair behind her ear. "So who are you nannying for? Are you still in the same town? What did you say it was? Maple Glen or something?"

"Sycamore Falls." I laugh. "And yes. I'm still here. One of the volunteers at the shelter asked if I'd be interested in nannying for her older brother. He's a doctor. Two kids. Seven-year-old daughter, almost two-year-old son."

She waggles her brows. "Is he single?"

"Of course you'd go there."

"Do you blame me? You know I'm a sucker for the boss-nanny trope. Forced proximity. Age gap. I can read that all day, every day."

"You're horrible," I respond nonchalantly.

But I can't ignore the warmth filling my stomach over the idea of a little boss-nanny action with Hayden. Of his unshaven jawline scraping between my thighs. Of his hands roaming my frame.

Which is the last thing I need to be thinking about right now, but I can't help it.

It's been so long since I've been with a man.

I make a mental note to find my vibrator and put it

to use… Especially if I'm to see Hayden in a suit every day. Or in gray sweatpants. Or even in jeans. I don't think the man has a single bad look.

"So…is he?" Emily cuts through my thoughts.

"Is he what?"

"Single."

I square my shoulders. "We didn't discuss relationship status."

"Well, is there a Mrs. Doctor?"

"No. It's only him and the kids."

"Divorced?"

I part my lips, considering her question.

"I don't think so. There's a sort of…sadness in this house." I lower my voice. "I think his wife may have passed away."

Emily's face softens. "That's heartbreaking."

"It is. And his daughter… She doesn't talk."

"Is she deaf?"

"No. Just doesn't speak. I'm pretty sure she can, but she just…doesn't."

Emily studies me with the same analytical gaze I've grown used to over the years. "You see yourself in her."

I exhale a long breath, leaning back against the headboard. "I know what it's like to have people look at you like you're different. After my surgery… Hell, even before when I was wondering if I'd ever step foot out of that hospital again… I hated it. Everyone tiptoeing around me. Treating me like I might keel over and die any second. The way people looked when they came to visit me. Like I was already dead."

"Most people don't know what to say," she offers sympathetically.

"I'm still the same person I was before."

She shakes her head gently, her painted red lips curving into a smile. "No. You're better. You finally stopped running yourself into the ground."

"Don't remind me," I mutter, my stomach tightening from the reminder of my old life.

How I used to work seventy or eighty hours a week trying to prove myself.

How I'd chosen success over relationships.

How I'd forgotten what's important in life.

Until I got the wake-up call I needed.

"How long are you staying?" Emily asks.

"I'm not sure. Maybe until the winds change."

She laughs. "Okay, Mary Poppins."

"You know I don't make long-term plans anymore. I'll stay until I'm ready to move on."

"Just promise me one thing."

"What's that?"

"That you'll still come home for my birthday. No way in hell am I celebrating the first anniversary of turning twenty-nine without you."

"I wouldn't miss it for the world."

"Good." She flashes me a smile. "I miss you. Miss having my bestie right around the corner."

"I miss you, too. But I need to do this. Need to have as many adventures while I can."

"I know," Emily responds with a long sigh.

She hates when I remind her of this, but it's the truth. Hell, I'm lucky to even be alive now, and it's only because someone with my same blood type was thoughtful enough to donate their organs before passing away.

Truthfully, I didn't expect to wake up from that surgery, not after learning all the risks involved. Even when I did, I expected my body to reject the donor heart, as my doctor warned could happen.

But it didn't. I survived.

Still, I know the statistics. Most heart transplants only last fifteen years before they start failing. Twenty years if I'm lucky. Thirty years if I'm *really* lucky. A follow-up transplant *is* possible, but there are greater risks. Greater complications.

Greater chance of rejection and ultimately…death.

This is why I quit my job at my father's law firm and used my savings to buy a van. So I can experience everything this world has to offer before my time is up.

"I think what you're doing is great," she adds. "I just worry about you."

"I'm fine. Promise. I'm taking all my meds every day like I'm supposed to. Plus, I'm nannying for a freaking doctor, for crying out loud."

"Does he know?"

"I'm not sure that's a topic of conversation for my first day of work. 'I know you just hired me, but about a year-and-a-half ago, I was diagnosed with arrhythmogenic right ventricular cardiomyopathy and would have died if I hadn't received a donor heart. But I'm fine now.'"

"Don't you think you should tell him? Just in case?"

"You worry too much." I avert my gaze, picking at a

pull in the duvet. "Plus, he treats me like there's nothing wrong with me. Like I'm not on borrowed time."

"Unlike me," she exhales.

"You don't do that. You just…care about me. That's all."

"And I always will." She wipes her eyes. "Enough of this. Tell me about the doctor. Is he hot?"

While this is the last thing I want to talk about, I can sense Emily needs a pick-me-up, so I give her what she wants.

It's not like I have to lie about it either.

"Let's just say I don't know which I like better," I begin with a mischievous grin. "Him in pajama pants, a suit, or gray sweatpants."

"Gray sweatpants? He actually wears gray sweatpants?"

I nod slowly, all too familiar with her obsession with hot men in gray sweatpants. She even follows several social media accounts devoted solely to this topic.

"And he looks damn good in them. Based on a cursory glance, he's definitely packing underneath them, too. See what saying yes can get you?" I giggle as a knock sounds at my door.

My stomach drops, heat blooming on my cheeks. How thick are the walls? Could Hayden have overheard what we were talking about? God, I hope not.

"I have to go," I whisper. "There's someone at my door."

"Keep me updated."

"I will. Love you."

"Love you, too."

I end the call and scramble off the bed, drawing in a calming breath before opening the door.

Hayden stands there in pajama pants and a t-shirt, looking just as surprised to see me as I am to see him. Which is odd, considering he's the one who knocked.

Then I realize what I'm wearing. Tiny shorts that barely cover my ass. Thin t-shirt. No bra.

And it's chilly.

Fantastic.

"Is everything okay?" I ask, aiming for casual, despite the fact that I can feel my nipples straining against my shirt.

He blinks, lifting his gaze to mine. "I just...wanted to thank you. For today."

"No thanks required. It's my job."

He shakes his head. "You did more than I asked. I can't remember the last time I actually ate with my kids, other than when my mom invites us over. So thanks for that."

"Of course."

He lingers for a beat, his eyes dipping to my legs again before slowly traveling back up my body, pausing on my chest. But not on my nipples. Instead, he's studying my tattoo.

Or, more accurately, the scar my tattoo hides.

I adjust my shirt in the hopes of covering it up. This is one of the reasons I got the tattoo once my doctor said it was safe to do so. I was so tired of people seeing my scar and feeling sorry for me.

Now, most people don't look past the intricate network of vines and roses snaking over my chest and along my collarbone, the scar blending seamlessly into the design.

But Hayden isn't most people. He's a doctor. And I can't shake the feeling he can see what I'm hiding.

"If you don't need anything else, I'm pretty beat. Jemmy tired me out today." I casually pull at the fabric of my t-shirt to cover up more of the scar. But by doing so, it reveals a sliver of my stomach.

"Right. Of course." He hesitates, studying me with unnerving intensity. "I just wanted to let you know I appreciate you. Even if I didn't show it yesterday."

"We're all allowed bad days. Good night, Hayden."

He nods, his gaze briefly lingering on my tattoo once more before meeting my eyes. "Good night, Rowan."

ELEVEN

Hayden

I stare at the ceiling as the sun creeps over the horizon, pale light bleeding through the narrow gap in the curtains.

My restlessness used to be caused by the kids — midnight fevers, bad dreams, Presley climbing into our bed with her stuffed unicorn tucked under her arm.

But that phase has passed.

The kids sleep just fine now.

I'm the one who doesn't.

Ever since Cora died, sleep has been…difficult. Elusive. Like something I no longer deserve.

After over a decade of sharing a bed with someone, it's a struggle to sleep alone. The bed is too big. Too cold. Too…empty.

In the weeks following her death, I'd often dream

she was still here, sleeping in the bed beside me, her skin warm, her chest rising and falling with her even breaths.

But her face was wrong. Blank. Still.

It was the same expression she wore when I was finally allowed into the ICU and they told me there was no neurological activity. No chance. No miracle waiting to happen.

The same expression she wore during the honor walk, the hallway lined with nurses, doctors, and staff as they wheeled her toward the operating room where she would give four people a second chance at life.

While her one chance was erased.

I've been on the other side of that conversation more times than I can count. I've delivered those words with practiced calm. Explained brain death. Advocated for organ donation. Tried to give them hope in its strangest, cruelest form.

Learning a loved one has died is never easy.

But after losing Cora, I wouldn't wish losing a loved one to brain death on anyone, even my worst enemies.

Because the body lies to you.

The chest still rises. The monitors still beep. The heart still beats. It gives you hope when every rational part of you knows better.

I knew it was statistically impossible.

Yet as I sat beside her for those few days while they coordinated her organ donation, I prayed for a miracle.

That sliver of hope still keeps me awake, even a year later.

Despite knowing the impossibility, I still wonder if I gave up too soon.

All because I saw her chest rise and fall.

That image will probably stay with me for the rest of my life.

Abandoning all hope of sleep, I throw the duvet off me to stand. Moving toward the windows, I pull back the curtains to allow some natural light into the room, hoping it will help clear away the cobwebs.

But as I do, my eyes fall on a figure in my back yard.

Rowan.

She's stretched out on a yoga mat, wearing dark leggings and a tank top that clings to her like it were made for her. She moves slowly, her body flowing from one pose to the next with ease.

The morning light catches in her dark hair, high-lighting her slender physique. And her tattoo. The vines and roses curl over her skin, beautiful and intricate.

From this far away, it looks like any tattoo.

But I know what I saw last night.

A scar covered by ink, deliberately disguised.

I probably never would have noticed it if she hadn't tugged her shirt higher. At first, I thought she was uncomfortable because it was obvious she wasn't wearing a bra.

And her nipples were rock hard.

But when she didn't attempt to cover her chest and instead kept tugging her shirt higher, I noticed a red scar.

Now, I can't stop thinking about it. Can't stop wondering what the scar could be from. I couldn't get a close look at it, so it could be from anything, from an accident requiring stitches to open-heart surgery.

Which is ridiculous, considering she's in her twenties.

Healthy. Vibrant. Standing barefoot in the cold morning air, doing yoga like she doesn't have a single care in the world.

I squeeze my eyes shut, shaking off my concern.

Whatever that scar is, it's none of my damn business. She's my employee. The reason for her scar has nothing to do with her ability to do her job.

I force my gaze from her, continuing through the room and opening the rest of the curtains. But as I reach the last window, movement catches my eye again, and before I can stop myself, I glance back at Rowan.

She folds forward, giving me the perfect view of her ass.

And god… What an ass it is.

I clench my jaw, every muscle in my body becoming rigid.

Including the one in my pants.

It's been a long time since I've wanted like this. Since my body reacted without permission. Grief and desire collide in my chest, confusing and unwelcome.

I close my eyes and press my forehead to the window, berating myself to get it together.

This is my employee, for crying out loud. She lives in my house. Takes care of my children. Not to mention, she's only a few years older than my younger sister.

My twenty-five-year-old younger sister.

And I'm on the other side of forty.

The reminder alone should be enough to kill the feeling.

It isn't.

My hand moves to the waistband of my pajama pants, and I wrap my fingers around my erection, giving it a few tugs. I moan, relief washing over me.

I should stop right now. The last thing I should be doing is jerking off while I watch my goddamn nanny do yoga as the sun rises in the distance.

But I can't look away.

And I can't seem to stop myself, especially as she lowers herself onto the mat, positioning herself on her hands and knees, her ass facing me.

It makes me imagine how she'd look if she were in the same position on my bed. Naked.

I rub myself harder, groaning at the image in my head.

What would she be like?

I may not know her all that well, but I have a feeling she'd be fucking incredible. She wouldn't be timid or shy. Wouldn't be remotely ashamed of exploring each and every one of her desires.

And I'd be more than happy to help.

She wouldn't just lie there and make me feel like she were counting down the seconds until it was over, like it felt Cora did those last few years of our marriage.

No. Rowan would have sex the way she seems to do everything in life.

Without restraint.

Without fear.

Without shame.

I'm so turned on, I can practically feel her clenching around me as she screams my name. In reality, it's my hand squeezing my dick and me who's moaning her name as my release overtakes me.

I frantically jerk at my erection while thick streams coat my pajama pants, my orgasm never seeming to end as I ride wave after wave of bliss.

When the haze lifts, I don't move for several seconds, breathing heavily as I struggle to wrap my head around what I just did.

What the fuck is wrong with me?

Maybe my mom's right.

Maybe it's time I put myself out there again. Even if I'm not ready for any sort of commitment, I could use some physical intimacy in my life… As evidenced by the fact that I just jerked off fantasizing about my kids' nanny.

I spin from the window and all but run into the bathroom, hastily shedding my pants and t-shirt, as if evidence of a horrific crime.

By the time I step into the shower, I'm wound tight with shame and guilt. The water is scalding, steam filling the room, but I don't care. I need the pain, the burning sensation anchoring me back to reality.

Once I'm dressed in my suit, I slip out of my room and hurry down the stairs, checking my watch as I turn the corner into the kitchen…

And run right into a tall, lithe body.

Instinct kicks in, and my hand shoots out, steadying Rowan by the hip.

She inhales sharply, her eyes flying to mine.

I should let go. Put as much space between us as

possible, especially when I feel that stirring in my pants, despite having just jerked off.

But my brain doesn't seem to get the message. Instead, my fingers move of their own volition, caressing the sliver of exposed skin above her waist.

For half a second, neither of us moves. She doesn't push out of my grip. And I continue to caress her soft skin.

She darts out her tongue to moisten her lips, and I snap out of my trance, dropping my hold on her as if I've been burned.

"Sorry," she says nervously, lifting the baby monitor. "Jemmy's stirring."

"Of course," I manage, allowing her to pass before rushing toward the coffee machine to make myself a cup.

Even then, the image of her lingers.

The warmth of her skin.

Her sweet perfume.

It's only been one day, and yet she seems to have already weaseled her way under my skin.

And I have no idea what to do about it.

TWELVE

Rowan

It's been over a week.

Long enough for routines to settle.

Long enough for the house to stop feeling foreign.

Long enough for me to feel like I've been here much longer.

Despite how much I'm enjoying my new job with these two amazing kids, I can't deny I'm looking forward to the weekend.

Two days of sleeping in. Letting my body recover. Maybe stopping by the shelter if I can carve out the time. I miss the dogs. Miss the way they love without expectation.

Maybe I'll eventually be able to convince Hayden to let me take Jemmy to walk the dogs. There's no doubt in my mind he'd love it. Jemmy seems to have the same thirst for adventure I do.

I want to do everything I can to nurture that.

Which is why I took a risk and asked — or, more appropriately, begged — Hayden to let me take Jemmy to story time at the library today.

He was reluctant at first, but I reminded him of the importance of socialization, even for young kids, so he eventually agreed and allowed me to take his spare car. Although he made me swear I'd keep my hands at ten and two on the wheel, that I wouldn't text, and wouldn't go even a mile over the speed limit.

He was definitely a bit overbearing, but it was worth it.

Jemmy loved every second of it. He even made some new friends, so afterwards we went across the street to the park to spend even more time with them.

By the time we got home, Jemmy was exhausted.

Getting him down for his nap was effortless. No fussing. No protest. Just a soft dinosaur roar and heavy-lidded eyes.

I close the door to his room and stand in the hallway for a second longer than necessary, listening to the hush of the house.

Silence like this is rare.

I consider napping myself, but I know if I lie down, I won't want to get back up. So after making myself a quick salad, I head toward the toy room and start picking up all the toys Jemmy took out to play with this morning.

It's not as bad as it usually is, since we were out of the house most of the morning. But I still spot a trail of cereal leading to a flipped-over bowl. I pick up what I can, but there are still crumbs, so I go hunting for the vacuum, finding one in the hallway closet.

After vacuuming the toy room, I decide to keep going. The living room. The hallway. The office. I never thought I would enjoy vacuuming as much as I do now. Maybe because I've been living in a van for the past few months, but there's something oddly therapeutic about sucking up all the dust and grime, leaving behind something clean.

Like a fresh start.

After I finish in the office, I bend to unplug the cord behind the desk, and my elbow hits a stack of folders, knocking them onto the floor, papers spilling everywhere.

"Crap," I mutter, hastily gathering them up and reorganizing them into a neat stack.

That's when I see it.

An envelope half-tucked inside a folder. Plain. Unassuming.

But the return address makes my chest seize so hard I forget how to breathe.

I know that logo. Know that nonprofit.

It's the one I worked with to send a letter to the family of the person who donated their heart to me.

I should forget I ever saw it.

Hayden's a doctor. There could be dozens of reasons he might have a letter from this nonprofit.

But my fingers move anyway, pulling out the envelope and lifting the opened flap to retrieve the contents.

My heart races, my hands becoming unsteady as I unfold the piece of paper.

And when I do, it feels as if all the air has been sucked from my lungs, the room spinning around me.

I know this letter.

I *wrote* this letter.

Every word. Every carefully chosen sentence. I can recite them from memory.

I'd spent weeks on it, knowing it might be the only opportunity I'd get to say what I wanted to.

And now I'm staring at those same words again.

Which could mean only one thing.

"No," I whisper, my throat tightening.

This doesn't make sense.

I don't want it to make sense.

Don't want to consider that the only reason I'm alive today is because Hayden lost someone.

Because Presley and Jemmy lost someone.

But I need to know.

Despite the voice in my head telling me to forget I ever saw this, I grab the folder and rummage through it.

More letters and cards.

But behind them all, I find a program.

The memorial for Cora Lawrence.

Her photo steals the air from my lungs.

Presley's eyes stare back at me. Jemmy's smile.

And then I see her date of death.

The same day as my rebirth, as I call it. The day I received the heart that's now beating in my chest.

I want to believe it could all be a coincidence, but what other reason would there be for Hayden to have this letter?

There's only one possible explanation.

Because his wife's heart beats inside me.

Every sound drops away except the thud in my chest, the rhythm that once belonged to her.

I'd imagined this moment before. Wondered what it would feel like to find out who my donor was.

I never imagined this.

Never imagined loving the children of the woman who saved my life.

Never imagined sleeping under the same roof as the man who lost her.

Never imagined thinking of them as my family.

The sound of the front door slamming shut startles me, snapping me out of my thoughts.

Presley's not supposed to be home for another half-hour.

I quickly shove all the papers back into the folder despite my shaky hands, returning everything to the desk.

Then I head down the hallway and into the living room just as Hayden storms toward the stairs.

He stops short when he sees me, his eyes on fire. "Where were you? Why weren't you answering your phone?"

I stare at him, dumbfounded. He asked me a question. I need to respond.

But I can't find the words.

Can't seem to do anything but stare at him.

At the man whose wife's heart is beating inside my chest.

It makes another wave of emotion well up inside me, but I do my best to push it down.

"My phone?" I manage to squeak out.

"Yes, Rowan. Your goddamn phone."

I blink repeatedly, searching my brain for an answer, still out of it.

"I… I must have forgotten it on the coffee table. I was cleaning before Presley got home—"

"You *forgot* it?" His voice cracks like a whip. "You were supposed to text me the second you got home with Jemmy. The fucking second. So I knew he was okay. So I knew he was safe. And you just…forgot?"

"I did text you."

I move toward the coffee table and grab my phone, my heart sinking when I see all the missed calls and texts from Hayden. Then I navigate to our text thread. But under my latest message is a red warning. The message never sent.

Shit.

"It didn't go through, but I texted. See for yourself." I show him my screen, but he doesn't seem the least bit satisfied.

"And you didn't think to make sure I received the message?"

"I… I'm sorry. But Jemmy's fine. You don't need to worry."

"I'm his father," he snarls, his imposing frame towering over me. "It's my job to worry. To protect them. To keep them safe. Are you always this fucking irresponsible?"

"I'm sorry," I say again. "I—"

"Don't." He holds up his hand, stopping me mid-sentence. "It's obvious this isn't going to work. I need someone who can follow instructions. Who I can trust. That's obviously not you." He stares at me for several long moments. Then he says, "You should go. Before Presley gets home."

I open my mouth, struggling to find the words to defend myself. To make him see he's being unreasonable.

But all I can see is Cora's face.

So I spin and hurry into my suite without saying another word.

I pack in a blur. It doesn't take long, since I don't have much stuff. Then I use my separate entrance to leave, saving me from having to see Hayden again.

As I climb into my van, I wipe the tears from my face, unsure if they're from getting fired, from not being able to say goodbye to Presley and Jemmy, or because of what I just learned.

THIRTEEN

Hayden

Rowan's taillights disappear at the end of the driveway, blinking once before the road curves and swallows her up.

For half a second, I wonder if I overreacted.

Then my chest tightens, the familiar vice grip settling in, and I shove the thought away.

I didn't overreact. It's my job to worry about my kids. To make sure nothing happens to them. To keep them safe.

I storm into the kitchen and open the cabinet over the fridge, grabbing the bottle of whiskey. I don't care that it's not even three o'clock yet. I need something to ease my frayed nerves, my hands still shaking, panic clawing at my chest.

When I'd repeatedly called Rowan and she never answered, I immediately went back there. To that moment. To the hospital hallway that smelled like antiseptic and burnt coffee. Watching a nurse wheel my daughter past me on a stretcher, her face scraped raw, her arm strapped into a makeshift sling.

I'm her father. An emergency room doctor.

Yet I'd never felt so damn helpless.

Useless.

Terrified.

I swore I'd never feel that way again. Swore I'd do everything in my power to keep Jemmy and Presley safe.

They're all I have left, and the mere idea of something happening to either of them claws at me.

So no. I don't think I was out of line.

I pour several fingers into a glass and bring it up to my mouth, taking a large swallow. Alcohol isn't the best coping mechanism, but I need it right now. Need to feel something other than…whatever this is.

As I slam back another large gulp, downing the remainder of the whiskey, the front door opens.

I return the bottle to the cabinet and head toward the foyer. But when Presley sees it's me instead of Rowan, her smile falters.

"Where's Rowan?" my mother asks from behind her.

"Why didn't Beckham or Haley pick up Presley?"

"Beckham couldn't get away from the vineyard, and Haley had to deliver a cake. Where's Rowan?" she presses again.

I part my lips, searching for the words I need. It's not the first time my mother's dropped Presley off from school to learn I've fired the nanny.

But this one feels different.

It shouldn't.

She wasn't in our lives for that long.

But she still managed to leave an impression. On Jemmy. On Presley.

And on me.

"Why don't you go grab a snack?" I say to Presley, hoping my mom will have some wise words to help me break the news to my kids.

But my daughter doesn't budge. Instead, she drops her backpack to the floor with a thud and crosses her arms tight over her stomach.

"Presley," I warn, an edge in my voice.

She still doesn't move.

Stubborn like her mother.

And me.

I blow out a breath and look at my mom. "It didn't work out. She left."

She lifts an eyebrow. "And whose decision was that?"

I steal a glance at Presley in time to see her eyes fill with tears. It twists something sharp in my chest. Makes it harder to admit what I'm about to.

"Mine."

The word barely leaves my mouth before Presley's tears spill over. Anger flashes across her expression, and she turns and storms up the stairs.

"Presley," I whisper-shout after her, her stomping feet echoing in the house. "Quiet. Your brother's napping."

She doesn't care. Her footsteps pound down the hallway, her bedroom door slamming hard enough that the walls seem to rattle.

I freeze, praying Jemmy sleeps through it.

Then the monitor crackles.

And he cries.

"Great," I mutter, dragging a hand down my face.

"That's karma," my mom says dryly.

"For what?" I ask, already heading for the stairs.

She follows close behind. "None of this would have happened if you hadn't fired Rowan. I thought she was doing well. The kids like her. Especially Presley."

I shake my head, but don't argue as I step into Jemmy's room.

He's standing up in his crib, his cheeks flushed, tears streaking down his face. I scoop him up, his small body warm and shaking against mine.

"Hey, Jemmy," I murmur, pressing a kiss to his hair. "Did the loud bang scare you?"

He nods, burying his face in my shoulder.

"It's okay. I'm here now."

He pulls back, sniffling. "Ro-Ro."

"I'm sorry, bud. But she won't be playing with you anymore."

His lower lip trembles as he sobs Rowan's name.

My mom appears in the doorway, arms folded. "Looks like you've got yourself in a pickle. Want to explain why you fired the one nanny your kids actually liked? Hell, the one nanny who actually seemed to like your kids."

"I already told you…" I carry Jemmy over to the changing table. "It didn't work out."

"Why?"

I toss the dirty diaper into the bin and use a wipe to clean him. "She took Jemmy to the library this morning and was supposed to text as soon as they got home. She didn't."

I leave out the part that she did text, but I never received it.

"When I called her, she didn't answer," I continue, dressing Jemmy in a t-shirt and pair of pants. "All I could think was that something happened. Thought I lost him too." I lift my son into my arms, holding him close, inhaling his fresh baby scent.

My mom's expression softens, and she steps closer, resting a hand on my arm. "You can't go there every time someone doesn't answer the phone. Jemmy's fine." She pinches his cheek, and he giggles. "Aren't you, little man?"

He reaches for my mom, and I allow her to take him, grateful he has at least one grandparent who showers him with love and affection.

"But what if he wasn't?"

"I get it," she sighs, arranging Jemmy on her hip as she heads out of his room. I follow her back downstairs. "I worried about you kids every day of my life. I still do. But sometimes, your protectiveness crosses into something else."

She steps off the stairs and into the living room, setting Jemmy down on the mat with his collection of dinosaurs. Then she faces me, dropping her voice.

"Did Rowan explain why she didn't text?"

I wince. "Technically, she did, and the message failed

to send. But she should have made sure it sent. And then she ignored all my calls and texts. Left her cell in the living room while she was cleaning, I guess."

Mom gives me a pointed look. "Do you think maybe you overreacted a bit?"

"There's no such thing when it comes to my kids."

"But is it worth it? Presley's been happier lately. Her teachers have noticed it, too. She's opening up again. Has even been playing with kids at recess instead of keeping to herself."

This information lands harder than I expected. "She has?"

Since we moved here, Presley's been shy. Reserved. Keeps to herself. I've sent her to therapy in the hopes she'd eventually come out of her shell, but nothing has worked.

Until Rowan entered our lives.

"I understand why you were concerned," Mom begins, "but you need to look at the big picture."

"This big picture?"

She nods. "As a parent, every decision you make is with one thing in mind."

"The best interests of the kids."

"Exactly. Based on what I've seen, having Rowan in their lives is definitely in their best interests. She made a mistake, one I bet she won't make again. Don't deprive your kids of a positive influence because you're bull-headed and stubborn." She holds my gaze for a beat, then her lips quirk up into a smile. "Plus, if you want Presley to forgive you anytime soon, I'd apologize, beg Rowan to come back, and offer her a raise."

"A raise?"

"Hazard pay for dealing with you." She winks, then pushes me toward the front door. "I've got the kids. Now go."

Before I know it, I'm being handed my keys and kicked out of my own home by my mom. I'm not sure I ever agreed to do this, but I don't have a choice now. Not if I don't want my kids to despise me for the foreseeable future.

I slide into my car, trying to figure out how to fix this. I start by trying to call Rowan, but it goes to voicemail after one ring, making me think she purposefully ignored my call.

I could stop here. Say I tried.

But Presley's expression replays in my mind. The way Jemmy called for Ro-Ro. The way Rowan brought light back into this house without even trying.

So I crank the ignition and drive away, praying it's not too late.

FOURTEEN

Rowan

"There's nothing you can do?" I ask, leaning against the counter and watching the mechanic tap away at his computer. "There isn't another tire place that might have what I need?"

Of course, this would happen now.

As I was trying to leave town with what little dignity I have left, my van lit up like a Christmas tree with a low tire pressure warning. Thankfully, the auto shop was only a block away.

I'd hoped all I needed was a patch. Not a full set of tires.

And definitely not have to wait until Monday or Tuesday.

"Sorry, ma'am," the mechanic says. "We don't get many vans like this around here. Mostly pickups and sedans. We can order them, but they won't be in until Monday."

I blow out a breath, frustration tightening my throat. But I force myself to swallow it down. I've dealt with worse than a flat tire. Way worse. I refuse to let this derail me.

Still, a small part of me wonders if this is the universe sending me a message that I'm not supposed to leave this town yet.

It looks like it's getting its wish. Because now I'm stuck here for an extra few days. I have no idea where I'll stay, but I'll figure it out.

I always do.

"Can I leave it here with you?" I ask. "I'd rather not have to drive it around with the tire like it is."

"Of course."

"Let me just grab a few things out of it."

"No problem."

I step into the chilly afternoon air and cross the parking lot toward the van. It doesn't take me long to grab what I need, since I'd packed all my stuff when I left Hayden's house.

Correction. When I was *fired*.

The word still stings.

I've never been fired before in my life.

Granted, I should have verified my text had been delivered. Just like Hayden should have seen it wasn't intentional.

But being the arrogant prick he is, he refused. It's probably for the best, all things considered.

I just need to get through the next few days and then I can be back on my way to my next adventure.

I grab my small suitcase and laptop bag, then climb out of the van. As I lock up, I hear footsteps behind me.

"Here are the keys," I begin, looking up. "It—"

I stop cold.

Because it's not the mechanic.

It's Hayden.

But his eyes are no longer full of anger like they were the last time I saw him. They're forlorn, his demeanor at odds with the serious and severe man he usually is.

"W-what are you doing here?" I finally manage to get out.

"Is everything okay?" He looks at the van, then back at me. "What's wrong with your van?"

"Flat tire," I explain. "I need to replace the front two, but they won't be in until Monday."

He nods, but doesn't say anything else. Just stares at me. For a split second, I wonder if he knows the truth.

Did he go into the office and notice the stack of folders was out of place? Did he look through the files and somehow connect the dots?

No. He couldn't have. There was no identifying information in that letter. Just heartfelt words and a sense of gratitude too big to truly capture.

"You still didn't answer my question," I state, placing my hands on my hips. "Why are you here?"

"I was looking for you. I called."

"I know," I snap, the words spilling out before I can stop them. "That's why you fired me, remember? I left my phone in the living room while I vacuumed so you wouldn't come home to a mess. I made a mistake. You've made your point, Hayden." I push past him, storming toward the building.

"I tried calling to apologize," he shouts after me.

I stop in my tracks, turning to face him. "Apologize?"

"I…may have overreacted." He takes a slow step toward me.

"You think?" I snip out.

"I just…" With a long exhale, he shakes his head. "Can we talk?"

A bitter laugh escapes me. "So now you want to talk? You didn't seem interested in what I had to say a few minutes ago."

"And I'm sorry about that. I fucked up. All I'm asking for is five minutes of your time. If you still hate me after listening to what I have to say, you'll never see or hear from me again. Just…give me a chance to make this right."

I should say no.

I've known guys like Hayden before.

I've *worked* with guys like Hayden.

Guys who never take responsibility for their mistakes.

Who are so set in their ways they refuse to admit when they're wrong.

After I got out of the hospital, I swore I'd never surround myself with anyone like that again.

But *is* he like that?

"Let me drop off the keys," I finally say.

Hayden blows out a long breath, his relief palpable. "Thank you."

I step inside and hand the mechanic my keys. After he promises to call Monday once the replacement tires arrive, I head back outside.

"Okay. Talk," I tell Hayden, crossing my arms in front of my chest.

He glances around, obviously uneasy about whatever he wants to tell me. "Do you want to go for a walk?"

I gesture to my suitcase. "I'd rather not drag that all over town."

"You can put it in my car. Afterwards, I'll take you wherever you want to go. Though I'm hoping it's back to where you belong."

"And where's that?" I arch a brow.

"You know where." He gives me a knowing look, and I can't ignore the strange fluttering in my stomach.

Since I first hopped in my van and put my old life in the rearview mirror, I didn't really care about belonging anywhere. I didn't *want* to belong anywhere.

Didn't want to put down roots.

But in only a matter of days, I've felt more at home with Hayden and his kids than I ever did back in Chicago.

Which is why I should walk away right now, especially knowing everything they lost.

But I can't seem to be able to.

Instead, I nod.

He takes my bags and carries them to his car. Once they're safe inside, he glances my way.

"Ready?"

I fall into step beside him, and we walk toward the historic downtown area of Sycamore Falls.

Now that it's approaching December, the storefronts are decked out for the holidays, green wreaths and red bows decorating the lampposts, making it look like something out of a Christmas card.

The sound of conversation and footsteps echo around us, but Hayden doesn't immediately speak. Instead, he remains silent for several minutes, his mouth set in a tight line, his brows furrowed, as if he's trying to figure out what to say.

"I know I can be…"

"Difficult," I offer. "Stubborn. Pigheaded."

He chuckles, and the sound settles in my chest.

In my heart.

His wife's heart.

"Yes. All of that," he agrees. Then his smile drops. "I lost my wife a year ago."

"I'm sorry." I keep my expression neutral, not wanting to give anything away.

"It was an accident," he continues. "A drunk driver ran a red light. T-boned her while she was taking Presley to dance class. Cora walked away with barely a scratch. Presley wasn't as lucky. I was working that night. We used to live in Chicago, and I worked in the emergency room at one of the busiest hospitals there. We were always getting car accident victims wheeled in." He shakes his head, briefly squeezing his eyes shut. "But nothing could have prepared me to see my own daughter being wheeled through those doors, her head and body covered with blood."

I can physically feel his fear. His panic. As if reliving that moment over and over again.

"Is that… Is that why she doesn't talk? Because of the accident?"

"No. She was talking as she came in, which was a relief. She kept telling me how much everything hurt, and I assured her she'd be okay. And she was. Had some broken bones and a concussion, but nothing permanent." He swallows hard. "But Cora…" His voice catches on her name.

"What happened? You said she walked away from the accident without a scratch."

"That's what I thought. She was walking and talking, so I didn't think anything of it. I told her she should get checked out to be on the safe side. She promised she would once Presley was out of surgery and she knew she was okay. I didn't push it. And I should have. If I had…" He trails off, his voice catching.

"She collapsed in the waiting room a short while later. At first, I figured it was just the adrenaline wearing off. But she never came back around. Never regained consciousness."

"Oh god…" I press a hand over my heart instinctively — *her* heart — feeling its steady rhythm beneath my palm.

Hayden's story is so sad. So tragic. To see her walking and talking one minute, thinking she hadn't been injured in an accident, to then watch her collapse and never wake up?

I knew the person who donated my heart had to have been declared brain dead in order for them to be able to retrieve her heart and transplant it into me.

But listening to the details knowing I have her heart is more emotional than I thought it would be.

"She had a brain bleed. Subdural hematoma." His voice fractures. "She was rushed into surgery to drain it, control the swelling. They couldn't. She died a few days later. Presley hasn't spoken since she said goodbye to her mother as they wheeled her into the operating room so they could donate her organs."

I hesitate for a beat. "Do you know who these people are?" I ask, praying he doesn't find my question suspicious, but I have to know. "The people who received her organs?"

"No. And I don't want to know," he declares with determination." I think… I think it would be too hard."

"How so?"

"I already lost her once. If I knew who received any of her organs and something happened to them… It would be like I lost her all over again."

I can understand why he'd feel that way. Transplants can add years you wouldn't have had otherwise, but they're not a permanent solution, especially for someone as young as me. I'll eventually need another transplant, where the risk of rejection or death is much greater.

It's why I left my job.

To live life while I still can.

"That's why I overreacted today. When I couldn't reach you…"

"You thought something happened," I finish as I stop walking.

He nods, facing me. "My brain immediately rewound to that day."

"I'm so sorry," I whisper. "I should have made sure my text went through."

"You made an honest mistake. I didn't handle it well. And I'm sorry. I don't deserve it, but I'd appreciate it if you'd give me another chance. If you'd give *us* another chance. If not for me, for Jemmy and Presley."

I flash him a teasing smile. "Are you using them to convince me to come back?"

"Is it working?"

"Maybe."

"I'll even pay you more." He laughs under his breath. "My mom says you deserve hazard pay for dealing with me."

I grin, meeting his dark eyes. "Your mother's a smart woman."

"She's the best. And is always right. But don't tell her I said that." He winks.

"Of course not."

"What do you say?" He steps toward me. "Will you come back?"

I shift my gaze away from him, taking in the sights and sounds of Sycamore Falls. Of the place I never meant to stay for more than a piece of pie.

But maybe there's a reason I'm still here.

Maybe all the times I've said yes were meant to lead me to this exact place.

To this exact moment.

To these people.

I return my eyes to his, the corners of my mouth curving as I respond, "Yes."

Not because I have to.

But because I *want* to.

Relief visibly rolls off Hayden, his shoulders relaxing. Before I can make sense of it, he wraps his arms around me.

I instantly stiffen, the feel of his body against mine sending sparks of electricity through me.

I've never had this kind of visceral reaction to a hug before.

Is it because the heart beating inside me somehow recognizes him?

Maybe that's why I've felt a strange pull toward him from the very beginning.

Because the way my body melts into him, the way being in his arms feels like home isn't normal.

But before I can attempt to figure out these warring emotions, he drops his hold on me, stepping back.

"Sorry. I don't know why I—"

"It's okay," I rush out, a sudden chill washing over me. "Should we head back?"

"Yeah."

It's silent as we walk in the direction of his car, both of us mindful to keep a respectful amount of space between us. Obsessively so.

But all I can think of is how perfect it felt to be in his arms for those few seconds.

FIFTEEN

Hayden

"Ro-Ro!" Jemmy squeals the second I step through the front door with Rowan.

Presley's head snaps up from where she's sitting on the floor beside him. For half a second, she freezes. Then she jumps to her feet and darts across the room.

Rowan barely has time to brace herself before Presley wraps her arms around her middle, holding tight.

"I missed you, too, sweet girl," Rowan says softly, kissing the top of Presley's head like it's the most natural thing in the world.

My chest immediately tightens at the sight of them together.

I've never seen Presley cling to anyone like this. Not my sister. Not my mom. Not even me. I still struggle to wrap my head around the fact that this woman was a complete stranger mere days ago.

But in that short time, she's ingrained herself into our lives to the point that my kids can't imagine life without her.

How is that possible?

Maybe that's just who Rowan is, easily able to draw people to her.

Hell, she drew me in, too, despite fighting it.

I'm *still* fighting it.

Every morning in the shower.

And sometimes at night, too.

Across the room, I catch my mother's eye.

She doesn't say a word, but the look she gives me is unmistakable.

I told you so.

I heave a sigh and look away.

She's right. I know she is. Watching Presley melt into Rowan like this makes it impossible to deny.

Rowan is absolutely in my kids' best interests.

Even if I'm starting to suspect she might not be in mine, simply because I can't stop thinking about her.

The way she moves through my house like she belongs here.

The way my heart speeds up the second she walks into a room.

The way my thoughts keep circling back to her, whether I want them to or not.

Maybe that's why I fired her earlier today.

Not because she messed up, but because she makes me feel things I'm not ready to feel.

Things I don't *want* to feel.

"Ro-Ro!" Jemmy calls again, toddling toward her with all the coordination of a baby giraffe.

Rowan laughs, and the sound fills the house, bright and warm. She gently untangles from Presley and crouches to scoop up Jemmy.

"Hey, bud."

He roars, throwing his head back dramatically.

"That's right," she says, grinning. "We can play dinosaur all you want. But right now, why don't we play something your sister wants to. Okay?"

"K," Jemmy agrees immediately.

She sets him down, and he bolts toward the living room, pointing at the bin of blocks. "Build house!"

Rowan glances at Presley for her approval.

Presley smiles and gives a small nod. Then she grabs Rowan's hand and tugs her across the room.

They all drop to the floor together, blocks scattering across the rug as Presley dumps them out. Rowan doesn't take over. She doesn't direct. She takes her cue from the kids. She lets Jemmy stack crooked towers. Lets Presley carefully reinforce them. Laughs when it all collapses.

My mom rises from the couch and crosses the room, giving Rowan's shoulder a squeeze. They share a brief look before my mom heads toward me.

Neither one of us says anything for several moments. We simply watch Rowan with Jemmy and Presley, another wave of giggles and laughter erupting when their next attempt falls to the floor yet again. But that doesn't deter them from starting over again.

"She looks so happy," Mom muses.

"I don't think I've ever seen Rowan not happy," I reply automatically.

My mom raises a brow. "I was talking about Presley."

"Oh." I clear my throat. "Right."

"But I find it interesting you thought of Rowan first."

"I didn't. I just…" I trail off.

"Whatever you say," she teases with a wink. "Do you need anything else?"

"The crisis has been averted for now."

"Then I'm going to head home." She grabs her purse. "Try not to fire your nanny again."

My eyes float to Rowan of their own accord. "I'm pretty sure I learned that lesson."

"Good. Because she's good for you."

"I see that now. I can't remember the last time Presley's played with Jemmy like this."

Mom shakes her head. "I'm not talking about the kids, Hayden. Although she's definitely amazing with them." She narrows her gaze on me. "She's good for you, too. You've seemed…lighter. Happier."

"I'm not sure about that. Not sure I *can* be happy," I admit.

"Why do you think that?"

I part my lips, about to respond, but Mom holds up her hand, cutting me off before I can utter a single syllable.

"I know what you're going to say. That you can't be happy because of Cora. Because it's only been a year."

I swallow hard. I can't deny she's right.

It's one of the reasons I keep cursing myself for the things Rowan makes me feel. Not just because she's technically my employee. But because I feel like I'm dishonoring Cora's memory by looking at Rowan the way I have been.

Hell, by looking at *any* woman.

But I haven't looked at any other women.

Only Rowan.

"I've been where you are, Hayden," Mom continues. "There was a part of me that thought I would dishonor your father's memory if I felt even a hint of happiness after losing him. But then I realized something."

"What's that?"

A nostalgic gleam fills her eyes. "He would have been livid if he learned I was moping around. He'd want me to live life to its fullest. He'd want me to laugh again. Maybe even love again."

I open my mouth to argue, but she cuts me off once more.

"I'm not saying you need to forget Cora. She's the mother of your children. A woman you loved for years. She'll always have a piece of your heart. But you *can* allow yourself to be happy. Okay?"

She may not come right out and say it, but I know what she's getting at.

That it's time for me to move on and find someone who makes me happy.

I'm not sure I'm ready for that.

Not sure I'll ever be ready for that.

But I'm not about to tell my mom that.

"Okay." I place a soft kiss on her cheek. "Thanks again. For everything."

"I'm always here for you."

I walk her to the door, giving her one last hug, then head back inside to watch my kids.

At least, that's what I tell myself.

In reality, I can't stop looking at Rowan.

At her wide smile.

The way she involves both Jemmy and Presley in their project.

The way her laughter rings through the air.

The way she makes these four walls *feel* like a home, instead of a place I live.

I pad toward them, keeping my steps soft so as not to interrupt Rowan and the kids. But Rowan senses my presence anyway, shifting her eyes to mine.

"I should probably start dinner." She starts to push to her feet.

"You don't have to," I say quickly. "I'll order pizza."

Jemmy cheers. Presley's eyes light up.

"I don't mind cooking," Rowan states.

"I appreciate that, but it's been a…trying day. You should take some time to relax."

"If you're sure."

"I'm sure."

"Oh. Okay."

She looks back at Jemmy and Presley, who both wear frowns.

"It's okay, you two. I'll be back tomorrow morning. This is your family time."

She tousles Jemmy's hair, and he giggles before

returning his attention to his blocks. Then she gives Presley a hug, promising to cook together tomorrow night before pulling herself to her full height.

She heads to the foyer to grab her suitcase, but I'm there in a heartbeat.

"I'll carry that for you."

"It's okay. I've got it. See you tomorrow." She continues toward the hallway leading to the in-law suite.

"Rowan," I call out, her name leaving my mouth before I can stop it.

She pauses, glancing over her shoulder at me.

I have no idea what I even want to say. It's almost like some other force took over, forcing me to stop her.

Maybe because deep down, I don't want her to leave yet.

"Do you… Do you want to join us?"

She doesn't say anything right away. Just stares at me.

I can't remember the last time I was this on edge around a member of the opposite sex. It was probably when I asked out Cora. But even back then, I didn't feel this unsettled.

"It's okay if you don't want to," I add quickly, a bout of nerves overtaking me. "I just thought—"

"Do you mind if I have pizza with you guys?" Rowan asks, directing her question at Jemmy and Presley.

Not surprisingly, both their faces light up with enthusiasm.

"I'd like that," she says, returning her gaze to mine. "Just give me a minute to unpack."

"I'll order the pizza. Do you have any preference?"

"I'm not picky. Whatever you like is fine with me."

"Okay."

As she walks away, I have to force myself to look somewhere other than her ass.

But I fail miserably.

SIXTEEN

Rowan

I finish shoving the last of my clothes into the dresser, then pull out a fresh t-shirt and a pair of yoga pants. Mere hours ago, I threw all my things into my suitcase, hoping to never step foot in this place again, too distraught and unsettled over the fact that the only reason I'm alive right now is because Hayden's wife isn't.

I almost didn't come back here with him.

But something made me say yes.

A part of me wonders if maybe Cora had something to do with it. If she led me here so her kids could have a piece of her back.

After I change, I check my reflection in the mirror and reach for my makeup bag before hesitating.

Am I doing too much?

Am I trying too hard?

Why do I even care?

I put on makeup for people all the time. Or I *used* to. These days, I don't care what anyone thinks. Life is far too short to give a shit about eyeliner symmetry.

Except I can't quite shake the way Hayden looked at me when he asked me to stay for pizza.

It didn't mean anything. It *can't* mean anything. He's my boss. I'm his nanny. He probably just thought the kids needed some stability after the emotional roller-coaster we've all been on today.

But the way he looked at me didn't feel like a boss asking his nanny to stay for dinner for the kids' sake.

I close my makeup bag after applying only a little gloss. Then I tug on an oversized sweatshirt and arrange my dark hair into a braid that falls over one shoulder. This version of me feels safer. Less flirty. More nanny.

Which is all I am.

I head back into the living room, expecting to find Presley and Jemmy entertaining themselves while Hayden cleans up or reviews patient notes, as is so often the case.

Instead, I stop short.

Hayden is on the floor.

Like, actually on the floor.

He's traded his suit for a pair of faded jeans and a t-shirt, and Jemmy is sitting between his outstretched legs, pushing toy cars down a mini slide. Presley has stacked blocks into a wobbly castle at the bottom. Every time a car crashes into it, Jemmy shrieks with laughter and Hayden cheers like his team just won the championship game. Even Presley claps wildly.

It's beautiful. And unexpected. I haven't been here

long, but I've never seen Hayden like this — loose, playful, fully present. It's also a little bittersweet, because their mom should be here, too.

She should be sitting on the couch, rolling her eyes at the mess, probably filming the chaos on her phone.

In a way, she sort of is here.

Her heart is with them, even if they don't realize it.

"Oh," Hayden says when he notices me. "You're back."

"I didn't want to interrupt. Whose idea was the slide?"

"Presley's."

I grin at her. "Good one."

She beams like she just discovered gravity.

"Pizza should be here in about ten minutes. Hope you like Hawaiian."

My nose scrunches before I can temper my reaction, and Hayden's expression falls.

"You said you weren't picky."

"It's fine," I insist with a smile. "If it's what the kids like, I'll eat it."

Out of the corner of my eye, I catch Presley's conniving grin, as if she's attempting to hold in her laughter. One thing is certain. That girl has a terrible poker face.

"You're messing with me, aren't you?" I place my hands on my hips. "You didn't order a Hawaiian pizza, did you?"

Hayden pulls himself to his full height. "I spent most of my adult life in Chicago. I may not be a native, but I'm pretty sure I'd be stripped of my association with that city if I ever admitted I liked pineapple on pizza."

"What *do* you like on your pizza?"

"I'm more traditional, I suppose. Pepperoni. Sausage."

"Thin crust or deep dish?"

"The correct answer is deep dish. All day, every day." He heads toward the kitchen. "Want a glass of wine? I've got red and white."

I hesitate, chewing on my bottom lip. "I shouldn't drink on the job."

"You're off the clock," he replies easily. "You're not here as the kids' nanny."

"Oh."

If I'm not here as their nanny, why *am* I here? I refuse to read into it too much. Like I told myself earlier. He probably just wants to give the kids some reassurance.

Still, a glass of wine sounds really good right now, if for no other reason than to relax me. My doctor did say an occasional glass is fine, as long as I'm careful. I've always been careful. So I nod.

"Red would be great."

I follow him into the kitchen and watch him uncork a bottle. His arms strain slightly when he moves, muscles on full display. My brain makes the deeply unhelpful observation that none of the doctors I've ever had looked like him.

If they had, maybe I wouldn't have been so desperate to get discharged.

I'd happily fake an illness in the hopes of Hayden giving me a thorough exam.

"Here you go." His voice cuts through, forcing me out of my thoughts, and I take the glass from him. "Hope you like it. It's from my brother's vineyard."

I arch a brow. "Your brother owns a vineyard?"

He nods. "Beckham's the owner of Vivanza. It's just outside of town."

"Doesn't another one of your brothers own a brewery?"

"Jude. Now if Finn or Dylan can start a whiskey distillery, I'd have all my bases covered." He flashes me a wink, and my god… It makes my girly bits go all aflutter, the hairs on my nape standing on end.

I need to get my hormones under control. It's probably because it's been so long since I've had sex. Hell, it's been a while since I've even had an orgasm. Lately, I've been so exhausted by the time I fall into bed, all I've wanted to do is sleep. I should probably rectify that, and soon.

Before I do something I'll regret.

"To second chances." Hayden lifts his glass toward me, and I meet his gaze, affection and sincerity swirling in his dark orbs. "Thanks for giving me one, Rowan."

"It's the least I can do."

I clink my glass with his and take a sip of the full-bodied red. But Hayden doesn't take his eyes off me, watching me with an intensity I feel deep in my marrow.

"It's not like I could leave town if I wanted to right now anyway," I add, trying to lighten the tension.

"Is that the only reason you agreed to come back? Because your van's in the shop?"

"No," I respond flippantly. "I said yes because I have to."

This causes a furrow to crease his brow. "You *have* to?"

"I had a bit of a…health scare a while back," I explain, not wanting to go into too much detail.

Not wanting him to put the pieces together.

"Is that the reason for the scar?" He glances at my chest.

I give him a subtle nod. "I'm fine now. Perfectly healthy. But it made me put things into perspective. I used to work sixty, seventy, even eighty hours a week."

"What did you do?"

"I was a lawyer."

"Wow. I did not expect that. Not that I don't think you're brilliant. I just don't know many lawyers who are…fun."

"I'll take that as a compliment." I wink, taking a sip of wine. "I thought success equaled happiness. I routinely turned down fun opportunities because of work. So after my health scare, I quit my job, bought my van, and decided to live life to its fullest, starting with having a 'Year of Yes'."

"And you just say yes to everything?"

I open and close my mouth several times, trying to figure out a way to explain this. "There are some limitations. Nothing illegal, of course. Also, nothing that could result in a long-term commitment. Whatever it is has to enrich my life, not diminish it. Some days the yes is something big, like potentially nannying for a grumpy, stubborn single dad."

I flash him a smile, and he chuckles, the laugh lines around his eyes crinkling.

"Other days, they're small things. Like saying yes to sunrise yoga. Or having pizza and wine with my boss." I lift the glass. "I started it as an extension of my life list."

"Life list?" He arches a brow.

"After my health scare, I made a list of all the things I once took for granted but never will again. Like watching the sunrise in the morning. Or a really good cup of coffee. The more things I say yes to, the more experiences I add to my life list."

He nods, seeming to process this. "Well, I'm glad you're here, even if it's only because you had to say yes."

"I would have said yes even if I didn't have to," I admit. "Then again, I'm not sure I would even be in this town if I hadn't spent the past several months saying yes. It's led me on quite an adventure."

"I'd love to hear all about it," he replies, taking a sip of his wine as his phone chimes. He pulls it from his pocket and looks at the screen. "Pizza's here."

"Great."

"Presley, grab your brother and help him get cleaned up," he calls out as he heads toward the front door.

I turn toward the sink and wash my hands. As I'm drying them off, Hayden rounds the corner, carrying two pizza boxes with a few bags placed on top. My stomach immediately rumbles from the delicious aroma filling the room.

"Do you need help with anything?" I ask as he pulls out a few plates.

"Actually, there is something you can do for me."

"What's that?"

"Nothing." He treats me to a gentle smile. "Just sit down."

I lower myself into the chair I've noticed is usually left empty and take a large gulp of wine, needing it to settle the butterflies flapping around my stomach. Thankfully, Presley and Jemmy come in seconds later. I instinctively jump up to help Jemmy into his high chair, but Hayden's beside me before I can.

"I thought you learned your lesson earlier," he murmurs as he sets Jemmy into the chair.

"What do you mean?"

"About following directions."

"I thought—"

"I told you to sit and let me take care of everything. So sit and let me take care of you for a change."

A shiver rolls through me, my core clenching from the timbre of his voice. It makes me wonder what he'd be like in the bedroom.

Would he chastise me for not following instructions there, too?

Would he punish me?

Would he call me a bad girl?

Better yet, would he call me a good girl?

This is the absolute last thing I should be thinking of right now, but I can't help myself.

Thankfully, Jemmy's excited squeals force Hayden's

attention away from me. I take a deep breath to calm my growing nerves.

"I know, bud. You want your pizza. Just give me a second to cut it up for you."

"I can do—"

I stop short, more than aware how Hayden will respond to my offer. Instead, I take another large swallow of wine, needing the burn to distract me from everything else.

"You're learning," he muses, throwing a wink my way.

Then he focuses his attention on cutting up a slice of cheese pizza for Jemmy.

"Would you like pepperoni or cheese, Rowan?"

"One of each."

"You got it."

After placing the pre-cut slices of pizza and strawberries onto Jemmy's tray, he sets a dish in front of me with my pizza, along with a bowl of salad. Once Presley has her own plate, he sits opposite me.

"Cheers." He lifts his wine glass.

Jemmy and Presley both raise their cups, and I join them, the four of us clinking our drinks together.

As I glance around the table, an unexpected warmth fills me.

This was once the life I wanted. The family. The noise. The chaotic dinners.

Since learning how dangerous pregnancy could be for me, I've made peace with letting that dream go.

But maybe I didn't have to.

After all, the universe sometimes has a funny way of giving us what we need, even if it doesn't look how we imagined.

And maybe being a part of this family, albeit temporarily, is enough for me.

SEVENTEEN

Hayden

I wake before my alarm, the house still cloaked in a fragile quiet that only exists right before dawn.

Today has been looming for weeks, weighing heavily on my mind.

Exactly one year ago, I watched as my wife was wheeled into an operating room so four strangers could have a second chance at life.

I'd rather mark the day with something Cora loved. Ice skating with the kids. Sledding until our fingers are numb. Decorating cookies with far too much frosting and sprinkles.

Instead, we'll spend the morning in a church pew, followed by a reception hosted by my father-in-law, where he'll keep an eagle eye on everyone to make sure they're grieving the way he'd want them to.

To make sure *I'm* grieving the way he wants me to.

I understand why he needs this. This is his way of honoring Cora's memory.

At first, I thought it's how I needed to honor her memory, too. Go to church services. Leave flowers at her grave. Mourn her every day.

And I do.

But I don't feel the need to put it on display.

I pad downstairs and start the coffee, the soft gurgle and hiss filling the kitchen. I run a hand over my face as I clear the proverbial cobwebs from yet another night of broken sleep. As I do, I glance out the window, spying a figure on the front porch.

Rowan's sitting on the swing, wrapped in a sweater, the rising sun painting her in soft gold. She looks peaceful. Serene.

Like nothing bad can ever touch her.

A smile pulls at my mouth before I can stop it.

It's been happening more and more lately, my body reacting to her before my brain can remind me why it shouldn't.

Weeks ago, she was a stranger I struggled to trust.

Now she's threaded through our lives so seamlessly I can't remember what the house felt like before her laugh echoed through it.

Jemmy lights up whenever she walks into a room, all smiles and giggles. He's not the only one, either. Presley's smiling again, especially when cooking with Rowan, both of them dancing to whatever music has captured their attention.

Lately, it's been Taylor Swift.

I've never had an opinion about her music, but now

I look forward to coming home just to hear Rowan belting "Shake It Out" at the top of her lungs as she dances with my daughter.

There have been a few times I was convinced Presley was about to start singing with her.

She hasn't yet, but that doesn't matter.

Rowan's teaching my daughter how to be heard again.

Despite my father-in-law's argument against Presley learning sign language, I agreed to let Rowan teach her. Presley's therapist believes it's a step in the right direction.

I think it is, too.

After my coffee finishes brewing, I prepare a second cup the way Rowan takes it. Then I pull my Northwestern sweatshirt over my head and step onto the porch.

"Do you mind some company?" I ask, holding up a mug. "I brought you a coffee."

"In that case, you're more than welcome," she replies with a smile, scooting over on the bench swing.

I sit beside her, our shoulders almost touching. The wood creaks softly as we rock, the scent of coffee mingling with pine and the cold morning air.

"I've never actually sat on this," I admit.

"You're missing out. It's one of my favorite things about your house. Tend the view… It's incredible."

I study her as she peers at the sun rising over the mountains in the distance, casting the world in various hues of pink and blue.

"Yes, it is," I agree.

But I'm not looking at the horizon. I'm looking at her.

At the way the sunlight catches in her dark hair, making it seem more reddish-brown.

At the tattoo covering up the scar I think about more than I should.

At how damn beautiful she is.

And not just on the outside either. But what I find most beautiful is her heart. She's so kind, caring, witty, charming. I'm drawn to her in ways I can't explain. Ways I shouldn't be, all things considered. But I can't help myself. It's why I've been inviting her to have dinner with us more and more, and not as our nanny.

Sensing my stare on her, she glances at me. I quickly look away and sip on my coffee, pretending she didn't just catch me checking her out.

"I can't remember the last time I watched a sunrise," I say, needing to fill the space. "Probably the day Presley was born. She came right after midnight. Cora was exhausted, so I stayed up holding her."

A few months ago, the memory would make my throat tighten. Hell, a few months ago, I wouldn't even be sharing this with anyone. But it feels good to talk about these things. To remember the happy times. Not dwell on the loss or grief.

"I watched the sun come up through the hospital window and was so damn worried I was going to screw up this whole parenting thing. That I'd fail Presley. That she'd hate me." I huff out a quiet laugh. "I still wake up with that fear. Guess it never really goes away."

Rowan nudges my arm gently. "You have nothing to worry about. You're a good dad, Hayden."

"Some days, it feels like I'm barely holding on, as you've seen for yourself."

"I think most parents feel that way. It's a scary thing. You go into the hospital just the two of you and leave with an extra human. Pretty sure they do more vetting when you adopt a dog than when you have a kid."

I chuckle. "I checked Presley's car seat so many times before we left the hospital. All Cora wanted to do was take a shower and lie down in her own bed. But I needed to make sure Presley would be safe. Then I drove so damn slowly on the way home. I bet I never went over forty. Even on the freeway."

Her laughter spills into the morning, and the unease that filled me when I first woke up slowly disappears.

This is exactly what I needed. A reminder that life isn't all loss and grief. That you can still find something to laugh and smile about, even on the worst days.

"I'm surprised you're up so early," I remark after another brief silence, the swing creaking beneath us as we continue to rock. "Especially on a day off."

"I'm a creature of habit. Plus, I can sleep when I'm dead." The instant the words leave her mouth, she winces. "Sorry. Probably not the best phrasing, all things considered."

"It's okay."

She meets my eyes, hesitating. "Are you ready for today? Is that even the right thing to say?"

"I'm not looking forward to it. But I've kind of grown numb to it. My father-in-law plans something like this constantly. Services. Memorials. He even turned the kids' birthdays into tributes to Cora."

Her jaw drops. "He did what?"

"These days, his sole purpose in life is to mourn his daughter every chance he gets. That, and remind me she's gone." I roll my eyes. "As if I could ever forget. It's more difficult on Presley than me."

"Would you…like me to come with you today?" she asks. "Not as your nanny. Just…emotional support. Especially for Presley."

I part my lips, about to tell her it's not necessary, but stop myself. Presley has certainly been off the past few days. More irritable. Less social. Her therapist explained anniversary events can be traumatizing for survivors, which is why she suggested doing something fun to make new memories of today.

I doubt it would go over well with Robert.

But if Rowan were there, it might make it a little more bearable for Presley.

"Are you sure?" I ask. "You don't have to."

"I *want* to. Want to be there for you." She lifts her gaze to mine, then quickly adds, "and them. I want to be there for them."

"I'd like that."

My gaze drifts over her face. Her vivid blue eyes. The curve of her cheek. Her full lips.

Over the past several weeks, I've thought about those lips more times than I care to admit. And every time, I've berated myself for doing so. For allowing my stare to linger on them too long. To imagine how they'd taste and feel.

And not simply because she's my kids' much younger nanny. But because of Cora. There's a part of me that still feels like I'm married to her and even thinking about another woman is cheating.

But every time I think that, I hear my mother's words in the back of my mind, reminding me that Cora wouldn't want me frozen in grief. She'd want me to live my life.

But with the nanny?

It's insanity. I should date. Distract myself. Do something so I'll stop thinking about Rowan nearly every second of the day.

But I get the feeling I could go out with every single woman in the area and I still won't stop thinking about Rowan.

Jemmy's babbling crackles through the monitor, forcing me back to the present.

"Duty calls." I stand abruptly.

"What time do we need to leave?"

"Ten. Service then lunch."

"I'll be ready." She pauses. "I don't have to wear black, do I? I'm not sure I own anything dark."

I chuckle. Of course she wouldn't have anything that's drab and colorless, not when she exudes life and vitality.

"Wear whatever you'd like."

"Okay. See you at ten."

"See you then." I hold her gaze for one more beat, then disappear inside, officially on dad duty.

[illegible] yet us [illegible] this was [illegible]

[illegible] of [illegible] [illegible] [illegible]
[illegible]

[illegible]
[illegible]
[illegible]
[illegible]
[illegible]
[illegible]
[illegible]
[illegible]
[illegible]
[illegible]
[illegible]
[illegible]
[illegible]
[illegible]
[illegible]
[illegible]

EIGHTEEN

Rowan

My bed looks like the aftermath of a fabric explosion.

Three sundresses. One denim skirt. A wrinkled maxi that smells faintly of campfire smoke. Nothing that seems appropriate for a memorial service.

Since I quit my job, my wardrobe has skewed aggressively casual. Practical. Easy to throw on and forget about. I haven't needed anything formal in months. Certainly not something to wear while sitting in a church full of people mourning the dead wife of the boss I can't stop thinking about.

Wanting to be there for Presley and Jemmy is one thing. Wanting to be there for Hayden, too? That's a complication I don't have the emotional bandwidth to unpack right now.

The last thing I should be doing is attending the memorial for the woman who gave me her heart. Especially when I've been carrying that secret around for nearly a month now.

And yet, it's also why I feel like I have to go.

To pay my respects.

To acknowledge the life that ended so mine could continue.

To honor her sacrifice, even if I'm the only one who understands it.

It's not exactly how I pictured spending my first "rebirth" day.

I originally planned on marking the day by saying yes to everything I could.

But I can't shake the feeling there's a reason I offered to go with Hayden. That it's important I be there today.

Pushing out a long sigh, I reach for the most conservative item of clothing I own — a red-and-blue floral dress that hits mid-thigh. It's not funeral black, but it's clean, ironed, and doesn't scream beach day.

After slipping on the dress, I take a minute to put on some eyeliner and lip gloss. Then I pull on knee-high black boots and shrug into my denim jacket before slinging my bag over my shoulder.

When I step into the living room, Presley's eyes immediately go to me. She launches herself at me, her small arms wrapping around my waist with surprising force.

I steady myself and give her a reassuring rub on her back.

She releases me and signs, *Are you coming?*

"I am."

She hugs me again, tighter this time, like she's afraid I might change my mind. As I give her another squeeze, my gaze lifts and collides with Hayden, who's studying us from across the room.

There's something different about the way his eyes linger on me today. Something unguarded. It sends a rush of sensation through me I can't name.

Excitement, maybe?

No. Absolutely not.

I'm about to go to his dead wife's memorial, for crying out loud.

Probably just nerves. Or guilt. Or the fact that I'm about to walk into a church for the first time in my life under questionable circumstances.

"We should get going," Hayden announces, tearing his gaze from mine as he lifts Jemmy.

I grab Presley's hand and follow him out the door.

The car ride is mostly quiet. Jemmy fills the silence with his running commentary — trees, trucks, dogs, truck again. His voice grows particularly excited when we pass the fire station. The bay doors are open, revealing a pristine red fire engine.

"Finn. Truck," he announces excitedly.

It doesn't matter that his uncle is on the fire department and lets him play on the fire trucks at least once a week.

Jemmy's eyes always light up when he sees them.

He may like them more than dinosaurs, and that's saying something.

"Yes, buddy," Hayden replies, his voice distant. "That's Uncle Finn's special truck."

I consider making small talk to cut through the heavy atmosphere in the car. But one glance at Hayden's profile as he drives — jaw tight, eyes fixed straight ahead — tells me this isn't the time to chat about how nice the weather is.

So I stay quiet and watch the town roll by.

After a few more minutes, the church comes into view, and he pulls into the parking lot. I look up at the imposing building, fidgeting with my hands in my lap.

"Are you okay?" Hayden asks as he kills the ignition.

"Fine. I just…" I lean closer, lowering my voice. "I've never been in a church before. How am I supposed to act?"

He huffs out a quiet laugh. "Just be yourself."

That doesn't feel reassuring, but I nod anyway, stepping out of the car and helping Presley, giving her a comforting smile. With her hand clasped in mine, we head into the church together.

The second we cross the threshold, the nervous butterflies dance in my stomach once more. If they ever stopped. Everything about this place feels off. And not just because I've always had a questionable relationship with any sort of organized religion. But it feels…heavy.

Too heavy.

The air smells like polished wood and flowers while voices murmur, grief compressed into polite tones and careful expressions.

Then I see her.

The portrait of Cora is massive, propped on an easel

at the front. I've seen her photo before, printed small on the program I found in Hayden's office. The quality wasn't all that great to begin with, and it had faded over time.

But this isn't.

She seems almost lifelike. Her dark hair falls in gentle waves past her shoulders, her green eyes full of life. Her smile is warm. Familiar in a way that makes my chest tighten. I never knew her, but seeing her like this hits me harder than I expected.

I glance at Hayden. His face is carefully blank, grief locked down behind months of training and sheer force of will. But his grip tightens around Jemmy, who stares at the portrait.

"Mama!" Jemmy announces.

"Yeah, bud. That's Mama."

"Heaven."

"Yeah. Mama's in heaven."

In a heartbeat, Presley wrenches her hand free from mine and bolts, weaving through the crowd before I know what's happening.

"Presley," Hayden whisper-shouts. "Get back here."

But she doesn't listen. She pushes through everyone and out the front doors of the church, running faster than I've ever seen her.

Hayden hurries after her, continuing to call her name while I remain frozen.

People stare at his retreating form as they lean closer to whisper amongst themselves, gossiping about the poor single dad who seems to have his hands full.

What do they expect when they have to spend the

day being reminded of the one person they'd give anything to have back?

I push through the crowd, ignoring the questioning looks.

The second I'm outside, I suck in a huge gulp of air, feeling like I can breathe again. If I felt suffocated inside those four walls, I can only imagine how Presley felt. I don't blame her for wanting to leave. Truth be told, I did, too.

I scan the area, spotting them almost immediately. Hayden stands beneath a giant tree, most of the leaves gone. And perched on one of the branches is Presley.

"I'm not going to tell you again, young lady," Hayden says, frustration evident in his voice. "Get down here. Right now. You're going to lose TV and tablet privileges for a week."

She doesn't budge.

His jaw clenches and he squeezes his eyes shut as Jemmy babbles, pointing to Presley and saying "monkey" before making the sound like a monkey.

"If you come down," Hayden begins, softer this time, "I'll take you to the toy store. You can pick out anything you want."

She looks at him, then gives a hard shake of her head.

I see it the second his patience snaps.

"You don't have a choice," he hisses. "If I have to climb up there and get you myself, I will. And you won't like what happens next. This is unacceptable. You're acting like a baby."

While I'd normally let him handle this on his own,

he's struggling. After all, I came today to help. It's obvious he needs it right now.

"Hayden."

At the sound of my voice, he spins toward me, his eyes blazing.

"Would you like me to try?" I ask cautiously.

"It's not necessary," he snaps. "She needs to act her age. None of us want to be here, but it's the right thing to do."

"Yes, but she's only seven." I grab a squirming Jemmy from his arms. "Everyone else here has had years to learn how to deal with grief. She's still figuring it out." My throat tightens. "Just…let me talk to her."

He doesn't say anything for several long moments, and I expect for him to tell me I have no idea what I'm talking about. Finally, he pushes out a slow exhale, his expression growing weary.

"Why is this so hard?"

"Life *is* hard," I offer. "But that's why I'm here. For you to lean on when shit gets hard."

"Shit." Jemmy giggles, cutting through the tension.

Hayden and I both freeze before our eyes slowly move toward Jemmy.

"Shit!" he repeats.

I shouldn't react. In my short time as Jemmy's nanny, I've learned he feeds off my energy. If I find something amusing or funny, he'll keep doing it. Which is why the best thing I can do to get him to stop swearing is pretend it never happened.

But I can't.

A laugh bursts out of me, completely inappropriate

and impossible to stop. Hayden joins in, too, his deep chuckle like music to my ears, especially right now.

"Shit! Shit!" Jemmy keeps exclaiming.

"I am so sorry," I gasp, my stomach hurting from laughing so much, tears streaking down my cheeks.

"Don't be. I think we needed this."

"We definitely did," I reply, stealing a glance at Presley. Even her shoulders are shaking with silent laughter.

"Shit!" Jemmy repeats yet again.

"That's not a nice word, bud," Hayden attempts to chastise.

"Ro-Ro."

"I know. Ro-Ro said it. But she's a grownup. That's a grownup word."

Jemmy looks between Hayden and me. Then a conniving grin tugs on his lips. "Shit."

Hayden sighs. "Great. Now I have to go into a church with a toddler whose new favorite word is a swear."

"I'm so sorry," I offer yet again, wiping away the tears of laughter still falling.

"I guess there are worse things."

"There are."

He draws in a deep breath, glancing at the church before returning his attention to me. "Do you think you—"

"I'll talk to her. Try to get her down from the tree and see if she'll give it another shot."

Relief covers his expression. "Thank you, Rowan. I appreciate it."

"It's my job," I respond dismissively as he takes Jemmy from me.

"No. It's not. So…thank you."

He meets my eyes, his attention seeming to focus on my mouth for longer than normal.

Then he turns and makes his way back toward the church.

NINETEEN

Rowan

I walk over to the tree and lower myself to the ground, stretching my legs out in front of me and resting my back against the trunk. I don't say anything right away. Just sit and run my fingers through the cool grass.

The sun peeks through mostly bare limbs and warms my face, taking the edge off the December chill. Not cold enough to be uncomfortable. Just cold enough to remind me I'm still here. Still breathing.

Still alive.

"I don't blame you for not wanting to be in there," I begin after a few minutes. "It was very…heavy."

I steal a glance up into the branches where Presley's hiding, but I don't push for eye contact.

"I'm not sure what's worse about these things," I continue. "Being reminded that someone you love is gone, like you need the reminder when every day already feels like one long reminder. Or everyone staring at you with that look of feigned sympathy, which is more like pity than anything else."

I shudder, rubbing my arms.

"For me, it's the pity. There's something about people looking at me that way that makes my skin itch. Someone thinking they're better off than you, so they should feel sorry for you. It's honestly the worst."

Silence settles between us again as a breeze blows through the air, causing leaves to skitter across the ground. There's a faint rustling, but even when the wind settles, it continues.

I lift my gaze as Presley carefully climbs down, her movements slow and deliberate. She drops the last foot to the ground and comes to sit beside me, hugging her knees to her chest.

I don't suggest we go inside. Instead, I stay right where I am, not wanting her to shut down again.

"I got sick a few years ago," I announce after a few moments. "Really sick."

Presley's head snaps up, eyes wide, fear flashing across her face so fast it almost knocks the air from my lungs.

"I'm okay," I rush to assure her. "I promise. I'm more than okay now. I had an incredible team of doctors just like your dad and they fixed me."

Her shoulders ease a little.

"But there was a brief time I didn't think I'd ever leave the hospital." I stare out across the grass, letting the memory wash over me without pulling me under. "A lot of people came to visit. And the way they looked at me…" I shake my head. "Like I was already dead. I hated it."

I twist my fingers into the blades of grass, tugging at them as I remember how awful that time in my life was. How it felt like every visitor who walked through the door wasn't there to see me but to pay their respects.

"But there was one person who never looked at me like that. My best friend, Emily. She never stopped believing I'd get better. And I think she's why I didn't give up." I laugh to myself.

"She used to play this game whenever she visited. She'd talk about all the things we'd do once I got better. At first, I refused to play along. I was convinced it was pointless."

Presley shifts her eyes to mine, listening intently to my story.

"But Emily didn't care. She'd rattle off ideas anyway. Like spending an entire day shopping without looking at price tags. Or hiring a limo to drive us around for no reason." I glance at her. "Or buying a van and traveling the country."

Presley's eyes widen.

"Every day she visited me and forced me to listen to what my future would hold, I felt a little less stuck. A little more hopeful. Eventually, I started making my own list. I called it my 'life list'. I even started journaling, as if I'd spent the day crossing off another item on this list. It didn't matter that I was stuck in a hospital bed with more wires attached to me than a science experiment and could barely stand without getting dizzy. I wrote about hiking to see the hidden waterfalls in Hawaii. Or seeing the catacombs in Paris. Or dancing on a float during Mardi Gras in New Orleans. And I didn't write about doing them someday. I wrote about each of these things as if I'd already done them. And do you want to know the crazy thing?"

Her brows knit together in a mixture of confusion and intrigue.

"It worked. What I thought was a pointless game gave me hope. I stopped feeling sorry for myself. Stopped thinking the world was unfair. Stopped thinking I was never going to get out of that hospital bed. To this day, I'm convinced Emily's game saved my life."

I give Presley a soft smile before shifting my gaze forward again.

"I know my situation is vastly different from yours." I steal a glance her way. "I didn't lose my mom."

Her expression drops, and she pulls her knees closer.

"But I like to think the people we love never really leave us. They're still here. Just in a different way than before. So maybe instead of sitting through that church service hating how everyone's looking at you, we come up with your own version of Emily's game."

She looks up at me again, her brows pulled in. Then she signs, *How?*

"You can pretend you're spending today with your mom," I suggest. "If she were here, what would you do?" My expression brightens. "Better yet, what would you want to do with her if today was a 'yes day'?"

She signs, *A yes day?*

"You've never heard of a yes day?" I gasp, scandalized, especially since my entire life has been one yes day after another since I got out of the hospital.

Presley shakes her head.

"A yes day is when parents have to say yes to everything you want. Within reason, of course," I add quickly. "No skydiving. Probably."

Her eyes light up as she signs, *Ice cream for breakfast?*

I grin. "Absolutely."

Cake for lunch?

"Mandatory."

She tilts her head. *Ice cream again for dinner?*

"Honestly, that feels like good planning."

She smiles. It's a small one, but it feels like a victory, all things considered.

"I know it's not the same as having your mom with you. But sometimes these little games help us get through the hardest parts."

She swallows hard, her lower lip quivering slightly.

"So…what do you say?" I wrap my arm around her. "Want to go inside and give it a try?"

She draws in a deep breath and shifts her gaze forward for a beat. Then she looks back at me and nods.

I pull her closer, leaving a soft kiss on the top of her head.

"I'm really proud of you, Presley. I may not have known your mother, but I know she'd be proud of you, too."

She pushes out a sigh as she rests her head on my chest.

Right over her mother's heart.

TWENTY

Hayden

The function room smells like roasted chicken, warm bread, and too much perfume.

It's the same private room at Matteo's where we gathered a year ago after Cora's funeral.

The same circular tables draped in white linen.

The same fluorescent lighting that felt like it was shining a light on all my inadequacies.

The same framed photograph of Cora propped near the entrance, her smile soft and familiar.

I linger in the corner, playing the part of the grieving husband like I have been for the past year when a pair of blue eyes lock on mine from across the room, a spark of something blooming in my chest.

Just like happens every time I've stolen a glance at Rowan over the past few hours.

She sits at a round table near the windows with my

mom and Dylan, the three of them bent toward Presley and Jemmy like it's the most natural thing in the world. Presley's smiling at something Rowan says, her hands moving animatedly as she signs. Jemmy babbles incessantly, like he's contributing meaningfully to the conversation.

The entire scene seems so…normal. Rowan doesn't look out of place with my family.

She looks like she belongs.

"Thought you could use this."

A bottle appears in front of me, and I glance up to see my brother, Jude, sidling up beside me.

"Thanks," I say, taking the beer from him. Of course, it's from his brewery.

I can't help but envy him. Envy all my siblings for having careers they love.

My brother, Beckham, is now the owner of a popular local vineyard. The expertise he has in cultivating grapes and turning them into wine is nothing short of remarkable.

Jude went to college for a bit but dropped out to pursue his passion…brewing beer. And his beer is now sold all over the country.

Finn is a lieutenant on the fire department, something he always dreamed of doing when he was a little boy.

Even my youngest sibling, Dylan, is chasing her dreams, having just started a private chef business with her friend from culinary school.

And then there's me… Working with my father-in-law at a small-town family medical practice.

It's a far cry from the emergency room at the busy Chicago hospital where I worked a year ago.

I take a long sip of beer, not realizing how much I needed it until the tension in my shoulders loosens a fraction. I can only imagine what Robert would say about me enjoying a drink during Cora's memorial.

Right now, I don't care.

"How are you holding up?" Jude asks, his voice filled with sincerity.

"Okay. All things considered."

"Good."

"I appreciate you being here. I know you'd probably rather be anywhere else. Hell, *I'd* rather be anywhere else."

"Even getting a root canal?" Jude retorts, tipping back his bottle.

"Definitely. At least there's Novocain involved. And if you really need it, laughing gas."

"How about doing your taxes?"

"Absolutely," I answer without a moment's hesitation. "And I'll raise you doing them by hand with no internet."

"Damn..." Jude exhales, chuckling under his breath. "How about a talent show on a cruise?"

I cringe. "Okay. That one might actually be worse than this."

"See? It's all about perspective." Jude bumps my shoulder lightly. "For what it's worth, I'm happy to be here for you. Even if I'd also prefer the root canal."

I give him a smile, grateful to have the family I do.

Because of the large age gap between me and the

rest of my siblings, I've always felt a little removed from them. I was packing for college when they were still in elementary school, so I never had a bond with any of them. Since moving back, that's changed. We've grown closer.

One of the few silver linings I never asked for.

I continue sipping my beer as I survey the room. I recognize almost everyone. Employees of the medical clinic. Longtime family friends. Members of Robert's church who never liked me much to begin with.

But as always seems to be the case today, my gaze snags on Rowan, a smile curving on my lips when I watch her play peek-a-boo with Jemmy.

I was somewhat surprised when she walked back into the church with Presley less than ten minutes after I left them. And throughout the service, Presley seemed…okay. She and Rowan kept exchanging looks, as if they were sharing an inside joke only they were privy to.

I didn't care as long as Presley was happy. And she is. I figured today would be like the funeral all over again. Or any of the other memorial services Robert has planned for Cora. Presley would spend the day with her face buried in her sketchpad, ignoring everyone until it was time to go home, at which point she'd lock herself in her room.

Instead, she seems happy. Or, as happy as she can be. Whatever Rowan said must have worked.

"Looks like your new nanny's working out pretty well," Jude remarks after a beat.

"Yeah. She's…great." I lift the bottle to my lips,

taking a sip to hide the smile that sneaks up on me as I watch her.

"That's something I haven't seen in a while."

I dart my eyes toward him. "What?"

"You. Happy."

The word makes me uneasy. There's still a part of me that doesn't think I deserve happiness.

But there's another part that can't deny I've had more moments of happiness over the past several weeks than I have all year.

And every one of them involves Rowan.

"Is there something going on between you and the nanny?" Jude asks in a low voice.

"What?" I tear my gaze toward him so fast it's a wonder I don't give myself whiplash. "No. Absolutely not."

"Are you sure?" He raises a single disbelieving brow.

"She's my employee. And she's thirteen years younger than me."

He doesn't say anything. Just keeps looking at me with that same skeptical look. As if he knows I'm full of shit.

"I mean, do I think she's attractive? You'd have to be blind not to. But that doesn't mean anything."

"Mmm hmm."

"What would you say if Dylan started seeing a guy my age?"

"She's an adult. She can make her own decisions." He shrugs, as if he's never put the fear of God into any of the unlucky bastards Dylan tried to date.

Which he has.

"Age is just a number anyway," he adds casually.

"I just lost my wife."

"A year ago."

I swallow hard, remaining silent.

"Granted, Robert would prefer you remain faithful to Cora for the rest of your life," he remarks.

"You're not wrong about that," I mutter, my gaze flicking to where my father-in-law stands across the room, his posture rigid, expression perpetually displeased.

"But is that what *you* want? Is that what Cora would want for you?"

I groan, taking another swallow of the beer. "You sound like Mom."

"As much as I hate to admit this, she's right. Do you really want to keep going on like this?"

"It's…hard," I admit, my shoulders sagging.

"I get it." His expression softens. "After Krista and I lost the baby, I didn't think I'd ever open my heart again. Didn't want to. Kept everyone out. Told myself it was safer that way. And then Abbey walked into my bar wearing a wedding dress."

A smile curves his mouth. He looks so different from the man he was less than a year ago. He was cynical. Bitter. Closed off.

Sort of like I am now.

"Some people just…get in," Jude continues. "Whether you want them to or not. I've learned that you can try to keep people out all you want, but there are some people who'll weasel their way in regardless. And when that happens, there's no fighting it."

With every word Jude speaks, I can't help but think of Rowan.

How she weaseled her way into my life so effortlessly.

How I think of her more than I should.

How I crave her presence to the point that I eagerly accepted her offer to come today.

I told myself it was to help with the kids. And while she definitely has, the real reason I wanted her here is for me.

"I just... I'm not ready," I say, averting my gaze. "It's too soon."

Jude tilts his head. "Are you saying that because it's true... Or because you don't think you're allowed to move on?"

I part my lips to remind him yet again that it's only been a year since I've buried my wife. But why do I think it's too soon? Because I truly believe it? Or because I feel like I'm dishonoring her memory by opening myself up to the possibility of someone new?

As if able to read my thoughts, Robert heads my way, seemingly on a mission.

Jude notices it, too.

"Something to think about," he says before stepping away, leaving me to deal with my father-in-law on my own.

"As if it's not bad enough you brought another woman to your wife's memorial, you're also drinking, too?" he snips out.

I pinch my lips into a tight line, swallowing down what I really want to say. I have to remember this is my kids' grandfather. And Cora's dad. She may not have had the best relationship with him for reasons I now understand, but he's still family.

"Rowan is the kids' nanny." I keep my voice as even as possible. "Nothing more."

"The people at the church don't know that. They see you walk in with an attractive young woman like that, one who your kids seem to adore and who's been living with you, and what other conclusion would they draw?"

"The correct one," I snap. "My kids adore her because she's a good nanny. And she lives in the in-law apartment in my house so I can handle any emergency calls that come in. If your friends draw the wrong conclusion, that's on them. Not me."

His eyes narrow. "And the sign language?"

My jaw ticks. Of course he'd bring that up.

"I told you it was a bad idea," he continues. "You're encouraging this…behavior."

"Behavior?" I scoff. "She's a child who experienced trauma."

For someone who's made a career out of supposedly helping people, he's always been narrow minded. Then again, Robert's from a different generation and mindset. He became a doctor because of the prestige attached to it. Unlike me, who worked my ass off to become a doctor because the perpetual idealist in me wanted to help people.

I still do.

"She needs to get over it," he says dismissively.

I find it amusing that the same man who'd have me remain celibate and grieve Cora for the rest of my life is the same man telling me that my daughter should get over losing her mother.

But Robert's always been a hypocrite.

"If she feels more comfortable communicating with sign language right now, I'm happy to support it. My priority is talking to my child, not dictating how she does it. To me, that's the most important thing, regardless of whether she uses her voice or not. She will eventually."

"Not if you keep giving her a reason not to," he sneers as he walks off.

I drain the rest of my beer, my chest tight with resentment.

I've spent years trying to prove myself to this man. And somehow, he still makes me feel like the teenage boy who wanted nothing more than to date his daughter.

But then I look across the room, my eyes landing on Presley.

She's smiling. Bright. Warm. Full of life.

Screw what Robert thinks.

Presley's happy for the first time in a year.

And maybe I finally am, too.

TWENTY-ONE

Hayden

"I'm glad today's over," I mutter as I sink onto the couch, the weight of the day rolling off me, especially now that Jemmy and Presley are both finally asleep.

Rowan offered to help get them ready for bed, but I told her to relax since it's technically her day off.

"I can imagine," she says, taking a sip of tea. "Your father-in-law is…"

"An asshole."

"That's one way of putting it," she retorts.

I lift the glass of scotch I poured after dinner, the amber liquid catching the glow from the TV. *Schitt's Creek* hums in the background, Moira's overly dramatic voice filling the space, but I'm barely paying attention.

"Has he always been that way?"

"More or less," I respond. "He's always hated me."

She scrunches her brows. "Why?"

I roll my shoulders, tension cracking through my neck. "Take your pick. First, because my family wasn't as well off as his. Then because I'm the reason Cora moved to Chicago instead of staying here to work at the family practice."

"Were you high school sweethearts?" she asks cautiously, seemingly unsure if I'm in the right mental state to talk about her today.

A year ago, I wouldn't have been. Hell, a few months ago, I wouldn't have been.

It stings a bit less lately.

"We were. I was a year older, which had its challenges, especially when I went to college in Chicago. Everyone talks about how young couples try to make long-distance work and fail in the first few months. That wasn't us. All my friends were hooking up with a different girl every night, but the only girl I wanted was Cora."

Rowan's full attention is glued to me. She's always like this. Whenever she's here, she's present. Not distracted by her phone or scrolling through social media. In fact, I've rarely seen her on her phone.

"Even though she stayed close to home for college, we made it work," I explain. "But when it was time for med school, she chose to go to Northwestern despite her father's wish that she go somewhere near here. But even he couldn't deny the prestige and bragging rights being accepted to Northwestern for med school would give him. So she moved to Chicago. A year later, I asked her to marry me. The rest, I suppose, is history," I finish with a sad smile.

"That's really sweet."

"It wasn't always easy. Two med students. Insane hours. Constant stress. But that didn't matter to us. We just wanted to be together."

"That's life, though, isn't it? Finding that one person you're willing to fight to be with, no matter the obstacles?"

"I guess it is." I shift my gaze forward for a beat before clearing my throat and returning my attention to her. "What about you? Any boyfriend I should expect to come visit?"

I take a slow sip of my scotch, my jaw ticking at the thought of someone else touching her the way I'll never be able to.

"Before I left, I was sort of seeing someone."

"Was it serious?"

She pushes out a nervous laugh. "You could say that."

"What happened?"

She hesitates, chewing on her lower lip. Which only draws my attention to them. Makes me wonder how they taste.

"We were engaged before my little health scare. I'm fine now," she adds quickly, like she did the last time she brought it up. "But when you go through something like that, you start re-evaluating things. I remember lying in that hospital bed, full of regrets. So I decided to Marie Kondo my life."

"Marie Kondo your life?"

She shrugs. "I got rid of anything that didn't spark joy."

"And this fiancé of yours?" I press tentatively. "Did he spark joy?"

I say a silent prayer that the answer is no. It's a ridiculous notion, but a part of me wants to be the one who does that for her.

"More like our priorities were no longer aligned." She swallows hard, and I sense there's more to her statement. "So we broke off our engagement."

"That must have been difficult."

"At first, it was. But now I'm grateful he showed his true colors. Life's too short for mediocrity. I mean, think about it." She turns fully toward me, her eyes bright. "The average life expectancy for women in this country is about eighty-one years. That's just under thirty thousand days. Sounds like a lot, right?"

"I suppose."

"But once you factor in how much of that is spent working and going to school, you only get a few thousand days to make it count."

There's a flicker of something in her expression. Something that looks like sadness. But it vanishes just as quickly.

"So many people stay miserable because they think there's no other option," she continues. "They stay with their spouse. They continue going to that boring job. They keep driving the reliable sedan. Not me. Not anymore."

I'm completely mesmerized by her. The way her

eyes light up. The way her hands move when she's passionate. I can physically feel her thirst for life.

But our circumstances are vastly different.

She has her entire life ahead of her. No responsibilities holding her back.

Not like me.

"You're young. You can just pick up and try something new. Not everyone has that luxury."

"I don't agree. Is it harder when people rely on you? Sure. But that doesn't mean you should stay unhappy." She folds her legs underneath her body, leaning closer, her attention fully devoted to me. "What about you? What sparks joy for you?"

"Sparks joy?"

"Exactly. Right now. This second. What makes you happy?"

"My kids," I say without a moment's hesitation. "Even if they frustrate me sometimes."

She grins. "Good. They get to stay."

I chuckle despite myself. "They'll be thrilled."

"What else?"

I shake my head, searching my brain for something else. But nothing comes.

"If you had a gratitude journal, what would you write in it?" she prods.

"A gratitude journal?"

"I write in mine every night nand come up with three things I'm grateful for."

"Don't you run out?" I ask, unsure if I'd be able to come up with three things to be grateful for total, let alone three things every day.

"No," she says. "Sometimes I repeat things because I'm feeling grateful for them again. It's not about novelty. It's about choosing to be grateful for the things in my life instead of wishing for something else. So your kids are one. What else?"

"My nanny," I say before I can stop myself. "I'm definitely grateful for her."

The air shifts, her eyes landing on mine. It probably only lasts a matter of seconds, but it feels like an eternity as her gaze holds mine, my admission hanging between us.

"I spark joy. Phew," she says around a nervous laugh, pretending to wipe sweat from her brow. "Guess I can keep my job for another day."

"I don't think it's possible for you *not* to spark joy in someone, Rowan."

She smiles, a blush blooming across her cheeks.

I shouldn't keep saying things like this. She's my nanny.

My *employee*.

But between the scotch, the anniversary, and Jude's voice echoing in my head, I find myself admitting things I shouldn't.

"One more," she says softly.

I part my lips, about to say my family.

"And it can't be a person," she adds, as if sensing what I'm about to say.

I snap my mouth shut and stare ahead. "I don't think there is anything else," I say with a self-deprecating laugh.

It's a bit of a rude awakening to learn there's

nothing else in my life that makes me happy. Nothing else I'm grateful for.

"What about your job?" she suggests. "Don't you enjoy what you do?"

"I…did."

"Did?"

"In Chicago. The ER. I loved it. The chaos. The pace. Never knowing what would come through those doors."

"It seems like a big change between a Chicago emergency room to a small town family medical practice."

"You have no idea."

"Then why are you working there? Why not work at an emergency room around here?"

"I figure taking over Robert's practice is the least I can do, all things considered."

She scrunches her brows. "What do you mean?"

"Because it's my fault his daughter's gone."

She straightens. "Why do you think that?"

"Because it's the truth."

"Did *you* hit her car?"

"No, but—"

"But nothing," she interjects. "It's not your fault."

I shake my head, refusing to agree with her. I can't. Not when I know I'm to blame.

"I should have insisted she get checked out after the accident. Hell, I didn't even examine her damn pupils, the easiest fucking thing to do to check for any sign of brain trauma. Instead, I let her sit in that waiting room while Presley was in surgery. By the time anyone realized what was happening, it was too late."

"It's not like you knew."

"I *should* have known."

My voice seems to echo in the stillness of the house, the ache in my throat and chest nearly unbearable. Not just for Cora, but for my kids.

"I'm a doctor, for crying out loud. I should have seen the signs. And now, because of me, my kids are going to grow up without a mother. Jemmy will grow up without any memories of her. All because I failed her. Failed them."

"Listen to me, Hayden."

She clutches my cheeks, not allowing me to escape this. I inhale a sharp breath at the feel of her touch, hating it yet craving it at the same time.

"You can't do this to yourself." Her voice is fierce, full of passion and life and everything I haven't allowed myself to experience for the past year. "You can't keep beating yourself up over this. I may not be as old as you are, but I know I wouldn't want to go through life with this much regret. This much guilt. You shouldn't either. And you definitely shouldn't let anyone else put that guilt or blame on you.

"Is what happened to your wife a tragedy? Of course. But your kids deserve better than a father who spends his days weighed down by guilt and regret. *You* deserve better than spending your days weighed down by guilt and regret. You deserve to be happy. To follow your dreams. To find those things that bring you joy. To—"

Before I can fully wrap my head around what I'm doing, I surge forward and press my mouth to hers, cutting her off mid-sentence, the words dying between us as our lips collide.

For half a second, she's still, her breath hitching softly against my mouth. In that fragile pause, every warning bell in my head goes berserk.

This is wrong. She's my employee. My kids are upstairs. It's the anniversary of my wife's death. I should pull back. Apologize. Pretend it never happened.

But the instant a tiny whimper falls from her throat, I forget everything other than her lips, warm and impossibly soft. I feel her kiss everywhere — down my spine, through my chest, loosening something that's been locked tight for so long I'd forgotten what it feels like to want.

I pull her closer, gripping her hips, like I'm afraid she'll disappear if I let go.

Like I'm afraid I will.

Her fingers curl into the front of my shirt, and the contact sends a quiet, aching need through me. She tastes of chamomile and something sweet. It's intoxicating in the most dangerous way.

For a few stolen seconds, the grief, the ache, the endless self-recrimination all go quiet. In their place is Rowan's breath mingling with mine, her mouth moving gently against mine.

For the first time in over a year, I don't feel like I'm just surviving.

I feel something warm. Real. Hopeful.

And that's what scares me the most.

Reality comes crashing back all at once, and I tear

away, jumping to my feet, my chest heaving like I've just surfaced from deep water.

I stare at Rowan's swollen lips for several protracted moments, horrified at myself. At how easy it was to forget. At how badly I wanted to stay suspended in that brief, reckless moment where the world didn't hurt so much.

"I shouldn't have done that."

I avert my gaze. If I don't — if I keep staring at the softness of her mouth, the faint flush in her cheeks, the proof that she felt it too — I fear I won't be strong enough to walk away.

"It's okay." She stands, stepping toward me. "I—"

"You're my nanny." My words come out sharp.

Too sharp.

But I need them to be. Need them to help re-build a wall between us before I do something I'll regret.

I don't look back as I climb the stairs, each step heavier than the last.

And when I pass a photo of Cora and the kids, the guilt and regret returns full force, reminding me why I don't deserve anything good.

Why I don't deserve Rowan.

TWENTY-TWO

Rowan

I wake up earlier than usual, the sky still dark beyond the window, the mountains nothing more than soft shadows against a midnight blue horizon.

Normally, I'd be outside by now, sitting on Hayden's front porch with a mug of coffee warming my hands, watching the sun creep up over the peaks. It's become one of my favorite rituals.

But this morning, I stay put.

I'm not ready to face Hayden. Not after last night.

Not after that kiss.

God. That kiss.

I squeeze my eyes shut, but it doesn't help. It's still there, the feel of his mouth against mine, warm and firm and desperate, like he'd been holding his breath for a year and finally let himself inhale. The way he held me. The way my entire body responded to him.

I've kissed plenty of men.

But I've never been kissed like that.

There was grief in it. And guilt. And longing so sharp it felt like it might slice us both open if we weren't careful.

But for one suspended, beautiful moment, I didn't care. I kissed him back without thinking about consequences or boundaries or dead wives whose hearts beat in my chest.

Instead, I let myself feel.

And it was everything I didn't realize I've been missing since I drove away in my van.

I roll onto my back and stare at the ceiling, exhaling slowly in an attempt to push down the unease about the situation.

Tomorrow will be easier.

Tomorrow, there will be kids. Schedules. Distractions.

Today, I need some dog therapy.

***

The shelter smells like wet fur and happiness that's been waiting patiently for a second chance.

I sign in, greet one of the shelter employees at the desk, and get paired with a spotted brown mutt who looks like he's part terrier, part something else entirely, and one hundred percent thrilled to be alive and about to get some much-needed fresh air.

"Ready for an adventure?" I ask Sergeant Puppers, clipping on his leash.

His tail thumps like it's trying to break free of his body.

Same, buddy.

Sycamore Falls is fully committed to Christmas now — garland strung between lampposts, wreaths on every door, twinkle lights framing every building. Store windows glow, and people actually stop to strike up a conversation.

Back in Chicago, I could walk for miles without anyone noticing I existed.

Here, locals ask about my day. About how I'm enjoying Sycamore Falls. About the kids.

It'll make it difficult to leave this place when the time comes.

And it will come.

It has to.

This isn't my home.

But is Chicago?

I'm not quite sure anymore.

After navigating through the sidewalks of the downtown area, I steer Sergeant Puppers onto a side street, allowing him to sniff any and everything that makes him happy. Who knows when he'll get the chance to go for a walk again.

As he follows his nose, we eventually end up outside a set of iron gates that open to a cemetery on a hill.

Every instinct tells me to turn around. To keep walking. To mind my own business. Instead, I allow the dog to pull me inside.

I walk slowly, reading names and dates, unsure what I'm looking for.

At least that's what I tell myself, even though I wonder if *she's* buried here. So as I meander along the paved path, I keep an eye out for any markers bearing the last name Lawrence.

I find Ryan Lawrence first. Died fifteen years ago. This must be Hayden's father. He hasn't spoken about him all that much, but Dylan mentioned he passed away when she was only ten.

I touch the cool stone, saying a silent prayer for a man I've never met, then continue on. A few rows later, I find yet another Lawrence.

Aspen Lawrence.

Who lived only two days.

My eyes burn with unshed tears over a life that never had a chance to become anything else.

Then I see it.

Large. Ornate. Impossible to miss.

Fresh roses rest against it, the red hue stark against the gray stone.

I approach slowly, my heart pounding with every step I take until I'm standing directly in front of it. I run my fingers over the letters of her name, my thoughts a jumbled mess. As if it wasn't enough to stare at a life-sized portrait of her yesterday. Now I'm standing in front of her headstone.

Still, like everything else in my life, I'm confident there's a reason I found this cemetery when I wasn't looking. Like some bigger force brought me to this exact spot.

"You don't know me, and I have no idea why I'm here."

My voice doesn't shake, which surprises me.

"Maybe it's selfish. Or maybe the universe is weird and likes irony." I huff out a breath. "I'm Hayden's nanny. Well, Presley and Jemmy's nanny. And they're kind of amazing." A small smile tugs at my mouth.

"Presley's art is unreal. When I was her age, I could barely manage a stick figure. But she notices things most adults don't. When she draws, it's like she's capturing how things feel, not just how they look. She's going to do amazing things. I can feel it. And Jemmy…" I shake my head as a laugh escapes.

"He's obsessed with dinosaurs. Like, truly believes he is one. Bath time involves a lot of roaring. Loud, very convincing roaring. I'm surprised the neighbors haven't complained."

I pause, as my smile fades into something gentler. Something sadder.

"They love their dad so much," I say softly. "They light up the second he walks into a room, even when he doesn't realize it. Or maybe because he doesn't think he deserves it."

I swallow, my gaze dropping to the roses at the base of the stone, wondering if he left them for her.

"He's kind and patient and exhausted in this quiet way that breaks my heart. He praises Presley's art like it belongs in the Louvre. He lets Jemmy climb all over him like he's a jungle gym, even when he's clearly running on fumes."

I glance at the gray sky, recalling our conversation last night. Everything he shared with me. The pain, the anguish, the blame. I feel the weight of it.

"He thinks he failed them. Failed you." My voice drops. "Blames himself for what happened to you. And the weight of that blame…" I push out a quivering exhale through the ache slowly building in my throat.

"I think he's convinced he doesn't deserve to feel anything good again. That he doesn't deserve to be happy. But if anyone does, it's him. And I know this is wrong. Know I shouldn't be telling you all these things, considering you were his wife. But when I'm with him, when I see him smile…a part of me wants to be the reason he smiles. And I hate myself a little for noticing him. For the way my chest tightens when I see him, or the way I want to reach for him when he looks like he's drowning in his own thoughts. In his guilt."

I press my lips together, breathing through the emotions overwhelming me as I think of Hayden.

"He deserves peace. And I wish… I wish he could forgive himself. Even a little." I stare into the distance, smiling sadly before clearing my throat. "But I'm not here to tell you about Hayden. I'm not sure why I *am* here. I guess I just wanted to say thank you. If it weren't for you, I wouldn't be alive." I press my hand to my chest, relishing in the steady thumping of my heart.

Her heart.

"I promise I'll take care of them for you. All three of them."

I touch my hand to the stone once more. Then I turn my attention back to Sergeant Puppers. "In the mood for a pup cup?"

He barks, enthusiastic and entirely unburdened. Truth be told, I feel slightly unburdened, too. Like sharing my thoughts and feelings with Cora's gravestone lightened my own emotional load.

With a firm grip on the leash, I start back the way we came, the cemetery still empty.

Except for a woman with almost white hair standing by Ryan Lawrence's headstone.

Hayden's mom.

I lower my head, attempting to slip past without her noticing me, not sure how I'll explain my presence in a cemetery. But then I hear her voice.

"Rowan? Is that you?"

I stiffen, cursing under my breath before facing her, feigning surprise at seeing her. "Mrs. Lawrence."

"I told you. Call me Danielle."

She approaches and wraps me in a warm hug. I can't remember the last time my own parents showed me affection like this. Yet this woman who is practically a stranger does.

"What are you doing here?" she asks as she pulls back.

I part my lips, struggling to come up with an explanation.

Visiting my boss's dead wife whose heart now beats inside my chest seems like…a lot.

"I've always found cemeteries interesting," I say dismissively. "That's not too morbid, is it?"

"Not at all. There's so much history here." She gestures toward a small hill in the distance, two massive oak trees standing like sentinels guarding a cluster of weathered, slanted stones. "That's where the founders of this town are buried. A lot of families are, actually. Generations worth."

My gaze drifts back to the headstone she'd been standing in front of moments ago.

"Is that your husband?" I ask gently.

"Yes." Her smile turns a little wistful but doesn't fade. "I like stopping by every so often. Updating him on how the kids are doing. That way, it doesn't feel like he's missing out on everything."

"Do you think he hears you?"

"I like to think so," she says after a moment's contemplation. "I know it might sound strange and a little *woo-woo*, but after I tell Ryan what's been on my mind, I feel…lighter. Less burdened."

I nod, knowing all too well how that feels.

It's how I feel right now, too.

"Well…" I adjust the leash in my hand. "I should probably get back. I promised this little man a pup cup before bringing him back to the shelter." I nod toward Sergeant Puppers. "I'm sure I'll see you sometime this week."

I head down the path leading toward the gate.

"What are your plans this afternoon?" Danielle calls out, stopping me.

I face her. "I'm not really sure yet."

Which is true. I'd considered checking out the Christmas Festival at Holley Ridge, since everyone in town seems to be buzzing about it, but I haven't made any concrete plans, aside from avoiding Hayden at all costs.

"If you're not busy later, it's Second Sunday."

I tilt my head. "Second Sunday?"

"It's a tradition I started a few years ago now that all my kids are grown and out of the house. I host a family get-together on the second Sunday of every month. Lots of food. Wine. Beer. It can get a little loud and chaotic," she adds with a grin, "but it's my favorite day of the month. I'd love for you to join us."

"I wouldn't want to intrude on your family time."

"Which is exactly why you should be there," she says without missing a beat. "You're part of this family now, too."

I haven't felt like I was part of a family in a while. You'd think when I was in the hospital, my parents would have visited me more often. My father had his personal assistant send flowers, but I could count on one hand the number of times either of them actually stopped by to see me. And when I told my father I was quitting the law firm to travel the country in a van, he thought I'd lost my mind.

He didn't understand how nearly dying could have changed my perspective on life. He figured I'd be happy to jump right back into my so-called career of working eighty hours a week in the hopes of becoming a junior partner in the next few years. Because that's what he did.

"I should probably check with Hayden to make sure he's okay with it."

Danielle waves a dismissive hand. "Who cares what he says? *I'm* inviting you." Her expression softens. "I hate the idea of you being left out. And it's not just immediate family. You've met Dylan's roommate, Claire, right?"

I nod. "We met up for a drink last weekend."

"She'll be there, too. Along with a few other family friends. Everyone's welcome at my table."

I open my mouth to protest again, but then I remember my rule to say yes, even if it scares me a little.

"Thank you, Danielle," I say finally. "I'd love to come. Do you need me to bring anything?"

"Just yourself," she responds with a wink, already turning away. "I'll see you later."

I watch her walk off between the rows of headstones, cursing my year of yes for the first time.

So much for having a day without seeing Hayden.

TWENTY-THREE

Hayden

My mother's driveway is already full.

Cars spill onto the street in both directions, like the whole damn town decided to show up today.

Over the past year, our family dinners have grown in size, like my mother's quietly been rebuilding something piece by piece. At first, it was just me, my kids, and my siblings.

Then Beckham got married, Haley and her daughter Maggie folding seamlessly into the mix. Jude met Abbey, and even without a ring, it's obvious she's not going anywhere. Finn finally stopped lying to himself about being in love with his best friend, and now Genevieve's pregnant, glowing, and somehow still laughing at his terrible jokes.

My immediate family may have shrunk after Cora

died, but my extended family grew. And it seems to keep growing.

I step out of my SUV, helping Presley down before slipping around to the other side to get Jemmy out of his car seat.

The moment I open the front door to my childhood home, I'm assaulted with a wall of sound. Laughter ricochets off the ceiling as someone argues about football in the living room. The smell of garlic, tomatoes, and fresh bread hangs thick in the air.

Jemmy squirms in my hold and I set him down. The second I do, he takes off running, Presley close behind.

"Slow down," I call, even though it's useless.

They don't even look back. They barrel down the hallway into their favorite room in the house.

The toy room.

I kick the front door closed behind me and take in the familiar surroundings. It's too big for one person, and I've told my mom that more than once. Suggested maybe it's time to downsize into something smaller now that we've all moved out.

But she always shuts me down. Says she wants us to know we can always come home. That this place still belongs to all of us.

I think the real reason is simpler.

This is the house she bought with my dad. Where they made memories.

She isn't ready to let go of those just yet.

Unlike me, who couldn't get out of Chicago fast enough. Who couldn't breathe in the house Cora and I shared without feeling like every room was accusing me of failing her.

I draw in a deep breath, then head through the foyer and into the living room, grateful for the distraction of being around my family.

Especially after last night.

After kissing Rowan.

I'd spent most of the night convincing myself it was a mistake.

That I was out of my mind with grief and I crossed a line I shouldn't have. One I won't cross again.

But that didn't stop me from replaying it in my mind all night long.

Her warmth.

The way she fit against me like she belonged there.

The soft, surprised sound she made when my mouth found hers.

It's a blessing in disguise she has the day off. It's given me space to figure out the best way to approach the situation when I see her next.

Although a part of me was disappointed when I didn't see her sitting on the porch this morning, bundled up against the cold like she usually is.

I say my hellos to my siblings and their spouses, accepting hugs, claps on the shoulder, familiar grins.

Well, most of them are familiar.

There's one face I can't quite place.

"You remember Joshua, right?" Finn says as he releases me from his hug, as if able to read my thoughts. "Dylan and Claire's friend."

Joshua stands, pulling himself to his full height, making me do a double take.

The Joshua I remember was a scrawny little boy who always hung around my sister and her best friend, Claire. That's not the case anymore.

"Of course." I extend my hand toward him. "How are you?"

"Doing well. Thank you."

"Dylan mentioned you're working at Holley Ridge with Claire."

"Sure am. Although not technically *with* Claire. She's in charge of marketing. I'm the head groundskeeper there now."

"What does that entail?"

"Landscaping and maintenance. Making sure the entire place looks pretty and runs smoothly."

I nod. That checks out. From what I remember, he always liked getting his hands dirty and fixing things that broke.

"If you'll excuse me, my mother will murder me if I don't go say hello."

Joshua laughs. "Fair enough."

I follow the sound of my mom's voice toward the kitchen.

At one point, she did all the cooking herself. Now Dylan's taken over most of it, experimenting with recipes she wants to test out for her private chef business.

I've never been happier to be a guinea pig.

"Hey, Ma," I start, turning the corner. "Sorry I'm late. We had—"

I stop short.

Because it's not only my mother and Dylan in the kitchen.

Rowan is here, too.

She's wearing a soft green sweater, her hair pulled back in a loose knot, light makeup on her face, along with a hint of gloss on her lips.

Her fucking lips.

I can't stop staring at them, especially now that I know how they feel.

How they taste.

What I wouldn't give to feel them again. To taste them again. To feel her body move against mine as her breaths intermingled with mine.

But I can't. I *won't*. She's my nanny. Nothing more.

"I assume Presley and Jemmy went straight to the playroom." Mom's voice forces me to look away from Rowan.

I move toward the refrigerator and grab a beer, even though I'd prefer something a bit stronger right now.

Something that burns.

"Of course they did."

"I hope you don't mind I invited Rowan," she remarks as I flick the top off the bottle and take a large gulp. "I ran into her at the cemetery this morning."

I nearly spit out my beer, fighting to force it down my throat. "The cemetery?" I look at Rowan. "Why were you at the cemetery?"

"I was walking a shelter dog. We were just wandering around and stumbled across it."

"Bark Twain?" I ask, remembering the dog she was

walking during our first meeting that resulted in me wearing my coffee.

"Thankfully, he's been adopted." She smiles, and I have to push down the warmth seeping through me from how damn beautiful she is whenever she does.

"Then who was it today? Bilbo Waggins? Winnie the Pooch?"

She tilts her head. "You remember the names?"

"It's hard to forget names like that," I say carefully.

What I don't say is I remember everything about Rowan.

The way she hums under her breath when she's distracted.

The way she dances when she doesn't think anyone's watching.

The exact curve of her mouth when she smiles, especially when she's trying not to.

I force my eyes away from her, aware of my mother's analytical stare scrutinizing everything I do or say.

"Do you need help with anything, Ma?"

"We've got it all under control." She flashes me a conniving grin, entirely too pleased.

"Okay."

I turn to leave, but as I do, my gaze snags on Rowan again. Our eyes meet for half a second, long enough for something to spark between us.

I quickly look away and hurry out of the kitchen, not breathing until I'm safe in the living room with my brothers.

But all I can think about is Rowan.

So much for spending a few hours with my family to distract me from her.

And the kiss I can't stop thinking about.

TWENTY-FOUR

Hayden

Dinner at my mother's house is never quiet.

Plates clatter. Glasses clink. Voices overlap in a dozen directions at once. Someone's always asking for the butter. Someone else is telling a story that gets interrupted halfway through. And there's at least one argument brewing over something inconsequential, usually sports-related.

Today is no different.

Yet somehow, despite the chaos, everyone's attention keeps drifting back to Rowan.

She's seated halfway down the table, her expression animated, obviously feeding off the energy of being in a room full of people.

"And then I realized I'd parked my van for the night in what I thought was a beautiful spot along the beach," Rowan says, laughing. "Turns out it was also the meeting point for a sunrise yoga class. At five a.m., someone rang a bell so aggressively I thought it was a tsunami alarm or something. I woke up convinced the world was ending. When I slipped out of my van to see what was going on, the instructor invited me to 'embrace the morning.' And because it's my year of yes…"

"You joined them?" Dylan asks with a single brow arched.

"I spent twenty minutes pretending to stretch while seriously considering whether crawling back into my van and driving off counted as personal growth."

The table erupts in laughter.

"Don't get me wrong. I love yoga. But there's a time and a place for it. And it's not five in the morning. But as I was attempting to contort my body into a one-legged pigeon pose, I don't know…" She pushes out a breath, a peaceful smile tugging on her lips. "There was something about doing yoga as the sun rose that sparked something inside me. So since that day, I've tried to start every day by doing yoga as the sun rises. I've added it to my life list."

"Your life list?" Joshua asks from beside her, leaning closer.

Closer than I'd like.

"It's sort of like a bucket list, I guess. But small things. Nothing like snorkeling the Great Barrier Reef or seeing the penguins in Antarctica, as awesome as both of those experiences would be. But my life list is more about finding joy in the little things. Like watching the sun rise every morning. Or slowing down and savoring that first cup of coffee. Or sleeping in on Sundays. Little things that can make your life feel…fuller."

I watch her without meaning to. The way her hands move when she talks, expressive and sure. The way her eyes light up when talking about the things that excite her.

She's everything I'm not.

"What about your family?" my mother asks. "They must miss you."

Something shifts in Rowan's expression. Her smile briefly falters. Her fingers tighten around her fork before she sets it down.

"I don't really have that kind of relationship with my parents."

"Oh. I'm sorry, dear," Mom replies.

Rowan shrugs. "My father was more upset I quit my job at the law firm where he's a senior managing partner," she continues. "Couldn't understand why I wouldn't want to work sixteen-hour days on the off chance I'd make junior partner someday. The truth is, I only went to law school because I thought maybe it would give us something in common. Maybe he'd like me more."

My chest tightens as I listen to her. She never told me about herself or her family. Then again, I never asked.

"My parents weren't around much when I was growing up," she explains. "I was basically raised by nannies. My mother was too busy with her socialite friends. And my father was always gone before I woke up, and didn't get home until after I went to bed. There was never any of this."

She gestures around the table — the noise, the closeness, the way everyone genuinely cares for each other, even if we get on each other's nerves at times.

It all clicks into place.

From the very beginning, Rowan pushed me to spend time with my kids. To sit down for dinner. To take mornings slow. I thought she was just trying to give them structure.

Now I realize she was trying to give them what she never had.

A parent who chose them.

"Well," my mother begins softly, "you're always welcome at my table. Consider yourself an honorary Lawrence."

"Thank you." Rowan gives her a sincere smile before shifting her gaze and landing on mine.

It lasts a heartbeat.

But in that single look, something passes between us. Recognition. Understanding. A quiet, dangerous intimacy that has nothing to do with the kiss and everything to do with what we see in each other.

"What's been your favorite place to visit so far?" Finn asks, and I force myself to look away.

"Sycamore Falls is definitely working its way to the top," she replies, and I feel that stupid, traitorous flare of something warm in my chest. "But before I came here, I'd have to say Santa Fe."

"Santa Fe?" Joshua presses.

"When I was a kid, I was obsessed with *Newsies*," she

explains. "Okay. I still am. And the main character is always talking about Santa Fe like it's this magical place where all his troubles would magically disappear. I'd never been, so I went."

"And?" Joshua asks, leaning in again.

And again, I have to resist the urge to shout at him to keep his distance.

"It was incredible," she replies. "The food. The art. The history. It felt…layered. Like the place had lived a lot of lives."

Joshua smiles. "Sounds amazing."

She meets his eyes. "It was."

I shouldn't care how he's looking at her. Or how easily she laughs at something he says under his breath. Joshua's a good person. One of my sister's closest friends. Practically family.

But I can't deny the truth.

I want to be the one who makes her laugh.

The one she curves toward.

The one who can touch her without it being wrong.

Jude nudges my knee under the table before leaning close. "If looks could kill."

I snap my gaze to him. "What?"

"The way you're shooting daggers at poor Josh."

"I'm doing no such thing," I respond, taking a long pull from my beer.

Rowan laughs again, unguarded and bright, and it's impossible not to look.

Or, more accurately, glare, especially as Joshua inches closer to her.

"They'd make a cute couple, don't you think?" Jude remarks.

"Who?" I ask, even though I know.

"Josh and Rowan. He's clearly into her. Has barely looked at anyone else since we sat down to eat. Then again, neither have you."

"I'm not into her," I say defensively. "And Rowan's free to date anyone she wants."

The words taste wrong. Bitter.

Because the idea of Joshua touching her, *kissing* her, sets something off inside me. Something hot and possessive.

I never felt this way about Cora.

Why do I feel this way about Rowan?

"I said the same thing about Abbey," Jude continues, not dropping it. "Our situations are pretty similar when you think about it. She was also my employee who lived with me."

"I'm not attracted to Rowan," I lie.

"Whatever helps you sleep at night." He pauses. "Want my advice?"

"No." I take another long gulp of my beer, trying to look anywhere but at Rowan. But my eyes keep finding her.

"Too bad," Jude retorts. "Stop telling yourself all the reasons you don't deserve to be happy and just let yourself be happy. However that looks for you."

I shift my eyes forward, immediately reminded of my conversation with Rowan last night. About the things that spark joy for me.

My kids.

Rowan.

And her kiss.

Hell, that kiss sparked more than joy. It sparked something I thought died with my wife.

Which is why I need to forget about it. Pretend it never happened.

Because it wasn't just one of the best kisses of my life.

It was the most dangerous, too.

TWENTY-FIVE

Rowan

A cheer rips through the crowded bar as someone belts out the chorus to "Livin' on a Prayer", most of them too drunk to care about pitch.

The large room is dim and sticky in that charming, well-loved way, neon beer signs buzzing against the walls. The air smells like spilled whiskey, citrus cleaner, and whatever's been frying in the kitchen.

After dinner, I'd been looking forward to curling up in bed. But when Dylan invited me to join her, Claire, and Joshua at a local bar for karaoke night, I knew I had to take the opportunity.

Despite everything I've done this year — sleeping in my van under desert stars, waking up in new states with no plan — I've never been to a karaoke bar.

So I said yes.

I also wasn't ready to go home yet.

Even with my own space, I can feel Hayden whenever I'm there, so I opted for a distraction.

And karaoke has definitely been an amazing distraction.

I haven't thought about that kiss once since I got here. It's hard to think about it when listening to a wide range of locals sing. Some people have been quite good. But others… Well, they don't seem to care how bad they sound. They're having fun. And that's all that matters.

"The show's on the stage. Not on those TVs," Claire says, nudging Dylan, who quickly tears her gaze away from the various screens hanging over the bar.

"I'm watching the show," she argues.

"Right," Joshua draws out with a playful roll of his eyes. "We know you better than that."

I steal a glance toward the bar, all three screens broadcasting the same hockey game. "Are you a hockey fan?"

"You could say that," Claire answers for Dylan. "Or a fan of a certain hockey player." She waggles her brows, bringing her drink to her lips.

"It's nothing." Dylan turns her attention to me. "Archer Ward grew up next door to us. He and Finn were close since they both played hockey together. That's all." She looks straight ahead, her expression distant.

I get the feeling there's a lot more to the story than she's telling me.

And based on her friends' expressions, there definitely is. But I don't know Dylan well enough to press.

So I return my attention to the stage just as the song ends, the entire bar cheering as if they just witnessed one of the biggest names in music perform instead of a local singing off-key.

"Next up is Joshua!" the MC announces.

We all clap as Joshua stands, mock-bowing.

"You better have chosen something good," he calls to Claire, wagging a finger.

Apparently, they have a rule whenever they come to karaoke together. You don't choose your own song. Someone else does. They told me I didn't have to play their game if I didn't want to. But who knows when I'll have the chance to do something like this again?

I've had to come to terms with the fact that life is short.

So I not only agreed to sing, but allowed Joshua to pick a song for me.

I just pray I don't regret it.

I take a small sip of my drink and look to the stage, waiting to see what song Claire chose. If the devious grin on her face is any indication, it's a good one.

The beat drops, and I can't help but burst out laughing when he sings the opening lines of "I'm Too Sexy".

And he's not embarrassed about it either. He struts. He owns it like it's an audition for a singing competition. Women whistle and catcall, and by the first chorus, the entire bar is on their feet dancing along with him.

As he circles his hips, Claire leans into me, laughing. "Now he's just showing off for you."

I blink, shooting my eyes toward her. "What do you mean?"

She gives me a pointed look. "I've known Joshua since we were in diapers. He's definitely into you."

"Into...me?"

"Of course."

"Oh." I glance back at the stage, her words making me view Joshua in a different light.

He's grinning and dancing like he doesn't have a single worry. Like the past doesn't weigh on him. Like joy is something he allows himself to have without apology.

Unlike Hayden.

"It's sort of why we invited you." Dylan nudges me. "Not that we don't enjoy your company," she adds quickly. "But we saw the way he was fawning over you the second you walked into my mom's house."

Claire smooths a dark curl behind her ear. "No pressure, of course. Just thought it would be a good opportunity for you to get to know each other better."

"Joshua is definitely..." I trail off, searching for the right word.

Not brooding.

Not guarded.

Not carrying the weight of the world on his shoulders.

"I don't think I've ever met a man willing to sing about being too sexy in front of a bar full of people and completely own it."

"That's Joshua," Claire says fondly. "He doesn't care

what people think. And he's loyal. One of the best people I know."

I shift my eyes back to the stage. "I can see that."

The song ends to thunderous applause. Joshua bows again, then hops off the stage, hugging a few people he knows as he makes his way back to us.

Before I can say anything, the MC squints at his clipboard again.

"All right, Rowan! You're up!"

My stomach drops. "I don't know if I want to follow that."

Joshua squeezes my arm. "You'll do great."

The way he looks at me should make butterflies explode in my belly.

Instead, there's only a small flutter.

Not like when Hayden looks at me.

Or when his mouth found mine and the world went quiet.

But that's precisely why I'm here. To forget that kiss.

"You better not have picked something cheesy," I warn as I head toward the stage.

Joshua grins. "You're about to find out."

I take the mic, my palms damp, heart racing. This is scarier than I expected. Scarier than sleeping alone in the desert. Scarier than quitting my job and telling my family I was leaving, despite their threats to cut me off financially.

The music starts and the opening notes to Lizzo's "Good as Hell" fill the bar.

At least it's something I know. And quite well. This has sort of been my anthem over the past year. Whenever I've doubted if I did the right thing by leaving the only home I've ever known to finally live my life, I put this song on and immediately feel better. On the surface, it's about a breakup, but for me, it's about rebuilding and choosing myself.

The first verse is a little shaky, but every time my nerves spike, I look at the table. Claire and Dylan dance while Joshua sings along, smiling like he picked this song just for me.

By the chorus, I smile too.

It feels…freeing. Like sunrise yoga. Like driving with the windows down and no destination plugged into my GPS.

When I finish, the bar cheers, and I jump off the stage.

Joshua pulls me into a hug. "That was great."

"It felt good," I admit. "Who knew singing in front of strangers could be so cathartic?"

"It's all about the song choice," he says, winking.

We stay a little longer, the high from performing keeping me going. But after a while, the adrenaline fades and exhaustion creeps in.

Once Claire finished her performance of "Father Figure", which Dylan chose for her, I push back from the table and stand.

"I'm going to call it a night. I have a full day of keeping a toddler entertained tomorrow."

"Would you like a ride home?" Joshua offers, pulling himself to his full height.

Claire drove me here since I took a rideshare to her mom's house for dinner.

While my van is convenient for traveling across the country, it can be a bit difficult driving it around town, especially squeezing it into tight parking spaces. Lately, I've been using Hayden's spare car to drive Jemmy to the library or the park, but I didn't feel right asking to borrow his car today, since it wasn't technically related to my job.

"You don't have to."

"I don't mind." Joshua shrugs. "I'm kind of tired, too, and it's on my way home. No sense taking an Uber when I drive right by your street."

"Oh. Okay. If you're sure."

Joshua gives me a small smile. "I'm sure."

I say my goodbyes to Dylan and Claire with promises to do this again sometime soon. Then I follow Joshua out of the bar.

Outside, the air is crisp and cold, invigorating in the best way. He steers me toward a pickup truck and opens the passenger-side door, helping me in before running around to get behind the wheel.

"It's so quiet," I remark as he drives through the mostly empty streets. If this were Chicago, it would still be bumper-to-bumper traffic.

"Small towns may not be for everyone, but I like it."

"Have you always lived here?" I ask, studying his silhouette. Strong jaw. Full lips. Thick, dark hair. And from what I was able to see during his performance earlier, he has a fairly built physique. He'd have to, considering he works as the head groundskeeper at the local inn.

"More or less. I went away to college for a year, but

then my mom was diagnosed with cancer so I came home and took care of her."

I nod, not pressing the topic further since I already know how that ended. His mother passed away earlier in the year.

"How about you?" he asks after a beat. "Where is home for you? I don't think you ever mentioned."

"My van seems more like home these days than anything else."

Or, more appropriately, Hayden's house does.

But it shouldn't. It's *not* my home.

I need to keep reminding myself of that.

"Where did you live before?" he asks.

I open my mouth, but hesitate. I haven't even mentioned to Hayden I'm originally from Chicago. It's not like I lied. It just never came up.

Although when he's brought up Chicago, I purposefully avoided telling him I also lived there, too worried he might put two and two together and realize the truth.

"Chicago, actually," I finally admit.

"Like Hayden," he muses. "Small world, isn't it?"

I glance out my window as the downtown area transitions into quaint residential neighborhoods. "It sure is."

Although he has no idea exactly how small.

We continue our conversation during the rest of the short drive, Joshua sharing stories about the town. About his job. About his mom. He even tells me how he's recently reconnected with the father he never knew he had, since he's the result of a one-night stand. But thanks to an ancestry kit, he found him.

"Thanks for the ride," I tell him after he pulls up to Hayden's house and helps me down from his truck. "And the introduction to karaoke. I had a lot of fun."

He gives me a warm smile. "Me, too."

I start up the driveway, but only make it a few feet when his voice stops me.

"Rowan."

I turn to face him as he approaches.

"Do you want to go out again next weekend? Just the two of us?" He takes another step toward me, his body a breath from mine. "I'd like to get to know you better."

I part my lips, not immediately responding. *Do* I want to go out with him?

I did enjoy spending time with him. He's fun. Full of life. Makes me laugh. And best of all, he's not some brooding grump whose personality can change in a heartbeat.

Maybe this is what I need. To spend time with someone else. Someone more appropriate. Someone who can help me forget about that kiss.

"I'd like that," I finally say.

"Great." Joshua's eyes light up in a way I don't think Hayden's ever have. "Are you free Saturday evening? Say around seven?"

"It's a date."

"Perfect." He leans in and brushes his lips against my cheek. "See you then," he murmurs in a husky tone that sends a slight shiver down my spine.

It's not the same as the shivers that overtake me whenever Hayden is close, but I need to stop comparing everyone to Hayden. He's my boss. Nothing more.

"See you then," I echo, turning from him once more and making my way into the house.

But as sleep evades me throughout the night, it's not Joshua's kiss I replay in my mind.

It's Hayden's.

TWENTY-SIX

Hayden

My alarm goes off in the dark, shrill and unforgiving. And entirely too early for my liking, especially after barely sleeping all night.

I scrub a hand over my face and stare at the ceiling. The house is quiet, wrapped in peaceful stillness. I used to love this time of day. It felt controlled. Predictable.

Now it feels like a countdown.

I've been dreading this morning since yesterday. Hell, since Saturday night when I made the colossal mistake of kissing Rowan.

Granted, I saw her yesterday, but there were other people at my mom's house. Noise. Distractions.

Today there's no buffer.

Nothing to distract me from what happened between us.

I swing my legs over the side of my bed and sit there for a moment, elbows braced on my knees.

For half a second, I toy with the idea of firing her. Telling her it's not working out.

But on what grounds?

Because I kissed her and can't stop thinking about it?

I doubt that would go over well.

Plus, she's damn good with the kids. Better than good. She's nurturing and patient in a way my kids haven't had in a long time.

Not since they lost their mother.

That's what matters.

That's all that *should* matter.

It doesn't stop me from remembering the way Rowan felt against me. The way her breath caught when I deepened the kiss. The way her fingers fisted in my shirt.

I quickly shut down the thought and jump to my feet, heading for the shower.

By the time I make my way downstairs, the house smells like pancakes and coffee.

Presley is at the table, her tongue peeking out in concentration as she colors something in her sketchpad. Jemmy is in his high chair, banging a plastic spoon against the tray in an uneven rhythm, singing along to whatever song is in his head.

Rowan is at the stove, her hair pulled up, a soft white sweater slipping off one shoulder, revealing her smooth skin. She flips a pancake with easy precision, then glances my way.

"Morning." Her tone isn't cold. But it's not warm, either.

It's more polite. Professional. As if reminding me of what our relationship is supposed to be.

"Morning," I reply, already moving toward the coffee maker.

Normally, I have no problem striking up a conversation with her. I'd ask her how she slept and what her plans were for the day.

I don't today, trying to keep our interactions to a minimum. All because I don't trust myself after that kiss.

And how I can't stop thinking about it. How I can't stop thinking about pinning her against the wall and tasting her again.

But this time, not stopping.

"Is that okay with you?" Her voice cuts through my thoughts.

I look her way, wondering how long I've been staring at my coffee mug.

"I'm sorry. What?"

"I was just saying I'm going to take Jemmy to the library for story time this morning. I wanted to make sure it was okay with you."

"Right." I shake off the fog and bring my coffee to my lips. "Yeah. That's fine."

"Thanks."

I turn from her and head to the table, like I usually do.

And like she usually does, she slides a plate full of pancakes in front of Presley before placing one in front of me containing eggs, toast, and sliced fruit.

But instead of joining us, she heads back to the sink, cleaning the dirty pans and bowls.

"Aren't you going to eat?" I ask, placing a napkin in my lap.

"I already did. You guys enjoy some time together before work and school." She gives me a small smile that doesn't reach her eyes.

Then she slips out of the kitchen.

The air instantly shifts. Like something essential has been removed.

I look down at my plate, then back toward the living room where she's picking up the toys I never got to last night. She moves efficiently. Quietly. Like she's trying not to take up space.

When I turn back, Presley is staring at me with something that looks a lot like accusation. As if she knows I somehow fucked up.

I did, but I'm not about to get into the details with my seven year old.

"Looking forward to school?" I ask her, clearing my throat.

She narrows her eyes, giving me pure attitude.

God help me when she's thirteen.

Sensing I won't get much response from her right now, I shift my focus to Jemmy. "Excited about story time?"

He points to Rowan's empty chair.

"Ro-Ro."

"Yeah. She's taking you to the library."

"No. Ro-Ro."

"She already ate, bud."

"Ro-Ro."

I drag a hand down my face and mutter under my breath, "I'm just batting a thousand today."

Presley snorts.

Not the reaction I was hoping for, but at this point I'll take it.

I slice into my eggs and eat faster than I usually do, just so this awkward breakfast can be over.

When I finish, I take Jemmy out of his high chair and set his feet on the floor. The instant I do, he takes off into the living room, toddling toward the bin full of toys Rowan just picked up, dumping them out.

"Bud, Ro-Ro just cleaned all those up."

"It's okay," she assures him with a smile. "I knew that would happen. But sometimes it's best to start with a clean slate."

"I suppose," I murmur. "Are you okay for a minute while I brush my teeth?"

"Of course." She waves me off, and I head upstairs.

When I come back down, I find her by the kitchen island, zipping up Presley's lunch bag while the kids play in the living room.

"You can eat breakfast with us," I say quietly. "And dinner. You may be their nanny, but—"

"You need time with them without me," she cuts in, her voice low enough that the kids won't hear. "The last few weeks… Some lines got blurred. I think it's important we re-establish boundaries."

The word sits between us like a wall. Boundaries. I know we need them. But it still stings to hear her say it.

"This will remind them I'm just their nanny," she adds. "I adore them. But I won't be here forever."

She says it so matter-of-factly, and something in my chest tightens, much to my surprise.

When I hired her, I knew she wouldn't stay forever. But in the short time she's been here, I've gotten used to her smile. Her laughter. Her excitement.

Maybe she's right. Maybe the best thing right now is to re-establish boundaries.

Start with a clean slate… Like Jemmy's toys.

"I understand. It's probably for the best."

She lifts her chin. "It is."

I hold her gaze for a beat, wanting to say something. But what?

That I don't want to re-establish boundaries?

That her kiss sparked something inside me and I want more?

That I saw Joshua drive her home last night?

That I watched from the window like some jealous teenager?

That I want to know if he got to brush his mouth against her skin?

If she smiled at him the way she used to smile at me?

That I hate how much the thought bothers me?

That I don't want anyone else touching her?

But I don't say any of that.

Because that would cross a boundary we're supposedly redrawing.

"Presley. Time to go," I call out, heading toward the mudroom.

She jumps up from where she was playing with Jemmy and hurries toward me. I hold her coat out for her, and she slides into it. Rowan joins us, helping her with her gloves and scarf before pressing a soft kiss to the top of her head.

"Have a great day at school."

Presley beams up at her.

It's simple.

Innocent.

And it hits me harder than anything else this morning.

There will come a day when Rowan won't be standing in this entryway.

Jemmy will adapt. He always does.

But Presley feels everything like it's magnified. Since the accident, it's like her heart is wired closer to the surface.

She'll be devastated when Rowan leaves, and I'll have to watch it happen.

Which is exactly why the best thing I can do — for my kids, for her, for myself — is to put space between us.

Redraw the lines.

Remind myself who she is.

Just the nanny.

Not the woman whose kiss still burns on my mouth.

Not the woman I lie awake thinking about.

Just. The. Nanny.

TWENTY-SEVEN

Rowan

I study myself in the mirror after applying a hint of gloss to my lips, butterflies stirring low in my stomach.

As sad as it sounds, this is my first real date since my rebirth.

Since the hospital.

Since I walked out of those sliding doors and decided if my life was going to be shorter than I'd planned, I was going to live it.

Buy a van. Drive. Wander. Say yes.

Over the past several months, dating hasn't exactly been a priority.

Maybe because of Landon and how he decided he no longer wanted to be with me since I couldn't give him kids, not without serious complications I'm not willing to risk.

Or maybe because I don't want anyone getting attached to me when I'm on borrowed time.

But tonight isn't about forever.

It's just dinner.

And if I'm being honest, it's also about distraction.

Because no matter how hard I try, my thoughts keep circling back to Hayden Lawrence.

This week has been trying, to say the least.

Not because he's been difficult. If anything, he's been the opposite. Professional. Respectful. Careful not to linger too long in my presence.

But I miss the easygoing routine we once had.

Miss the lively meals with the kids.

Miss sitting with him once the house has grown quiet at night.

Miss seeing him smile.

Headlights sweep into the room, and I glance out the window to see Joshua's truck pull up. I take one last look at my reflection — sweater dress, knee-high boots, hair loose. Content with my appearance, I grab my coat and head for the door, slipping out through the separate entrance so I don't have to walk through the house.

Don't have to face Hayden.

Cold air greets me immediately, smelling of pine and chimney smoke. Everything I've come to love about Sycamore Falls.

Joshua is halfway up the porch steps when I call out, "Hey. I'm here."

He turns, a smile spreading across his face. "Were you waiting outside?"

"There's a separate entrance to the in-law suite," I explain, hooking a thumb in its direction.

"I see." He skims his eyes over me, lingering on my legs long enough to make me feel appreciated. "Are you ready?"

"Yes."

When we arrive at Holley Ridge a short while later, it looks like something out of a postcard. I've driven by this place a few times, but have never actually stepped foot on the property. It's unlike anything I've ever seen.

Lights wrap around every railing and tree branch, reflecting off the lake beyond. Snow-capped mountains rise in the distance. But even with the Christmas festival drawing crowds, the restaurant itself is hushed — soft music playing overhead, candles flickering on each table.

"This is beautiful," I tell Joshua after our wine is poured. "Have you worked here long?"

"Since I turned sixteen. At first, it was just seasonal. They hold a harvest festival with a pumpkin patch and tractor rides during the fall before switching gears and decorating for Christmas. That was before they built this inn and restored the barn for weddings. After that, I started working full time, doing various odds and ends before Parker made me her head groundskeeper."

"It sounds like you love it," I remark thoughtfully.

"I do." His expression brightens. "It might sound cheesy, but I've always loved this place. Always loved what I do. It may not be as prestigious as being a lawyer or doctor, but I really enjoy working here. Love taking care of the grounds. Love that every day is different."

"Prestige doesn't matter," I tell him with a slight roll of my eyes. "I think a lot of parents put pressure on their kids to follow a certain path. In my opinion, a high-paying or prestigious job doesn't equal success. I hated being a lawyer. It was never my dream, just something I did because I thought it would make my father proud. It took a health scare for me to realize I'd wasted years of my life trying to make my father give a shit about me when the only thing I was good for in his eyes was continuing his legacy. So I left."

"Have you spoken to your parents since then?" Joshua asks.

"I've sent them a few postcards from my travels, but I haven't reached out. Maybe it sounds selfish, but this journey has been about protecting my peace and cutting people out of my life who don't do that."

"Like your parents."

"Exactly." I take a sip of my wine. "They'd probably lose their minds if they learned I was working as a nanny right now. But I actually like it better than working at that stuffy law firm. If anything, that job prepared me for this one."

Joshua furrows his brow. "How so?"

"Many of my clients acted like toddlers when they didn't get their way. Toddlers, at least, can be reasoned with. Grown adults? Not so much."

He laughs, and the sound winds its way deep inside me. He's so carefree and open. He shares things, doesn't hide his emotions.

Unlike Hayden, who seems to keep his feelings locked up tight.

Throughout dinner, our conversation continues. To my surprise, there's no shortage of things to talk about. It feels like I've known him much longer than the few days I have. He seems interested in everything I have to say.

He asks questions. Listens. Doesn't interrupt. Doesn't compete.

When he talks about his mother, about losing her, his voice softens but he doesn't shut down. There's grief there, but also gratitude. Acceptance.

Unlike Hayden, who carries his grief like penance. Like if he ever loosens his grip on it, he's betraying his wife.

It's refreshing to see someone have a healthy relationship with grief, if there can ever be such a thing. But Joshua doesn't allow the loss to weigh him down. Instead, he remembers the good times he shared with his mom.

By the time we finish eating, the restaurant is nearly empty. I have no idea how long we sat there, but it must have been hours. He's a breath of fresh air, especially after the awkwardness with Hayden.

"Want to take a walk?" Joshua asks as we make our way back toward the lobby. "You can see the lights."

"I'd like that."

"This way." He touches a hand to the small of my back and guides me toward a pair of double doors leading to a veranda.

Outside, Christmas lights twinkle along the path, reflected in the thin sheen of frost on the grass.

"I can see why you love this place. And this town.

I've definitely enjoyed my time here. The people I've met have been incredibly welcoming."

He arches a brow. "Present company included?"

"Present company definitely included."

I draw in a deep breath, tilting my head back to admire the towering Norway spruce against the inky night sky. Everything's so clear. So peaceful. Unlike back in Chicago.

Just then, a few snowflakes drift lazily down from the sky, landing on my cheeks.

"It's snowing," I whisper, doing a slow circle as flakes start falling more steadily. "It's beautiful."

The world feels softer. Quieter. Like we've stepped into a moment that doesn't belong to anyone else.

"It is," Joshua says.

But when I glance at him, he isn't looking at the sky.

He's looking at me.

The lights reflect in his dark eyes, and for a second, something shifts in my chest.

Maybe it's the cold.

Maybe it's the way the snow settles in his hair.

Maybe it's the magic of Christmas in a town that feels like the first home I've ever had.

Or maybe I'm just tired of thinking about Hayden.

Whatever it is, I take a step toward Joshua.

Then another.

"Can I tell you something?" I murmur, my voice throaty.

His eyes drop to my mouth before lifting again. "What's that?"

"I've never been kissed in the snow."

"Didn't you live in Chicago?"

I nod. "Sad, isn't it? There were countless opportunities, but I never took them."

"Should we do something to correct that?"

"It *is* on my life list," I tell him.

"Before or after sunrise yoga?"

I laugh. "Definitely before."

"Well then," he hums, stepping closer, "let me help you cross it off."

The teasing note in his voice fades into something softer.

His hand finds my waist, warm and steady, fingers splaying slightly as he draws me toward him. Not rushed. Not hesitant either. Just certain.

Snow gathers in the dark strands of his hair. A flake melts against my cheek, cool against overheated skin. My breathing is shallow and uneven as his thumb traces a slow arc against my hip.

He lifts his other hand, brushing a stray curl away from my face. His knuckles skim my jaw before his palm settles there, cradling. Guiding.

The air between us feels charged with the kind of excitement that usually makes everything sharper — the lights brighter, the air colder, the promise sweeter.

I wait for that familiar rush, the tightening in my stomach, the electric pull that makes the rest of the world fall away.

Joshua leans in, and his breath ghosts over my lips, warm against the winter air.

Finally, his mouth touches mine.

Soft.

Gentle.

Careful.

His lips move with practiced ease, coaxing rather than claiming. He tightens his grip on my waist, pulling me flush against him as flakes drift down around us like we're inside a snow globe.

It's romantic.

It's sweet.

It's…nice.

But I don't want nice. I want passion. Want my body to light on fire.

I want Hayden.

I quickly silence the thought as I kiss Joshua back.

When he parts his lips, I follow, our tongues brushing in a brief, exploratory sweep.

And I still feel nothing.

No lightning strike. No loss of gravity. No hunger consuming me.

Just a kiss beneath falling snow.

When he finally pulls back, he rests his forehead against mine, his breath mingling with mine in visible puffs.

"I could keep doing that all night. But I have to work tomorrow." He pulls away, meeting my eyes. "Maybe we can do this again?"

Even though the kiss didn't undo me, I nod. "I'd like that."

But as we walk back to his truck, my hand tucked

into his, I wonder if I said yes because I genuinely *want* to see him again.

Or because I'm trying to erase Hayden's kiss from my mind and body.

But I have a feeling I could kiss a thousand men under a thousand snowflakes, and I still wouldn't be able to forget the way Hayden Lawrence kissed me.

TWENTY-EIGHT

Hayden

The house is dark except for the lamp in the corner of the living room, the amber glow reflecting off my glass as I take another large swallow of scotch.

I should have gone to bed hours ago, but I wanted to enjoy a quiet house.

At least that's what I told myself at ten. Then again at eleven.

Now it's after midnight, and there's only one reason I'm still awake.

And it's not to enjoy a quiet house.

It's because Rowan still isn't home from her *date* with Joshua. She left with him hours ago. How long do dates last these days? I wouldn't even know. It's been over twenty years since I've been on one.

I consider calling her to make sure she's okay. But what if I interrupt something?

The image comes uninvited. His hands on her body. Her legs wrapped around his waist. His mouth pressed against hers.

My jaw tightens, and I jump to my feet, storming into the kitchen and pouring another scotch. The liquor coats my stomach, dulling the edge of jealousy, but not killing it.

Headlights suddenly flash through the window, and my body reacts before my brain does, propelling me back into the living room. I peek through the blinds but stay just out of view, pressing myself against the wall like some kind of stalker.

Joshua steps out first, hurrying around the truck in order to open Rowan's door for her, offering his hand like the perfect fucking gentleman.

This would be easier if he were an asshole.

But Joshua's always been a good guy. Left college during his first year to come home and take care of his mom after she was diagnosed with cancer. That still doesn't stop the red-hot jealousy from shooting through me.

As they get closer, I notice Rowan glance toward the house.

Toward this window.

I shift back instinctively, as if she somehow knows I'm watching her.

Which is ridiculous. It's dark. She can't see me.

Instead of heading for the front door, she steers him toward her separate entrance. I gave her the code so she could come and go without feeling like she lived under my roof.

I regret it now. Because now I can't see or hear a damn thing.

All I can do is wait.

And wait.

And wait.

How long does it take to say goodnight? It shouldn't take this long.

Unless…

I squeeze my eyes shut, praying she doesn't invite him inside.

Or worse, to stay the night.

Would she do that?

I run a hand through my hair and start pacing. I told her she was free to have people over so long as it wasn't during working hours and they were respectful.

I never considered a man might spend the night.

Finally, the sound of footsteps cuts through my thoughts. I look out the window in time to see Joshua head toward the driveway.

Relief crashes through me so hard I have to brace myself against the wall.

But as he walks beneath the porch light, I notice his mouth is shinier than it was before.

Like he's wearing lip gloss.

Rowan's lip gloss.

I should let it go. It doesn't matter.

She's my employee. Just my employee. My kids' nanny.

That's exactly what I tell myself as I stride down the hall.

It's what I tell myself as I lift my hand.

And it's what I tell myself as I knock.

It's not until the sound echoes around me that the realization of what I'm doing finally hits me. I should turn around, go to bed, and forget about Rowan.

But before I can, footsteps approach and the door opens.

Rowan appears in a sweater dress and knee-high boots, her cheeks flushed from the cold, hair slightly wind-tossed.

God, she's beautiful.

"Did you kiss him?" I blurt out.

She blinks, obviously taken aback by my question.

"That's none of your business, Hayden. What I do during my personal time is precisely that. Personal."

"Just tell me," I push, despite knowing better. "I need to know."

"Why do you care?" She crosses her arms. Defensive. Beautiful. "You're the one who pushed *me* away. You don't get to act jealous now that I'm seeing someone else. It doesn't work that way."

"I know." I drag a hand through my hair, tugging at the ends. "Do you think I wanted to push you away? Fuck, Rowan. I haven't been able to stop thinking about that damn kiss since Saturday. Every time I'm around you, it replays in my head. This week has been torture. All because of how incredible it felt to finally kiss you."

"Then why did you push me away?"

Because you're my kids' nanny.

Because you're younger.

Because people would talk.

Because I lost my wife.

Because wanting you feels like betraying her.

All the reasonable answers line up neatly in my head.

All the excuses I've repeatedly told myself.

But none of them come out.

"Because you scare me," I admit.

My confession causes her to inhale a sharp breath. I'm not sure if it's the substance of the words or the fact that I didn't give her the same excuse I've given myself all week.

"You have since the beginning," I continue when she remains mute. "There's something about you. When you're around…" I shake my head, unsure how to describe it. "I feel…at peace. For the first time in a long time. You make me feel things I shouldn't. Not after—"

"Who says?"

I blink. "What do you mean?"

"Who says you're not supposed to feel what you do? Is there a rule somewhere?"

"I lost my wife."

"I'm aware." Her voice softens, yet her eyes don't waver. "But where's the rule that says you have to mourn her forever? The rule that says you have to stop living because she isn't? The rule that says you have to stop feeling?"

I open my mouth, but no words come.

For the past year, I've been living according to invisible rules. Expectations. Behaving like I believed a grieving husband should. Sacrificing the things a single father should.

But the truth is, I'm so goddamn tired.

Tired of feeling like I'm betraying Cora's legacy if I don't mourn her every second of every day.

Tired of being made to feel like I'm less than if I move on.

Tired of feeling like I don't deserve to be happy.

"Aren't you tired of not feeling?" Rowan continues, stepping toward me. "Of barely living? Don't you—"

Before she can utter another syllable, I crash my mouth against hers, as if some other force is at play. Or maybe this is simply me finally making a decision instead of blindly going through life. I don't care why or how. All I do care about is that the second our lips meet, something inside me snaps into place.

She gasps softly, and I deepen the kiss, my hands framing her face like I'm afraid she'll disappear.

God, I missed this. Missed her. Missed the taste of her. The warmth. The way everything else — the guilt, the expectations, the fear — falls away when she's in my arms.

When I'm kissing her, there's no past. No future. There's just this. Just us.

She pulls away first, breathing hard as we stare at each other for several protracted beats.

"Are you…okay?" I ask when she doesn't immediately do or say anything.

"I guess I'm…waiting."

"For what?"

"For you to tell me this is a bad idea and we shouldn't do this."

I let out a shaky breath. "It *is* a bad idea. And we definitely shouldn't do this."

"But?" She arches a brow, sensing there's more.

I slide an arm around her waist, pulling her flush against me, feeling the steady beat of her heart against my chest.

"But I'm ready to take a page out of your book."

"How so?"

I swallow hard as I stare into her brilliant blue eyes. It feels like I'm standing at the door of an airplane about to take a giant leap of faith, all the while praying my parachute deploys. But for the first time in over a year, I refuse to let fear or guilt overpower my needs.

"I'm ready to stop living by everyone else's rules. I'm ready to start saying yes again. I'm ready to say yes…to you."

Then I slam my lips against hers once more.

TWENTY-NINE

Rowan

This is completely reckless.

Not because he's my boss.

Not because of blurred lines.

But because of the secret I'm keeping.

The letter in his office. The one I never should have read. The one that told me whose heart beats inside my chest.

I should stop this.

Tell him the truth.

Instead, as his tongue swipes against mine, I allow myself to be selfish. To drown in the way my body responds to Hayden's kiss.

It's exactly what I wanted to feel earlier. What I searched for with Joshua…and couldn't find.

Now that I have, I don't want this to end anytime soon.

Hayden backs me into the room, kicking the door shut behind him. His touch is firm and resolute. Like he's done fighting himself.

He presses me against the wall, one hand gripping my thigh and hooking it around his waist. When he rocks against me, hard and unmistakable, a broken cry slips from my throat.

Every nerve ending feels awake, as if something long dormant just sparked back to life.

He pulls his mouth from mine and buries his face in my neck, his teeth grazing over sensitive skin. My head falls back against the wall, allowing him better access.

"I kissed him," I pant.

The confession spills out before I can stop it.

He stills slightly, but doesn't stop kissing me. "Is there a reason you're telling me about kissing another man right now?" He nips at my skin, pain mixing with pleasure in an intoxicating combination.

"I just…" I close my eyes, trying to steady myself as his mouth drags lower, over my collarbone, along my scar. "I kissed him because I wanted to erase you." I dig my fingers through his hair. "Wanted to forget what your kiss made me feel. Or maybe I hoped I'd feel the same thing with someone else."

He lifts his head, his lips hovering just above mine. "And did you?"

I swallow, searching his eyes. "I could probably kiss a thousand men and never feel what I do when I'm with you."

Something dark and hungry flashes across his face.

Then his fingers tangle in my hair, and he claims my mouth again, deeper this time. Desperate.

"Hold on," he murmurs roughly against my lips.

"What do you—"

Before I can finish, he lifts me effortlessly, my legs instinctively wrapping around him. I cling to his shoulders as he carries me toward the bed, my heart racing so hard it feels like it might burst through my ribs.

But even when we reach my bed, he doesn't put me down. Instead, he kisses me. Slow. Sensual. A taste of what's coming.

"I could do this for hours," he breathes against my mouth.

"You won't hear any complaints from me."

"Duly noted."

He presses another kiss to my lips before carefully lowering my feet to the floor.

"Sit." The word comes out soft, yet commanding at the same time.

I obey, lowering myself onto the mattress, my eyes never leaving his.

And his definitely don't leave mine. Almost like he's worried I'll disappear if he looks away.

He drops to his knees in front of me and takes one of my boot-clad feet in his hands, slowly lowering the zipper. The boot lands on the floor with a thump, my sock soon following.

His fingers skim over my ankle, his touch achingly gentle, almost reverent. The pad of his thumb traces the delicate bone, then glides upward in a slow, measured path that makes my breath hitch.

He's just touching my leg.

But my body reacts like he's struck a live wire.

Heat blooms wherever his skin meets mine, spreading outward in ripples. My stomach tightens. My toes curl.

Then he leans in.

The first press of his lips against my ankle is soft. Warm. Unhurried.

I inhale sharply.

He lingers for a beat longer than necessary, and I can feel the shape of his mouth against my skin. The subtle movement as he exhales. The faint scrape of stubble that sends a delicious shiver down my spine.

Slow, deliberate kisses mark a path up my calf. My muscles tremble beneath his touch, and I grip the edge of the bed, attempting to ground myself.

He pauses below my knee, pressing a kiss there before letting his lips drag lightly over the sensitive skin at the back of it. I gasp softly, surprised at how intimate something so simple feels.

He doesn't miss it.

He inches higher, his mouth trailing upward along the inside of my thigh. The air feels cooler where he hasn't kissed me yet, and the contrast makes every touch burn hotter.

My body tightens in anticipation, thighs instinctively parting a fraction more, welcoming him to continue his exploration.

He presses another kiss. Then another. Each one higher than the last. Each one making my breath grow more uneven.

My core clenches in anticipation, a slow ache building that makes it almost impossible to stay still.

"Hayden…" I whimper.

He hums against my skin, the vibration traveling straight through me. When his mouth hovers inches away from where I need him most, he pauses.

Doesn't touch.

Just waits.

My heart slams against my ribs.

My breath stalls in my lungs.

Then at the last second, he retreats.

"Tease," I groan.

His brow lifts. "Me?"

"You know you are."

"How so?"

"Because you were so close."

"Close to what?" His wicked smile nearly undoes me.

God, I love this version of him.

Playful. Confident.

I wonder if this is who he was before everything shattered.

But I push the thought away. This isn't about his past. Or mine.

It's about right now.

This moment.

"Tell me," he murmurs as he removes my other boot with the same maddening slowness, his mouth traveling upward again. My body feels hypersensitive, every brush of his lips magnified.

"Tell you what?" My voice is unsteady.

"What I was close to." His fingers slide higher, pushing my thighs apart. "Tell me where you want me to touch you."

I swallow hard as heat floods my face.

I've never been good at this part. Never been encouraged to give voice to my wants and desires.

But this is what my year of yes is all about. Doing things the old Rowan never would have. Saying yes to new experiences, even if they scare me.

Granted, when I decided to embark on a year of yes, I didn't exactly foresee it requiring me to tell my boss in explicit detail what parts of my body I want to feel his mouth on. But I've learned the universe works in mysterious ways.

"Your mouth," I say in a shaky voice. "On me."

"My mouth *is* on you," he teases.

"I'm not talking about my leg."

"Then tell me where."

"My pussy," I whisper. "I really need your mouth on my pussy."

"And I'm dying to taste you, Rowan." His expression darkens with hunger. "Now lie back."

I do as he commands, my back sinking into my mattress.

Several seconds pass as I wait to feel him, the anticipation unraveling me. Finally, he brushes several kisses up the inside of my thigh, inching closer and closer to my center.

But instead of feeling his mouth on me, he moves to my other thigh, teasing and torturing me with more kisses.

"Hayden," I groan in frustration.

"Yes?"

"Please."

"Please what? What do you need?"

"I need you to make me come. I'm so turned on, it fucking hurts."

He dips his gaze toward my panties. "I see that."

Biting his lower lip, he smooths his hands up my thighs. When he rubs his thumb over my panties, I nearly come off the bed.

"I *feel* that," he adds, continuing to torture me through the thin material.

"Then feel more of me. Feel *all* of me. Taste all of me."

"Yes, ma'am." He grips my panties and slides them down my legs before pushing my thighs even wider.

But he doesn't move. Doesn't dive in for a taste.

Instead, he just admires me.

I should feel exposed. Vulnerable.

But there's something about the hunger and greediness in his expression as he stares at me that turns me on even more.

"You're so wet," he murmurs.

"It's all for you. Now taste me."

He takes his time inching toward me. And when he finally drags his tongue up my center, the sound that leaves me is raw.

Relief. Pleasure. Release.

"Fucking delicious."

I can't respond, too lost in sensation as he glides his

tongue over me. He moves with confidence, with focus, like he's learning me. Like my reactions matter.

When he sucks my clit into his mouth, I have to grip the sheets below me to remain grounded when it feels like I'm flying.

"You like that?"

"God, yes," I exhale.

"Well, let's see how you respond to this."

He returns his lips to me, sucking my clit again. But this time, he slides a finger inside, stretching and massaging me.

I squeeze my eyes shut, trying to make sense of the way my body responds, but I'm already looming perilously close to the edge of oblivion.

"That's it, baby," Hayden grunts as I pulse against him, a slave to sensation. "Fuck my face. Rub your cunt all over me."

I wasn't sure how Hayden would be in the bedroom. But I didn't imagine this. No one I've been with has ever been this vocal. This open. This unashamed. And it turns me on in a way I never expected, no longer able to contain my reaction.

I cry out his name, tugging and pulling at his hair as I convulse through one of the most intense orgasms I've ever had.

It's not just physical.

It feels like something breaks open inside me.

When the tremors finally subside, he moves up my frame, kissing a slow path back to my mouth.

"Want a taste?" he asks.

"Yes."

He covers my mouth with his. But unlike all the previous times he's kissed me, this one is unhurried. Intimate. Sharing.

The taste of me on his lips sends another wave of heat through me.

"My turn," I say when he pulls back.

"For what?"

I lean forward, brushing my lips along his jaw before catching his earlobe gently between my teeth.

"To taste you. Can I do that, Hayden?"

His grip on my face tightens. "Fuck, yes."

THIRTY

Hayden

I slam my mouth against hers, and the second she opens for me, I'm done for.

It's not just the taste of her.

Or the way her body curves into mine.

It's the sound she makes.

Soft. Wanting. Unfiltered.

And I hate that I imagined Joshua hearing that sound. Hate that I let the thought fester until it drove me down this hallway like a man possessed.

Jealousy isn't something I'm accustomed to.

Either is desire.

I should stop. I'm more than aware this is wrong on so many levels.

Or is it?

Like Rowan said earlier, who says this is wrong, other than the fact that she's technically my employee?

Why shouldn't I do what I want?

Why shouldn't I do the things that bring me joy?

And being with Rowan brings me joy.

Kissing Rowan brings me joy.

Burying my face in her pussy definitely brings me joy.

When I tear my lips from hers, she gently pushes against me to stand before extending her hand toward me. I take it, allowing her to pull me to my feet.

All I can do is admire how damn beautiful she is, the dim light in the room casting shadows over her.

"Can I?" she murmurs, reaching for the hem of my shirt.

I swallow hard. "Yes."

She tugs the t-shirt over my head before tossing it onto the floor. As she drinks me in, I can't help but feel exposed.

I like to stay in shape, but I'm not in my twenties anymore. Not like Joshua.

But as her eyes trace over me, all I see is desire.

Her hands glide over my chest in appreciation. She isn't pawing at me like this is some frantic thing we have to finish before we come to our senses. She's exploring. Mapping. Memorizing my body with quiet focus. She doesn't skip anything. Doesn't rush past imperfections.

She lingers.

And that's what makes this dangerous.

Her hands slide lower, tracing the ridges of my abs. Slow. Intentional. She's watching my face as she does it, like she's studying my reaction. Cataloguing the subtle shifts — my jaw tightening, my breath growing heavier, the way my stomach contracts under her fingertips.

Her touch isn't just turning me on.

It's waking me up.

For years I've existed in muted tones. Grief dulls everything. Even pleasure.

But this?

This is color flooding back in.

"Can I?" she asks again, teasing the waistband of my sweatpants.

"Yes."

She peppers kisses along my collarbone and down my chest as her fingers disappear into my pants, each swipe causing the muscles in my body to tighten. When she brushes against the tip of my erection, I groan.

"Payback's a bitch, isn't it?" Rowan croons into the crook of my neck. "This is what you get for teasing me."

"But I made it worth it for you? Didn't I?"

"You did." She brings her lips to mine. "Now I plan on returning the favor."

I expect for her to finally push my pants down. Or at least grab my cock.

Instead, she steps back, putting space between us.

Frustration builds, making me wild with need. Making me want to throw her onto the bed and fuck her until the entire town knows she's mine and only mine.

With her eyes trained on me, she reaches for the bottom of her dress and pulls it over her head before unclasping her bra, dropping it to the floor.

My breathing increases as I sweep my appreciative gaze over her body. She's beautiful in a way that hits me harder than I expected. Sure, her curves are incredible, her skin soft. But what has me desperate to drown in her and never come up for air is her strength. In the way she stands. In the way she doesn't flinch under my gaze.

And just like she took her time running her hands along my body, I take my time drinking her in, too. Her dark waves falling gently over her shoulders. Her soft skin inviting me to feel her. Her intricate tattoo blooming over her chest, a stunning design of thorns and roses.

"You're fucking beautiful," I exhale, threading my fingers in her hair and covering her mouth with mine.

She moans into me, our tongues tangling as she teases my waistband again. I'm on the verge of pushing my sweatpants down myself, forcing her to her knees, and making her suck me off.

But before I can bring that fantasy to fruition, she finally pushes them down my legs.

I kick them to the side as she hoists herself onto her toes. "Can I touch you?"

"God, yes."

"Good."

Her mouth is warm as it touches mine. And when I feel her hand wrap around my length, I can't help the moan that breaks free, weeks of restraint and hunger rolling off me in waves.

"Tell me something, Hayden."

I squeeze my eyes shut, fighting against the raw need overwhelming me as she strokes my erection, especially when her thumb brushes over my tip.

"Yes," I grit out, bringing my gaze to hers.

"When's the last time a woman touched you like this?"

"Years," I answer before I can think about what I essentially just admitted.

I brace for her questions about how that could be, unsure if I'm ready for that conversation. How Cora and I may have been married, but the romance fizzled out ages ago. How we had become more like roommates who had kids together.

But she doesn't press the subject.

"And when's the last time you felt a woman's mouth on your cock?"

"Even longer."

"Well, then…" She slowly lowers herself to her knees. "Allow me to change that."

Every muscle in my body tightens as she continues to stroke my cock, bringing her mouth toward me.

And when she teases my tip with her tongue, I have to fight against coming right away, my body begging for the release it's been deprived of for far too long.

She slides her tongue up and down my length, torturing me even more, every second a battle of restraint. When she finally takes me in her mouth, it feels like the floor's given out beneath me, the room spinning.

For the first time in quite a while, my brain goes quiet. I'm no longer thinking about my failures. My duties. My obligations. All I'm thinking about is Rowan and how fucking amazing her mouth feels on me.

I look down at her, the sight of her on her knees with her mouth full of my cock turning me on even more. I bring my hands up to her head, guiding her, gently thrusting in time with her motions.

"God, Rowan. Your mouth is dangerous."

She moans around me, the vibration propelling me higher and higher. I notice her squeeze her thighs together, obviously just as turned on as I am.

"Touch yourself," I demand. "I want to watch you fuck yourself as I fuck this mouth."

I have no idea what's come over me.

I'm normally not like this. At least, I wasn't with Cora. I loved her, but I never felt this unyielding hunger that tapped into my baser desires. Not like I do with Rowan. Maybe it's because it's been so long, but I get the feeling it goes deeper than that.

Which is why I should stop. Not take this any further.

But I can't stop now, especially as I watch Rowan spread her thighs and lower her hand between them, a moan falling from her as she rubs her clit.

"That's it, baby," I groan as I move faster, gripping her head harder. "Get yourself off. Fuck that greedy little pussy."

She moans again, and I nearly lose it when she slides a finger inside, followed by another. Her slickness echoes around me, combining with the sound of me driving in and out of her mouth.

Her breathing increases, and I'm desperate for her to let go, unsure how much longer I can hold off. Finally, she releases a cry and her body trembles through another orgasm. I don't wait for her to fully come down before hauling her to her feet.

She blinks, obviously disoriented. "What's wrong?"

I answer by slamming my lips to hers, my chest heaving.

"Nothing. Except if you kept doing that, I was going to come in your mouth. And I need to be inside you."

I trail my hand along her hip, sliding it between her legs. She whimpers again as I slowly rub her clit.

"Can I do that, Rowan? Can I fuck you?"

She flashes me a playful smile. "I'd be disappointed if you didn't."

"And I wouldn't want to leave you disappointed." I touch a soft kiss to her lips, then my expression falls. "Except…"

"What is it?"

"I don't have any condoms."

"It's okay. I have an IUD."

I push out a long breath. "That's music to my goddamn ears."

I crush my mouth against hers and steer her toward the bed, lowering her onto the surface and settling between her legs.

"I haven't done this in a while," I say when I pull out of the kiss. "I might be a bit out of practice."

She runs her fingers through my hair, urging my lips back toward hers. "If the way you fucked my mouth is any indication, you'll do just fine. Now Hayden…"

"Yes?"

She curves toward me, taking my earlobe between her teeth. "I need you to fuck me."

"Yes, ma'am."

I straighten to kneel between her legs and bring my

erection up to her. She's so wet. So warm. And the way her breathing increases as I tease her sets me on fire yet again. The pure hunger. The unabashed way she shows her desire. I've never experienced anything like it.

"Let me feel you, Hayden," she begs. "I'm losing my damn mind."

I know how she feels. Because I'm out of my mind, too.

I ease inside of her, warmth enveloping me with every inch. Nothing's ever felt so damn perfect.

Once I'm fully seated, I release a shuddering exhale as I cover Rowan's body with mine, linking my hands with hers.

"You okay?"

She smiles up at me. "Better than okay."

"You feel fucking incredible, Rowan."

She wraps her legs around my waist, dragging her nails up my spine. "Then feel more of me."

She doesn't have to ask me twice. I move in and out of her, slow at first, needing to savor every tremor, every moan, every tug of my hair.

"Harder," Rowan begs, attempting to move her hips faster against mine.

"In time," I promise with a kiss. "Let me enjoy this. Enjoy you."

I straighten, continuing my languid rhythm. Then I wet my thumb before bringing it to her clit and rubbing circles in time with my motions.

"Oh, god." Her eyes flutter closed.

"Give me what I want and I'll give you what you want."

"And what do you want?"

I curve toward her. "To feel your pussy clench around my dick. Give me one more orgasm and I'll fuck you so hard you'll feel me for days."

She meets my gaze. "I don't know if I can. Don't know if I have any more orgasms left."

"I know you do." I capture her mouth in a brief kiss before straightening once more. "Now give it to me."

I increase my motions, thrusting into her with more intensity. She moans and closes her eyes, gripping the sheet below us.

"Eyes on me, Rowan. I want you to look at me while I fuck you."

"Yes, sir," she responds with a smirk, snapping her eyes to meet mine.

I harden even more, raw need taking over as I move inside her with more fervor.

And she doesn't look away. She stays with me with each desperate thrust. Each ragged breath. Each strangled moan.

I see it the moment she's on the verge of falling over the edge, her eyes going wide, her lips parting.

So I thrust faster, rub her clit harder.

"Come on, baby. Don't fight it. Let me feel you. Give me your pleasure."

Her back arches off the bed as she screams my name, the sound seeming to echo throughout the house.

Normal, sensible Hayden would stop this for fear she may have woken up the kids.

Instead, I cover her mouth with mine, swallowing her moans.

"Are you trying to wake up the entire neighborhood?" I tease as I continue moving, the feel of her clenching around me driving me wild.

"Stop fucking me so good and I won't scream like that."

"Never, Rowan. I'll never stop giving you what you need. What we both need." I lift her legs over my shoulders and angle toward her once more. "What we both deserve," I finish before pistoning into her, pinning her wrists to either side of her head.

The sight of her, hair splayed on the pillow, wrists pinned to the bed, eyes locked on mine pushes me over the edge.

I try to bite back my own cry of pleasure, but it's impossible, her name leaving my mouth on a groan as I come undone. It's not just explosive.

It's overwhelming.

Like something locked tight in my chest has finally been allowed to run free.

When I have nothing left, I collapse onto the bed and pull her against me, both of us struggling to catch our breath.

"That was…" I shake my head, not even having the words.

"Amazing."

"It definitely was."

I hold her for another minute, savoring in the feel of her body against mine. How perfect she fits. Then I carefully extricate myself from her, pressing a kiss to her head.

"One second."

I slip into the bathroom and grab a washcloth. When I return to her, she reaches for it, but I shake my head.

"Let me." I push her legs apart and clean her up, albeit begrudgingly.

There's something about seeing my cum dripping from her that ignites something primitive and possessive inside me.

Makes me want to claim her again.

After I finish, I toss the cloth onto the floor, my gaze snagging on my clothes.

"It's okay," Rowan assures me.

I whip my eyes back to hers. "What do you mean?"

"I don't mind if you want to go sleep in your bed. All things considered, you probably should."

"You won't be upset?"

She stands, moving toward me.

"I didn't fuck you with any hopes of a relationship, Hayden. I know what this is and what it isn't. I slept with you because it made me feel good." She lifts her lips into a smile. "No need to make it more complicated or awkward than it has to be.

"Too many people focus on the future. Making plans instead of just focusing on the now. So let's not do that. Let's just enjoy ourselves if and when the mood strikes. No promises or expectations for more."

"I can't remember the last time I wasn't obsessed with the future," I reply around a chuckle. "Or the past."

She erases the remaining space between us. "Then let me show you how good it can be to only live in the now." Her voice turns sensual and throaty as she traces circles along my neck. "To be present."

She nibbles slightly on that spot right beneath my earlobe, and my erection returns to life. Something I didn't think possible so soon.

"You're making it really hard for me not to think about the future." I thread my fingers through her hair, bringing her lips back within an inch of mine. "To not fantasize about the next time I'm inside you."

She mischievously waggles her brows as she steals a glance at my dick. "Why does it have to be in the future?"

I hesitate, torn between doing what I should and what I want.

As seems to be the theme tonight, I silence the voice telling me to be responsible.

Instead, I do what *I* want, steering her back toward the bed and sinking deep inside her once more.

THIRTY-ONE

Rowan

Soft rays of sun peek through the blinds, stirring me from one of the most restful nights' sleep I've had in a long time. I stretch against the sheets, and an ache blooms between my thighs, along my hips, even on my ass. The things I did last night… The things I felt…

I stare at the ceiling and wait for the guilt to arrive.

It never does.

Old Rowan would have been spiraling by now. Making exit strategies. Creating lists of reasons this is reckless. Inappropriate. Complicated.

Old Rowan would have insisted we never do it again.

But this Rowan knows better. Knows how fragile life truly is.

Why shouldn't I grab joy when it offers itself up in broad shoulders and sinful dimples?

Granted there's the small matter of the secret I'm keeping that can complicate things.

But only if I let it.

Like I told Hayden… We're not building a future together. As far as I'm concerned, there *is* no future for us. This is temporary. Nothing more.

He needs someone to infuse a little life back into him. Someone who makes him smile. Who makes him laugh. Who makes him feel all the things he's deprived himself of this past year.

I'm more than willing to volunteer for the position, especially after the way he made me feel last night. My god… The man was incredible.

I had a feeling it would be, especially after that kiss. You don't have such a strong, visceral reaction to something as innocent as a kiss and end up unsatisfied in bed.

And Hayden definitely satisfied me. If my count's correct, by the time he finally went back to his bedroom at around three this morning, he'd satisfied me five times.

I've never done anything five times in one night except binge a Netflix show.

As much as I want to sleep, my body's on a schedule, thanks to the medication I need to take.

With a quiet groan, I push the covers off and pad into the bathroom. The tile is cool under my feet as I retrieve the little container I keep tucked behind my toiletries — my collection of orange bottles with labels I've memorized by heart.

My morning companions for the rest of my life.

I swallow them one by one with water, the routine as

automatic as brushing my teeth, before lifting my eyes toward the mirror, studying my reflection.

Flushed cheeks. Kiss-swollen lips. Hair wild and unapologetic.

I look…happy.

Which is strange, since I've spent the last several months following whatever brought me joy.

But a delicious piece of pie isn't the same as the things I experienced last night with Hayden.

After pulling my dark hair into some sort of messy bun, I tug on a pair of soft sleep shorts and an oversized tee, then head toward the kitchen.

The house is quiet this early in the morning, the sun starting to filter through the windows, washing everything in pale gold. The air smells faintly like laundry detergent and something distinctly Hayden — something woodsy and clean.

As I step into the kitchen, I expect it to be empty.

Instead, Hayden's standing by the sink, staring out the window.

Shirtless.

Of course, he's shirtless.

The morning light catches along the planes of his back, highlighting the broad line of his shoulders. He looks almost contemplative, like his thoughts are weighing him down. My stomach immediately dips.

Does he regret it?

Regret me?

But when he turns and his eyes land on mine, a slow, devastating smile spreads across his face.

No regret.

Just heat.

He crosses the room in three easy strides and pulls me into him.

We didn't discuss the limitations of whatever this is. I figured it would be a friends with benefits situation. Or, more accurately, boss with benefits. We'd satisfy our cravings when the mood strikes, but that's it. I certainly didn't expect him to wrap me in his arms and bury his face in the crook of my neck.

But that's exactly what he does. And I didn't realize how much I'd been craving this simple contact until this moment.

"You're up early," I say. "I thought you'd sleep in today."

"I woke up with a massive hard-on," he murmurs, peppering soft kisses along my neck. "I wonder why."

"I wonder." I tilt my head, giving him better access because apparently I have no self-control.

He slides his hands under my shirt, his palms warm against my skin. "It could be because I'm a guy and sometimes my dick does what it wants."

"It's a possibility," I breathe, my body coming to life with every gentle caress.

"It could be because it wanted attention this morning." His thumbs trace upward, and my breath hitches as he nears my breasts.

"Could be."

When he ghosts a finger over my nipple, I can't reel in the whimper that escapes, desire flooding through me, especially between my legs.

"Or," he says, his voice deepening, "it could be because I had a dream."

"What kind of dream?"

"One where I threw caution to the wind and finally did what I've been wanting to do for weeks."

He squeezes a nipple, and I release a desperate moan, which he swallows with a kiss.

"I got to touch you," he murmurs, his lips grazing my jaw. "Taste you. Fuck you."

"It wasn't a dream," I whisper.

"Thank god." He slams his mouth against mine, yanking my body against his.

Despite the desperation in his hold, his kiss isn't rushed or frantic. It's slow and claiming and warm. His hands continue roaming my frame, moving toward the waistband of my shorts, and for a moment, I forget we're standing in the kitchen of the house where I'm technically employed.

Until Jemmy's babbles sound from the monitor, calling for his dada.

Hayden groans against my mouth, but doesn't immediately release me. Instead, he rests his forehead on mine, staying in this moment, his thumbs absent-mindedly brushing my hipbone.

"My friends always said kids are the most effective form of birth control," he mutters. "Turns out they weren't lying."

I laugh, still somewhat breathless from his kiss. "They always have terrible timing, don't they?"

"The worst." He drops one last kiss to my lips before reluctantly stepping back. "Guess I'm on duty."

"Do you want——"

"It's your day off," he interrupts before I can finish my question. "Go do something fun. Walk dogs. Do yoga. Whatever it is twenty-nine-year olds do." He flashes me a smile before his expression shifts into something darker. "Just promise me one thing."

"What's that?"

He leans in, brushing his mouth along the sensitive spot below my ear. "Promise you won't touch yourself today."

My stomach somersaults.

"I want all your orgasms. Every single one. Okay?" He pulls back slightly, one brow raised in challenge.

The audacity.

The confidence.

The very unfairness of how good he looks saying that.

Finally, I nod. "Okay."

"Okay." He touches a gentle kiss to my forehead. Then he turns toward the stairs.

"Hayden?" I call out before he can disappear.

He pauses, glancing over his shoulder.

I give him a coy smile, nibbling on my lower lip. "What if I break my promise and get myself off?"

His eyes darken, and he stalks back toward me slowly. Deliberately. Like a predator who knows exactly how this ends.

Without breaking eye contact, he turns the volume down on the monitor. Then he grips my hair, forcing my head back, firm and controlled.

My god… This man.

For someone who hadn't had sex in over a year before last night, he has some serious game.

"If you do," he says quietly, his mouth hovering just shy of mine, "you'll be punished."

My heart pounds so hard I'm confident it's about to burst out of my chest.

"Promise?" I whisper.

His hold tightens, just enough to remind me he's in control of this moment.

Of me.

"Absolutely." His breath brushes over my lips, warm and slow, and I swear I can taste him in the air between us. My entire body is strung tight, every nerve ending waiting for impact.

The space between us feels heavy and charged. I can see the faint stubble along his jaw, the way his pupils have blown wide, the slight flare of his nostrils like he's breathing me in.

The restraint is exquisite torture.

His thumb brushes lightly along my scalp, almost soothing, completely at odds with the way he's holding me, my body humming with anticipation so sharp it's almost painful.

"You have no idea how hard it is not to kiss you right now," he murmurs, voice low, almost reverent.

"Then kiss me."

His nose grazes mine, and I brace for the crash of his mouth against mine.

But instead of closing the distance and giving me what I'm silently begging for, he releases my hair.

The loss of contact is immediate. Cool air where his warmth was. Space where his body had mine caged in.

I sway forward slightly before placing my hand on the counter to steady myself.

He steps back like a man who knows exactly what he's doing.

Like a man who understands the power of anticipation.

He lets his gaze drag over me — slow, heated, promising. Then he turns, leaving me alone in the kitchen.

I stare at the space where he just was, my heart racing.

It's official.

This just became the longest day of my life.

THIRTY-TWO

Rowan

There's a festive hum in the air as I steer a sweet little beagle mix through historic downtown Sycamore Falls. The sidewalks are busy but not chaotic — couples bundled in scarves, kids clutching hot chocolate, shop doors chiming as people pop in and out with full bags and wide smiles.

It's nothing like Chicago.

There, I'd keep my head down. Earbuds in. Anonymous in a sea of rushing bodies.

Here, I make eye contact. I say hello to Grandma Estelle outside the café and wave at a little boy I recognize from taking Jemmy to story time.

After only a few months, I know names. I know stories. I know who just got engaged and whose son made varsity.

I know which chapters in Grandma Estelle's latest book have the spiciest bits.

I almost feel like I belong.

Almost.

I refuse to admit I actually do.

Because I'm not supposed to belong.

I'm not supposed to plant roots or grow attached to towns with charming downtown stores and handsome single dads.

I'm just supposed to follow my joy.

Which is exactly what Groucho Barx is doing, his nose to the pavement as he drags me toward the bakery like he's on a mission from God.

"You are not subtle," I inform him.

He sneezes and doubles down, attempting to pull me inside.

"Fine. I'll get you a pup cup on the way back."

His ears lift and his tail wags. With the future promise of a treat, he allows me to steer him away from downtown, the noise fading behind us. Unlike last week, I make a deliberate turn that avoids the cemetery.

Especially today.

What would I even say if I stood in front of Cora's headstone?

Hi. You don't know me, but your husband is extraordinary in bed. And don't even get me started on that thing he does with his tongue. You know what I'm talking about.

Not exactly appropriate.

Instead, I follow a quieter street until we reach a

small park a few blocks away. With almost everyone downtown or at the Christmas festival, the park is essentially empty, allowing me to unclip Groucho's leash to let him run free, as if he doesn't have a care in the world.

As if he's not worried about when the next time he'll be able to do this might be.

This is what I admire about animals. They don't worry about things in the future. Their sole focus is on what's in front of them right now. And right now, Groucho's sole focus is on chasing after the tennis ball I throw across the field.

I inhale a deep breath, savoring the simplicity of this moment.

Cold air in my lungs. Sunlight filtering through bare branches. A dog losing its mind over felt and rubber.

Then my phone rings, cutting through the peaceful silence. I reach for my cell, Emily's name popping up on the screen. I almost don't answer.

Not because I don't want to talk to her. But because I have no idea what I'm going to say.

It's why I've been avoiding her since I found the letter all those weeks ago.

I've sent her the occasional text, assuring her I'm okay and have been really busy with the kids. But I can't put this off forever.

So instead of sending her to voicemail, I answer.

"It's about damn time you picked up," she says immediately. "When you first left, we talked daily. I was practically your emotional support human. Or therapist. Or life coach."

"All of the above," I reply with a smile. "And I'm

sorry. I'll do better. But in my defense, I wasn't responsible for keeping two kids alive back then."

"Speaking of which… How's that going?"

"Good," I say automatically. "Great, really."

There's a brief pause on the line. The kind only your best friend can weaponize.

"What aren't you telling me?"

I part my lips, unsure how to begin updating her on everything. If I even want to. But I've been keeping the truth locked inside for too long now. At first, I didn't think it mattered. Convinced myself I could just pretend I never saw that letter.

But last night changed everything, even if I tried to convince myself it didn't. We still crossed a line.

And I'm still keeping a huge secret from Hayden.

One that's getting heavier and heavier with every day.

"Things have gotten…interesting."

"Oh, my god. You banged your boss."

"Emily!" I spin in a slow circle, scanning for witnesses. Just a jogger in the distance and a squirrel whose sole focus is on stuffing acorns into its mouth.

"You did, didn't you? I can hear it in your voice."

I try to suppress the smile stretching across my face, but fail miserably. "You're right. I did."

"It's about damn time!" she shrieks so loudly I have to hold the phone away from my ear. "This is what you wanted when you left. Find your joy, remember?"

"I found more than joy with him," I admit, my cheeks warming despite the cold. "It was… incredible. I didn't know sex could be like that."

"Because you weren't with the right person. Now you are."

"We're just having fun. Living in the—"

"In the present. Yes, yes. I've heard the speech." She sighs. "But you've been there two months, Ro. The longest you've stayed anywhere else was, what? Eight days?"

"Ten," I correct.

"There's a reason you're still there. Maybe *he's* the reason, but you're too scared to admit it."

"He's not… It's not…" I trail off, my body physically fighting against saying the words.

"What were you saying?" she taunts.

It's a good thing she didn't do a video call. Lord knows what she'd see on my expression if she did. She would have probably already figured out the truth.

I blow out a long breath as I bend to retrieve the tennis ball Groucho just dropped at my feet. Then I throw it once more before returning my attention to Emily, bracing myself for this conversation.

"He might be *part* of the reason I stayed."

"I knew it!"

"But not how you think." I pause, chewing on my bottom lip. "I found something when I was cleaning one day."

"Okay…"

"It was a letter, Em. *My* letter."

"What do you mean? What letter?"

"*The* letter."

I don't have to embellish for her to know what I'm talking about.

Emily sat with me as I wrote every draft of that letter. Watched me rewrite sentences until my writing was barely legible. You'd think someone who used to write motions and legal briefs could handle a personal letter.

But nothing I've ever written felt as heavy as this one.

As *important*.

"Why would he have—" she begins, but stops short. "His wife."

"I have her heart."

It's the first time I've spoken the truth out loud to anyone, and it feels both freeing and suffocating at the same time. Because the person I want to tell doesn't want to hear them.

"Oh, my god," Emily whispers, momentarily speech-less, a feat for the woman who always knows what to say. "Does he know? Your hottie, single-dad, fuck-buddy boss?"

I laugh, grateful for the break in tension. If there's anything Emily's good at, it's cutting through a difficult situation.

"He has a name. It's Hayden. And no."

I fall onto a nearby bench as the wind picks up slightly, rustling dry leaves across the grass.

"He told me he doesn't want to know who received her organs. Because if something happened to them, it would be like losing her all over again. In his mind, he'd rather enjoy the peace of mind in knowing his wife saved four lives and leave it at that."

"But doesn't your situation complicate things?"

Emily replies softly. "It's not like you're a stranger. You're living in his house. Taking care of his kids. Sleeping with him."

"I know. And a part of me wants to tell him," I admit as Groucho sprints back toward me with the ball in his mouth. "But I also want to respect his wishes. He's been stuck living in the past for so long, but is now becoming more present. I don't want to do anything to pull him back, ya know? Plus, I won't be here forever. Soon, the wind will change, and I'll fly away to my next destination."

I expect her to laugh at my Marry Poppins reference.

She doesn't.

"But you like being there. Like being with *him*."

"We agreed," I tell her. "We're simply enjoying ourselves whenever the mood strikes. No future."

"What happens if you want more with him? If you want a future? Or if he does?"

"He won't. He—"

"You can't control what he feels or thinks," she interjects.

She's right. I can't. But I *can* control what I feel and think.

"I can't think about a future with him. *Won't* think about a future with him. He's already lost his wife. I'm not selfish enough to make him get attached to me, only for him to lose me, too. Because he *will* lose me."

"You don't know that. You could defy the odds and outlive us all."

I smile at her optimism. Normally, I'd hold on to the

same hope. But I'm more than aware that a heart transplant isn't a fairy tale. It's a borrowed miracle with a timer no one can see.

"We both know the statistics. I'm lucky if I live to see fifty. I've made my peace with that."

Mostly.

Some days.

Other days, the weight of it wears on me.

"The best thing for me to do," I continue, forcing a brightness into my voice I don't entirely feel, "the *only* thing for me to do is live in the present. Because making plans for a future I know I won't be a part of? It's too hard."

The line goes silent, and I sense she wants to argue with me.

But she knows better.

And she also knows the reality of my situation, despite her hopes I'll somehow defy the odds.

"So I'm just going to keep living in the now. Collect moments. Collect joy. Collect really, really good orgasms."

It's silent for a beat. Then Emily snorts a laugh. "Well, if this grand philosophical acceptance includes mind-blowing sex, I fully support it."

I giggle, the heaviness easing just enough. "It absolutely does."

"Good." She's silent for a beat. Then she asks, "You're okay, though?"

"I'm okay," I assure her.

And not to make her feel better. But because I feel okay. Better than okay.

Not fearless.

Not invincible.

But choosing joy anyway.

And right now joy looks a lot like a beagle demanding a pup cup and a single dad who promised to punish me later.

I'm more than okay with that.

THIRTY-THREE

Hayden

I'm awake before my alarm.

That part isn't new. Sleep and I have had an uneasy relationship for years now. I usually lie in bed for hours staring at the ceiling, counting the cracks in the plaster, waiting for obligation to drag me upright.

This morning is different.

There's a restless energy in my chest. Not regret. Not grief. It's something warmer.

Something…happier.

I swing my legs over the edge of the bed and head downstairs, telling myself it's to enjoy the quiet before the kids wake up.

In reality, it's because I want to try to steal a few minutes with Rowan.

The house is mostly dark, the sun just beginning to

peek over the horizon. And when I turn the corner into the kitchen, something loosens in my chest at the sight of the brunette by my coffee maker, preparing herself a cup.

This quiet domestic scene — Rowan wearing an oversized t-shirt, her dark hair rumpled from sleep — feels dangerously intimate.

Because it's a scene I wouldn't mind waking up to every morning.

I pad quietly toward her and loop an arm around her waist, drawing her body into mine, her back to my front.

She melts into me, and I brush my mouth along the curve of her neck, slow and unhurried. Her skin is warm, smelling faintly of lavender.

"Did your…problem wake you up again?"

I chuckle as I gently thrust against her. "What do you think?"

"I think it's a strong possibility."

"Any interest in helping me take care of it?"

I slide my hand down her stomach, my fingers disappearing into her shorts. When they land on her center, she moans, leaning her head back against my chest.

"In return, I'll help you take care of your problem, too."

She moves with me as I circle her clit, spreading her wetness around. "I'm really enjoying these added perks of my employment."

"As am I." I spin her around, crushing my lips to hers, our kiss hungry and frantic, as if it's been ages since we've felt each other, instead of mere hours.

Her hands curl into my shirt as I guide her back a step, then another, until her hips meet the island. She smiles against my mouth like she knows exactly what she's doing to me. That she's made me lose all sense of reason.

Yet I don't care.

In one swift move, I yank her shorts down and force her around once more, pressing her stomach flat against cool marble. She spreads her legs in invitation, and I bring my arousal up to her, teasing her.

"You're already so wet."

Rowan glances over her shoulder at me. "And you're already so hard. Now let me help you take care of that."

"Gladly."

With one desperate thrust, I push inside her.

She bites back her moan, her hands flying out to grip the counter.

It takes everything I have not to cry out myself. There's nothing like being inside of this woman. I've never felt anything so damn perfect. So damn right.

I know I shouldn't feel these things. Know this entire situation is reckless.

But I can't stop myself. Don't *want* to stop.

Instead, I let myself sink fully into the present.

Not thinking about tomorrow.

Not thinking about consequences.

Not thinking about how this ends.

I stay in the moment with her.

Her body moving against mine.

Her moans echoing in the silence.

Her breath hitching as she gets closer and closer to falling over the edge.

"Come on, Rowan," I groan, on the verge of losing control. "Don't fight it. Let me feel you."

I bring my hand to her clit and rub as I continue thrusting into her.

A soft moan slips free, and she moves against me with more urgency, her muscles growing rigid until her body convulses, her fist in her mouth muffling her cries.

"God, I love watching you come. Love feeling you lose all control. Because you've made me lose all damn control, too."

I grip her hips and drive into her over and over, every muscle in my body tightening, desperate for the release only Rowan can give me. Electricity courses through my veins, and I have to bite back the roar begging to be set free as waves of bliss wash over me, stronger than anything I've ever experienced.

I curve toward her, leaving soft kisses along her shoulder blades, addicted to her in a way I never thought possible.

Once I have my breathing under control, I ease out of her and grab a fresh towel from the drawer. I help her upright, then clean between her legs.

"I can do that, you know," she states.

I lean down and touch a soft kiss to her forehead. "I know. But I like taking care of you."

The words come easier than they should.

And that's what unsettles me.

Because I do like taking care of her.

Like being with her. Like the passionate, intense

moments when we can't seem to satisfy our cravings fast enough.

But I also like these quiet, tender moments when we've satisfied our urges and can be at peace with each other.

I toss the towel onto the floor and pull her against me, wrapping her in my embrace and enjoying this moment of peace. Of tranquility.

Something I never thought I'd have again.

Then the baby monitor crackles to life.

"Ro-Ro. Ro-Ro," Jemmy babbles.

Rowan pushes against me, and I reluctantly let her go.

"Guess I'm officially on the clock," she sighs, grabbing her shorts and sliding them on.

"Sorry if I cut into your 'me time'."

She grins, hoisting herself onto her toes and planting a soft kiss on my lips. "I can think of a lot worse ways to spend my mornings than with your cock inside me. Feel free to cut into my 'me time' again tomorrow morning."

"But isn't that the future? I didn't think we did that. I thought we were only focusing on the now. Living in the present. Not making any plans for the future."

"I'm not making plans. More like…manifesting."

I arch a single brow. "Manifesting?"

"Exactly. I know I wouldn't mind having a cock first thing tomorrow morning so I'm sending good vibes out to the universe to deliver me one…in whatever form that may be."

I tug her against me, nipping at her neck. "The only cock you'll be getting tomorrow morning is mine."

"Then it's working already." She brings her lips toward mine, and I brace myself for her kiss.

But it never comes.

Instead, she slips free, flashing me a grin before walking away, swaying her hips as she goes just to torture me.

THIRTY-FOUR

Hayden

When I step into the office later that morning, I'm surrounded by the familiar smell of antiseptic and coffee, the fluorescent lights humming overhead.

Normally the sound grates on me. Today it barely registers.

Everything feels lighter. How could it not after this morning? Hell, after this weekend?

"Good morning, Margaret," I call out as I pass the reception desk.

She looks up and blinks, staring at me as if I've grown another head.

"What happened to the real Dr. Hayden Lawrence? Because you are definitely not him."

"What are you talking about?"

"For the past year, I've seen you walk through those

doors. Seen you drag your sulking butt to your office. And not once have I seen anything remotely resembling a smile crack on that pretty face of yours."

"I…smile," I attempt to argue in my defense.

"I'm not talking about that tight, polite one you give your patients. I'm talking about a *real* smile. One that makes me think you're so full of joy you can't help but *to* smile."

At her words, I immediately think of Rowan and how she lives her life following joy everywhere she can.

Margaret leans forward, lowering her voice. "Did you meet someone?"

I open my mouth to respond, pausing just long enough for her to notice.

"Oh, my god." Her eyes widen. "You did."

"I didn't say that."

"You didn't have to." She beams, as if I just told her we were doubling her salary. "Don't worry," she adds quickly. "I won't tell Robert. I keep telling him you need to move on. That it's the healthy thing, but you know how he is."

Do I ever.

Control disguised as concern.

Grief weaponized as loyalty.

"Sorry to disappoint you, Margaret, but I haven't met anyone new."

It's not a complete lie. Rowan isn't new.

She's been in my house for months. In my life in quiet, unassuming ways. Sitting on the floor with Jemmy. Braiding Presley's hair. Folding laundry in the living room.

But something shifted this weekend.

And I don't regret it for a second.

Margaret studies me a moment longer, then places her hand on mine, squeezing. "Whatever it is, I'm happy for you. It's good to see you actually…living again. Happiness looks good on you."

I don't respond. Instead, I just give her a small nod and continue down the hallway.

I usually dread this walk. Dread staring at Cora's portrait as I head toward my office. Am normally overcome with guilt and grief.

Not today.

Today, I pause in front of it and look into her eyes, seeing her in a different light.

Like a weight's been lifted off her, too.

I slip inside my office and exchange my winter coat for my white jacket. Then I sit at my desk and open my laptop to review a few case notes.

As I do, my cell phone buzzes. I grab my glasses and put them on, clicking on the message.

A selfie fills the screen. Rowan and Jemmy pressed cheek to cheek. Jemmy's curls are a mess. Rowan's smile is wide and unguarded.

ROWAN:

Smiles for Daddy.

Warmth spreads through me, slow and steady. It's ridiculous how something so simple can do that. I tell myself it's because of how happy Jemmy looks. And that's part of it.

But it's not the only reason for this feeling that's overtaken me.

A knock sounds, tearing my attention away from my phone just as the door opens.

Robert stands in the doorway, his analytical stare studying me.

"You seem…happy," he says, as if the mere notion leaves a bad taste in his mouth.

I lower my glasses. "Just had a nice weekend."

"Hmm." He narrows his gaze on me.

He's searching for something. Evidence of betrayal maybe.

For a flicker of a second, I wonder if he can see the truth on me. If he can tell the reason I'm so happy is because I got laid again. If he can sense I was unfaithful to his daughter.

But I wasn't unfaithful.

Cora's gone.

That truth used to feel like a blade. Now it feels like something else. Permission, maybe?

Or maybe I've finally reached acceptance.

"I spoke with the pastor," Robert announces after a beat. "We're arranging a service in Cora's memory on the twenty-first of next month. I've reserved the function room at Holley Ridge for afterwards."

I frown. "We just had her memorial. A week ago."

His eyes sharpen. "January twenty-first is her birthday. Or did you already forget?"

The air in the room cools several degrees, the uneasiness I always feel in his presence creeping in.

I haven't forgotten. He won't let me. But I don't say that.

"Is this really necessary?" I ask.

His face reddens, his jaw tightening. "Is it necessary to pay tribute to your wife? To honor her memory?"

"I didn't mean it like that. I just..." I blow out a breath, briefly closing my eyes to collect my thoughts. "It's difficult for the kids, especially Presley. If it weren't for Rowan—"

"I'm glad you brought her up," Robert interjects. "This time, it's for family and close friends only. No additional attendees or...plus ones."

"Rowan isn't an additional attendee or a plus one," I say carefully. "She's my kids' nanny."

"People are still talking about why you brought a date to your wife's memorial."

I'm about to remind him once again that she wasn't my date. That she helps with the kids and it could be good to have her there, especially if he insists on them attending, but I don't. He'll only read into it more than he should.

I'm not sure I want Rowan there anyway. Especially now.

It was different when she was there as emotional support for Presley.

Now that we're sleeping together, inviting her to my dead wife's birthday memorial seems a little strange.

"She won't be there," I assure him.

A flicker of satisfaction crosses his face. "Good."

"If you'll excuse me," I say calmly, returning my glasses to my face and gesturing toward my laptop, "I need to review some case notes before seeing my first patient."

He lingers a second longer, searching my face for something. Probably the same unbearable guilt that's weighed me down since Cora's death.

He won't find it.

I refuse to continue burdening myself with the past.

In just one weekend, Rowan's taught me the importance of letting things go.

I can only imagine what one month with her will do.

Do I *have* a month with her?

I don't know.

And I'm surprisingly okay with that.

I've always lived my life structured. One milestone after another. High school. College. Med school. Residency. Marriage. Children. Promotions.

Always moving forward.

Never remaining still.

Then Cora died, and everything stopped.

I've been standing in the wreckage ever since.

Until Rowan.

When I'm with her, I'm not calculating what's next. I'm not replaying what I should have done differently.

I'm just there.

Enjoying the moment.

Although, I am very much looking forward to later tonight when I can feel her again.

"Of course," Robert says finally. "I'll let you know more details once I have them."

I give him one last nod before he retreats into the hallway.

When the door shuts behind him, I release a slow breath.

My chest doesn't feel tight.

My hands aren't shaking.

I don't feel like I've failed some invisible test.

Instead, I feel…steady.

Robert can cling to the past if he wants. Build shrines and host services and replay what-ifs until the end of time.

But I have two children who need a father who's present.

And that's exactly what I plan to be.

THIRTY-FIVE

Rowan

"I thought I saw you walk in."

At the sound of the familiar voice, I come to an abrupt stop in the produce section of the local grocery store, my cart loaded with everything I need for the dinner I'm planning to make with Presley later.

Today seems like a day to celebrate. Then again, in my humble opinion, we should celebrate every day. But it feels like a good day to make a big Mexican feast.

So after taking Jemmy to the library for story time, I stopped to pick up some things I'd need.

The last thing I expected was to run into Joshua.

Truth be told, I haven't thought about him once since he dropped me off Saturday night.

Every spare inch of mental space has been consumed by Hayden.

The way he looks at me.

The way his smile brightens his face.

The way he touches me like he's rediscovering something he thought he'd lost.

The way I feel when I'm with him.

I quickly push down the thought, devoting my full attention to Joshua. He looks like he just stepped out of a catalogue of small-town book boyfriends — flannel shirt, slightly messy hair, faded jeans tucked into a pair of work boots.

"Oh, hey. Sorry. I didn't notice you. I was distracted trying to choose the perfect..." I trail off and pick up the closest vegetable.

And when I see what I end up with, I'm horrified at the double meaning.

"You got distracted looking for the perfect eggplant?"

"Sure did."

"I can understand that. Finding the perfect... eggplant is definitely important."

"It certainly is."

In more ways than one.

We stare at each other for several seconds, the eggplant still in my hand as Jemmy babbles at all the different foods he sees, naming them the best he can, although he's come up with quite a few interesting nicknames. Tom-toms for tomatoes. Yummies are grapes. But my personal favorite is probably broccoli, which he calls mops because they remind him of a mop.

"Well..." Joshua clears his throat, "I just wanted to say hi. I'm picking up a few things for Holley Ridge, but I need to get back."

"Okay. Well… Hi."

He steps closer, his eyes trained on me. "Hi."

I swallow hard. "Hi."

"Hi," Jemmy interjects, waving a hand in Joshua's direction.

"Hey, Jemmy." Joshua shifts toward him. "High five?"

He slaps his palm against Joshua's with dramatic enthusiasm.

"Wow," Joshua says, shaking his hand, feigning pain. "You're getting strong."

A week ago, I would have swooned at how great Joshua is with little Jemmy.

That was before I knew what it was like to be wrapped up in Hayden's arms. Before I knew exactly how his body felt against mine. Before I knew what kind of inferno his touch could ignite inside me.

Joshua turns his attention back to me now that Jemmy seems pre-occupied with listing off the produce once more. "I had a lot of fun Saturday."

"I did, too."

It's not a complete lie. I did enjoy my time with Joshua.

It was easy. Comfortable. Safe. But it was forgettable.

"What are you doing this Saturday night? Are you free?"

My expression immediately falls.

While Hayden and I aren't exactly in a relationship, I still don't feel right stringing Joshua along. Like I've repeatedly said… Life's too short to waste on mediocrity. And Joshua doesn't make my heart race.

Not like Hayden.

"Listen, Joshua…," I begin.

"That doesn't sound good," he says with a self-deprecating laugh.

"I'm sorry." I wince, worrying my bottom lip.

I've always hated breakups.

It's probably why I never broke up with Landon when I wanted to. When every voice in my head told me he wasn't the right man for me. That I deserved someone who'd scale mountains to be with me. Who wouldn't cut bait at the first sign of trouble.

"I really like you. And I had fun. But I don't think it's fair to keep going out with you."

"You're friend-zoning me," he says gently.

"I guess I am. Maybe if things were different…" I shake my head, pushing away the thought. "But the truth is I only agreed to go out with you because I was trying to…forget about someone else."

He studies my face carefully. Not defensive. Not angry. Just…curious.

"Did it work?"

I slowly shake my head.

Not even close.

If anything, going out with him made the truth I'd been fighting crystal clear.

"Me neither," Joshua admits on a long exhale.

My brows knit in confusion. "What do you mean?"

He runs a hand through his dark hair, a sheepish smile tugging on his lips, revealing those adorable dimples.

But they have nothing on Hayden's.

"There's this girl. Well, girl isn't exactly the word. She's…" He huffs a laugh. "She's older."

"How much older?" I ask, unable to stop myself.

"Old enough that she used to babysit me."

"Wow."

"I wasn't in diapers or anything," he adds quickly, stealing a glance at Jemmy. "But she grew up next door. I had the biggest crush on her when I was little. Thought it was just an innocent childhood infatuation. But she came home for the holidays after learning her husband's been cheating on her. I guess seeing her again has made me realize it wasn't just an innocent infatuation."

"And you thought going out with me would help you forget about her," I say, all too familiar with his thought process.

"Terrible strategy."

"It is," I agree with a sigh. "I've learned the heart wants what it wants and doesn't care about reason or circumstance."

"You're right about that." He stares into the distance for a beat before returning his attention to me, extending his hand. "Friends?"

I push out a sigh and place my hand in his. "Definitely."

"Good." He leans in and presses a chaste kiss to my cheek.

"Kiss, kiss," Jemmy says excitedly. "Kiss, kiss."

We break apart, laughing.

"Sorry, bud," Joshua says to him. "Didn't mean to steal your woman."

"These Lawrence men can be extremely possessive," I joke, then immediately wish I could take back my words.

"Is that right?" Joshua arches a brow.

"I, uh. I didn't… That came out wrong."

"It's okay. Your secret's safe with me." He winks, then leans closer. "Although I'm not sure how much of a secret it is, considering it looked like Hayden was ready to murder me just for talking to you last weekend." He steps back, flashing me a smile. "See ya around."

Then he disappears down the aisle, leaving me speechless with an eggplant still in my hand.

I don't even need eggplant.

But I take it as a sign and put it in my cart anyway.

THIRTY-SIX

Rowan

Steam filters out of a pan on the stove, the aroma of cumin and chili powder surrounding me as Taylor Swift belts about revenge and grudges from the speaker.

I tried to convince Presley to let me put on something more on-theme for enchilada night, something with Spanish guitar or at least a little salsa flair, but she crossed her arms and signed, *Reputation*.

A girl after my own heart.

She stands beside me on the step stool, her dark hair pulled back, humming as she spoons the chicken, cheese, and bean mixture onto a tortilla. It's off-key and barely audible, but it's there.

I pretend not to notice.

If I look at her too long, if I make it a thing, she might retreat. So I roll the tortilla tight, tuck it seam-side down into the baking dish, and let her hum.

"Something smells delicious."

At the sound of the deep, husky voice, a jolt of electricity shoots through me. I attempt to school my expression when I see Hayden turn the corner, but it's a losing battle. Especially when I'm greeted by his devastating smile.

Normally when he comes home from work, he looks burdened. Like the day beat every last ounce of life out of him.

Not today.

Today, he looks lighter.

"Hope you don't mind," I say, wiping my hands on a towel. "I was in the mood for Mexican. Presley's helping me make enchiladas."

He steps closer, close enough that I catch the clean scent of soap and the office — something sterile layered over something uniquely him.

"Sounds delicious."

His fingers wrap around my upper arm, giving it a gentle squeeze. His thumb brushes once, almost absently, before he pulls away.

The contact is brief.

But not brief enough.

Presley definitely notices.

Of course she does.

She notices everything.

And when she returns her attention to me after Hayden presses a soft kiss to her head, she gives me a playful waggle of her brow.

What? I sign.

She replies, *Nothing.*

She continues spooning the mixture onto the tortillas, which I roll up tight before adding to the tray.

Then she nudges me to get my attention.

It's okay if you like him.

I glance at Hayden as he picks up Jemmy and peppers him with kisses. And my ovaries combust just watching him.

Presley tugs on my arm, forcing my eyes back to her. It's *really* hard to focus when Hayden is in the same room.

It's not like that, I sign back quickly.

I typically speak my responses to her, but I'd rather keep this conversation between us… For now, anyway.

Presley narrows her eyes. *So you don't do crush business?*

I choke back a laugh, recalling Hayden's niece, Maggie, using the term.

We definitely do crush business, but I'm not about to tell her that.

He's my boss, I sign in reply.

Presley gives me a look that essentially says, "I'm seven. Not stupid."

That's not an answer, she signs.

"Just fill those enchiladas, please."

She playfully salutes and goes back to work. But there's a knowing smirk on her face.

As we cook to the soundtrack of Taylor Swift's revenge era, I can't help but smile at how much Presley's changed since I first met her.

I'm going to miss spending time with her when I

leave. Cooking dinner together. Dancing to music. Teaching her things I was never taught when I was her age.

A tiny voice sounds in the back of my head, reminding me I don't have to leave, but I quickly silence it.

This isn't forever. This isn't my family. It's Hayden's. They've already been through enough. Already buried one wife. One mother.

I won't put them through that again.

"Do I have time for a quick shower before dinner?" Hayden asks, cutting through my thoughts.

I look up and meet his eyes. "Of course. Take your time."

"I won't be long." He flashes me the smile that makes my knees weaken every single time, my pulse still fluttering long after he's disappeared from view.

With a long sigh, I turn back, only to come face-to-face with Presley making exaggerated kissing faces at me.

I don't have it in me to deny it. I simply shake my head and continue rolling up the enchiladas.

By the time Hayden comes back downstairs, the enchiladas are in the oven, and Presley has taken Jemmy into the living room to play for a bit before dinner, giving me time to fluff the rice.

Which is what I'm doing when I feel him behind me.

Not hear.

Feel.

The subtle shift in the air. The heat of him. The

awareness that makes the tiny hairs all over my body stand on end.

"Miss me?"

His voice is low. Sensual.

Dangerous.

"No more than usual," I reply, trying to play it cool as I turn to face him. "Although I did see a very impressive eggplant at the grocery store earlier. It reminded me of you. Or, more accurately, your dick."

He throws his head back, his laughter echoing through the house.

"I'm not sure if I should be flattered or…"

"Oh, you should be. It's thick. And long. And it's curved at just the right angle. I bought it as a souvenir."

He shakes his head, his laughter continuing to rumble through him. "Of course you did." Then he erases the space between us, his hand settling on my waist. "I missed you today."

"I missed you, too," I admit around a sigh.

He leans down and brushes his mouth over mine. It's gentle. Tender. Testing. For a split second, I want to melt into it.

Instead, I press my palm to his chest and create space.

"What's wrong?" He eyes me in concern. "We're alone."

"I know." I glance toward the living room, confirming the kids are occupied. "But Presley's already picked up on…whatever this is. She asked if I like you."

He waggles his brows. "And do you?"

I playfully swat his arm. "I'm trying to be serious."

"So am I. My ego is extremely fragile."

Despite myself, I laugh.

I adore this version of him. The playful one. The man who isn't carrying the weight of the world on his shoulders. The carefree man he must have been at some point in his life.

"I think it's probably best if we keep our hands to ourselves when the kids are around. It's already going to be difficult for them when I leave."

At the reminder, his expression falls, and I hate that I'm the cause of it. But my plans haven't changed. I'll eventually leave, and Hayden will find a new nanny. Maybe someone like me but with more stability.

Someone without a ticking clock.

Although, the mere thought of it makes something hot and sharp bubble inside me.

"I just think it will be a lot less confusing if we tone down the PDA," I finish.

He pushes out a long breath, running his fingers through his still-damp hair. "You're right. I'll keep things professional when they're around."

"Thank you."

I turn back to the stove, fluffing the rice, even though it doesn't need it.

"But for the record," he murmurs, stepping close again, "I'm going to PDA all over you the second those kids are asleep."

Before I can react, his palm lands against my ass with a firm smack.

I whirl around. "Hayden!"

He's already backing away, looking far too pleased with himself.

And I hate that my first instinct isn't to berate him or remind him of what we just discussed.

It's to count down the hours until bedtime.

THIRTY-SEVEN

Hayden

Six conversations overlap in my mother's dining room, bouncing off the pale yellow walls and the antique china cabinet she refuses to replace. Forks scrape plates. Someone laughs too loudly. Jemmy babbles incessantly to my mom, and she hangs onto every word he speaks.

Same table. Same faces. Same heavy oak chair beneath me.

Everything else is different.

A month ago, I sat in this exact seat with my jaw locked so tight it ached. Every time Joshua leaned toward Rowan, every time she laughed at something he said, it killed me. Made me rage with jealousy. Because *he* could touch her. Could make her smile. Make her laugh.

I couldn't.

Or so I thought.

Today, Joshua is still part of whatever animated conversation Rowan's having with Claire and Dylan, but he doesn't touch her arm when he talks. Doesn't lean too close. Doesn't linger.

Every few minutes, she steals a glance my way, a myriad of unspoken words in that one look.

A part of me wonders if Joshua knows, since he seems to keep his distance, especially whenever he notices me looking at Rowan. But if he's figured it out, he hasn't mentioned it.

Regardless, one thing is certain.

This past month has been one of the best of my life.

Quiet laughter during dinner. Making Rowan come after the kids are asleep. Stolen kisses in the kitchen.

It's been…easy.

After a year of wearing my grief like a badge of honor, I feel lighter. I sleep better. Laugh more.

All because of Rowan.

It doesn't even bother me that any day she could decide she's had enough of us and leave.

Do I *want* her to leave?

Of course not.

But I'm not obsessing over the future.

Hell, I'm not even obsessing over the past anymore.

For the first time in ages, I'm just here.

Present.

Free.

"Is that a smile I see?"

Jude's voice cuts through my thoughts, and I quickly school my expression, pretending I wasn't just smiling at the mere thought of the things my employee did to me before the kids woke up this morning.

"What are you talking about?" I bring my beer to my lips and take a sip. "Good batch, by the way," I say, referring to the beer.

But he doesn't take the bait. I should know by now he wouldn't.

"What's going on with you?" He leans back in his chair. "You seem…different."

"I'm not different," I respond dismissively. "Just enjoying my beer."

Jude scrunches his brows, studying me with even more intensity. "The Hayden I've seen moping around the past year hasn't enjoyed *anything*. Which begs the question…" He brings his thumb and forefinger up to his chin. "What precisely are you enjoying now?"

I avert my gaze, stealing a glance at Rowan as I do. "I don't know what—"

"A-ha!" His voice echoes through the room, everyone pausing their conversations to look his way.

"Sorry." He clears his throat. "Just figured out a crossword clue from this morning. Those Sunday puzzles can be brutal."

My mom gives him a skeptical stare, but eventually shrugs it off and returns her attention to Jemmy.

Once the noise returns to its normal fevered level, Jude leans toward me. "You're fucking the nanny."

I choke on my beer, coughing as I struggle to catch my breath.

"What?" I manage to say after a few seconds. "I don't know where you got that."

"Allow me to present Exhibit A."

"What are you?" I snort. "A lawyer?"

"Better. I own a bar. Have spent thousands of hours pouring beers for people who tell me their deepest, darkest secrets. I'm everyone's favorite therapist. And over the years, I've learned how to read people. Better yet, I'm able to read the tension between people." He gives a subtle nod in Rowan's direction. "Last month, the tension between the two of you was fucking intense. It screamed, 'I can't have her, but I'll murder anyone who even looks her way.'"

Heat creeps up my neck, but I play it off. "That so?"

"Case in point…the death glare you shot poor Joshua every ten seconds. But this month? It's different. No death glare."

"Because there's nothing—"

He holds up a hand, cutting me off.

"Ah, ah, ah. I'm not finished." He brings the bottle back to his lips and takes a long swallow. "As I was saying, there's no death glare this month. And the tension isn't giving off those territorial vibes. Instead, it's oozing with 'I just had her and I'm counting down the seconds until I can have her again.'"

He waggles his brow, and I shake my head. But he's not wrong.

I *am* counting down the seconds until I can be alone with Rowan.

"You can't even deny it. You've got it bad."

There's no sense in lying to him. If there's anyone I can talk to about this, it's Jude. He's one of the few people who can truly understand what I've gone through this past year. He suffered a loss, too. A different kind of loss, but a loss all the same. He wrestled with guilt, regret, and grief, just like me.

Struggled to move on. Until Abbey.

"We're just having some fun. That's all."

"Famous last words." He tilts back his beer bottle and takes a sip.

"We agreed. No plans for a future. We're just having some fun while she's here and when the arrangement no longer works out or it's time for her to leave, it ends and we go our separate ways."

"Are you sure about that?"

"It's not like we're dating or anything," I attempt to argue. "It's just sex."

"It's never just sex, brother."

He glances toward the other end of the table where Abbey sits with Finn and Genevieve.

"I said the same thing about Abbey. We were just having some fun while she figured out what was next for her." He leans closer and drops his voice. "And do you know what I did last weekend?"

"What?"

"Went ring shopping."

"Wow. That's great, Jude." I give his shoulder a squeeze. "I'm happy for you."

"Thanks, man. I never thought I'd be here again. Not after everything I went through with Krista. I figured that part of my life was over. But when you meet someone who makes you feel like yourself again? Like the version of you that existed before the worst thing happened?" He narrows his gaze on me. "That's not something you walk away from lightly."

My chest tightens as the sound of Rowan's laughter filters through the air. It's bright and unguarded, and it hits me harder than I expected.

I remember the man I was before my entire life was consumed by grief and regret. The man who laughed easily. Who said yes more than he said no.

I've seen glimpses of him lately.

"We're not—"

"I get it," Jude cuts through before I can repeat yet another bullshit lie. "It's terrifying. You went through something horrific. Lost your wife and are now raising your kids on your own. It makes sense that you wouldn't want to put yourself in a situation where you or your kids might go through anything remotely similar. I was in your shoes, too. Was so fucking scared of loving someone and losing them again that I shut out everyone. And I almost lost the best thing that's ever happened to me because of it."

I nod, all too familiar with what he's talking about. How he let Abbey leave, then flew across the country to admit he fucked up.

"But maybe instead of insisting something could never be, you keep yourself open to what might be. I've seen a change in you over the past few months. I've seen the old Hayden again. My *brother*. Maybe I'm wrong, but I have a feeling that girl has something to do with it. Hell, she has *a lot* to do with it."

I don't argue. Because I know she does.

"You don't let something like that walk away without

a fight, man. Haven't you punished yourself long enough?"

The noise around us swells again. Silverware. Laughter. The hum of family. But I don't hear any of it.

Instead, my sole focus is on Rowan as she signs something to Presley. Something amusing, because Presley's mouth curves into a wide smile, something she rarely did a few months ago.

For a second, the future flashes before my eyes. Coming home to a quiet house. No music playing in the kitchen. No vivacious girl dancing between checking on Jemmy and teaching Presley how to cook.

I've told myself I'll be okay when she leaves.

That it won't bother me.

But the mere idea of walking into the house without her there feels unbearable.

And that scares me more than anything.

THIRTY-EIGHT

Rowan

"Don't you dare slam that door again, young lady!" Hayden's voice cracks through the house like thunder, colliding with the sharp bang of wood, and I freeze inside the great room.

Lately, I've been starting my day on the front porch, but I knew today might be difficult for everyone, considering it's Cora's birthday. So I went outside to do yoga to give Hayden some space, all things considered.

And apparently walked in on World War III.

I have a pretty good idea of what caused it, too.

As expected, Hayden's father-in-law has arranged another memorial service honoring Cora's memory, followed by a luncheon. While I disagree with constantly having to attend these memorials, it's not my place to say anything.

Although it's been a struggle to bite my tongue.

Especially with how Presley's been unravelling all week. She's been short-tempered and withdrawn. Hell, she hasn't even wanted to help cook dinner, something that's usually the highlight of her day.

I try to slip through the living room unnoticed, hoping to disappear into my bedroom and give Hayden space to handle it, but he storms down the stairs at the exact moment I pass them.

His jaw is tight, eyes on fire, muscles rigid with frustration. Grief. Helplessness.

He looks like the Hayden from months ago.

The one who lived permanently on edge.

But when he sees me, his expression shifts, the tension falling from his shoulders.

He crosses the space between us in three strides and pulls me into his chest.

Hard.

For a second, I hesitate.

We've been careful lately. No lingering touches in the open. No blurred lines in front of the kids.

But today isn't a normal day.

So I wrap my arms around him and give him the comfort I sense he needs.

"Rough morning?" I murmur.

Hayden blows out a humorless laugh. "You have no idea."

His hand slides up to cradle the back of my neck, thumb brushing beneath my ear.

"But it's better now." He tilts my chin up and presses the softest kiss to my mouth.

It's barely there, but it melts something inside me all

the same.

God, I love this man.

The thought sneaks in before I can stop it. I didn't mean it like that. I care about him. Want him to be happy. But I don't love him.

I *can't* love him.

"Is Presley being difficult?"

On a long exhale, he steps back, still keeping one hand on my hip, as if he needs the reassurance I'm here.

"She doesn't want to go today."

"She hasn't been herself all week. Even her teachers noticed."

"I know." He releases me and drags a hand over his face, fatigue etched into every line. "But I need to be there. And if I need to be there, she does, too."

"Is this really the best thing for her?"

His eyes flick up to mine.

I normally don't question his decisions as a parent. But we're not talking about signing Presley up for art classes or letting Jemmy have a play date.

This is bigger than that.

And it's been affecting Presley's mental health.

"I'm not a professional," I continue softly, "but reminding her of the accident and losing her mom as much as your father-in-law does can't be good for her. She makes so much progress, then it's like we rip off the scab and she bleeds all over again."

Upstairs, there's another muffled thud followed by an angry stomp. Hayden squeezes his eyes shut, his frustration evident. But it's mixed with something else, too. It reminds me of the despair I saw that first night. When he absentmindedly commented how he thought he'd have his shit together by now.

"It's her mom's birthday," I say, running a reassuring hand up and down his arm. "She doesn't need church services and speeches. Maybe she needs something lighter. Maybe… Maybe I should watch them today."

He shoots his gaze to mine. "It's your day off."

"I don't mind. I love spending time with them. We could do something fun. A yes day of their very own. Let them pick what they want to do."

He hesitates, and I expect him to say no. Remind me of Presley's obligations. Of all the reasons why she needs to sit in a church today instead of being a kid.

"Actually… I think that's a really good idea."

I blink, surprised. "You do?"

"I do." He chuckles. "Although their grandfather won't be happy…"

"When is he ever?" I mutter under my breath, then wince. "Sorry. I didn't mean that."

"Yes, you did. And it's okay. I'm willing to bear the brunt of Robert's ire if it means Presley can have a good memory of today. She deserves it."

I touch a hand to his bicep. "You all do. You could have a yes day, too."

A small smile tugs at his mouth as he pulls me back into his arms. "I wish I could."

He lowers his lips to mine and kisses me again. There's no urgency in it. Just the same connection I've grown to crave over the past several weeks.

"Maybe I can have a yes night with you later," he

murmurs against my lips as he tugs me closer, slowly circling his hips so I can feel his erection.

"What would that entail?"

"I'm not quite sure. But I have all day to come up with my list." He waggles his brows, giving me a mischievous smile.

"When you put it that way," I begin, hoisting myself onto my toes, "how can I possibly say no?"

He covers my mouth with his one last time, our tongues briefly touching. Then he steps back, already squaring his shoulders, preparing to face the storm.

As I watch him climb the stairs, warmth blooms in my chest, and I wonder how much longer I can keep pretending this is just temporary.

Keep pretending my heart doesn't ache at the idea of not seeing these people every day.

Keep pretending I'm not in love with my boss.

THIRTY-NINE

Hayden

The church parking lot is already half full when I pull in.

Black sedans. Polished SUVs. People dressed in subdued colors moving slowly across the pavement.

The brick building looms in front of me, its white steeple cutting into a picturesque blue sky.

My phone buzzes in my pocket, and I retrieve it, finding a message from Rowan.

It's a photo. Presley is mid-laugh, a smear of chocolate ice cream on her upper lip. Jemmy's entire fist is buried in a bowl of whipped cream. Rowan's arm stretches into frame, holding her own ridiculous sundae stacked with gummy bears and sprinkles.

ROWAN:

Ice cream for breakfast = Yes Day win!

I trace my eyes over the photo, my heart squeezing at how happy Presley is.

This morning she wouldn't even look at me. Wouldn't put her shoes on. Slammed her door hard enough to rattle the house.

And now she looks…light.

Alive.

I glance back at the church, and my jaw tightens.

For the past year, I've told myself that showing up to these memorials is how I honor Cora.

How I prove she still matters.

But sitting here, staring at a picture of my daughter covered in ice cream at nine in the morning, I realize something I've ignored.

I've been honoring the dead at the expense of the living.

By clinging to what I lost, I've been missing what's right in front of me.

Missing mornings like this.

Missing the chance to make new, happier memories with my family.

Before I allow the guilt and regret to overwhelm me yet again, I throw the car into reverse and leave the past in my rearview mirror.

Where it belongs.

***

The bell above the diner door jingles when I step inside, and I'm immediately surrounded by the aroma of coffee, bacon, and maple syrup. On a Sunday morning, the place is buzzing with people, but it doesn't take me long to find who I'm looking for.

Presley is still eating her ice cream, although it looks like she's slowing down. Jemmy's singing a song about dinosaurs while Rowan attempts to clean the whipped cream off his hands, but she doesn't seem aggravated or frustrated by the mess. She sings along with him, a bright smile on her face.

I don't approach right away.

I just watch them, wanting to freeze this moment.

Presley hasn't looked this carefree in months. Maybe longer. For the first time since the accident, she truly looks happy.

And Rowan...

God.

She looks like she belongs with them.

With me.

Like she's a part of this family.

A part of our life.

Jemmy giggles as Rowan continues trying to clean him, his eyes finding mine.

"Dada," he says excitedly, clapping his hands.

"I know, buddy," Rowan replies, wiping at his face. "He's sad he can't be here. But he's going to try to join us later on. Okay?"

"No." Jemmy shakes his head fiercely, pointing a chubby finger at me. "Dada."

Rowan and Presley both turn.

The moment Rowan sees me, her entire body stills, her mouth parting slightly.

I've never seen her speechless.

Until now.

I walk toward the booth, my shoes echoing softly against the tile.

She blinks, like she's trying to process whether I'm real. "What are you doing here?"

"I couldn't let you three have all the fun without me."

"So you're not going to the…thing today?"

There's something vulnerable in her question. Like she's bracing for disappointment. For me to tell her I'm just stopping by.

I shake my head and smile. "I'm exactly where I need to be." I hold her gaze, allowing her to see the truth in my words.

Then Presley jumps to her feet and wraps her arms around my waist, ice cream and all.

I don't even care. I pull her close, breathing in sugar and strawberry shampoo and the moment I almost missed.

My past will always be part of me.

Cora will always be part of me.

But this — sticky fingers, loud laughter, ice cream before ten in the morning — this is my life now.

And I'm done watching it from a church pew.

FORTY

Hayden

By the time we pull into the driveway, the house is dark except for the porch light.

Presley is slumped against the car window, a smear of powdered sugar still faintly visible on her cheek from the funnel cake she insisted counted as a "late lunch." Jemmy's mouth hangs open in his car seat, fingers still curled around the cheap plastic dinosaur he refused to part with at the arcade.

Ice cream for breakfast turned into the park. The park turned into letting Presley pick the loudest, most chaotic trampoline park in the area. That somehow turned into pizza at the arcade.

We walked a shelter dog named Groucho Barx. Played mini golf. I let Presley bury me in snow at the playground like she used to when she was four. I pushed

Jemmy on the swings until my arms ached and he shrieked with laughter.

For the first time in over a year, it felt like we were a family again.

Except Rowan isn't technically part of that family.

But she was woven through every part of today.

And with every passing day, it's getting harder to imagine my life without her in it.

I step out of the car quietly and open Presley's door first. She doesn't stir when I lift her into my arms. She's getting heavier these days. Taller. Growing faster than I'm ready for.

Rowan moves around to the other side and carefully unbuckles Jemmy, pressing a soft kiss to his temple before lifting him, his head lolling against her shoulder.

I carry Presley upstairs and somehow manage to wrestle her into pajamas without waking her fully before pulling her blankets over her. I brush her hair back from her face and press a kiss to her forehead. Then I quietly close her door and head toward Jemmy's room, planning to take over for Rowan.

But when I reach his doorway, I pause at the sight of her holding Jemmy close, swaying as she hums. His head rests on her shoulder, one tiny hand tangled in her hair.

There's something so natural about the way she moves. The way she leaves a soft kiss on his head. The way she carefully lowers him into the crib, resting her hand over his heart for a beat.

It does something to me.

Not lust.

Not even desire.

Something bigger.

Something I'm scared to name.

She turns and startles slightly when she sees me watching. Then a small smile tugs on her lips, and she slips into the hallway, closing Jemmy's door quietly behind her.

"Well," she says softly, walking into my embrace. "Have you decided?"

"On what?"

"Your own yes day." She rises onto her toes and brushes her lips against mine. "Or, more accurately, yes night. What's first on your list?"

"Well, I've had some time to think about it. Came up with quite a few ideas throughout the day."

"Is that right?"

"It is. But after much deliberation, I've decided there's really only one thing I want tonight."

"And what's that?" Her lips hover over mine. "Your wish is my command."

I hesitate, unsure how this will go over. What I'm about to ask of her is different from anything we've done before. It's a risk.

But I'm all about taking risks and breaking the rules today. Why stop now?

"You," I tell her. "In my bed. All night long."

She stiffens, pulling back, her eyes searching mine with confusion.

"I want to fall asleep with you beside me," I continue, keeping my gaze trained on her. "And wake up with you in my arms."

She parts her lips, but no response comes. I can physically feel her reluctance. Her hesitation.

I get it.

This crosses a line we agreed we wouldn't cross.

I'm not just asking her for sex tonight.

I'm asking for more of her.

All of her.

"Please, Rowan." I step toward her, erasing the space between us. "Give me one full night with you. It's the only thing I want. Just you. Please. Say yes."

Her breath leaves her on a shaky exhale as she closes her eyes.

For a second, I think she's going to insist she can't. Remind me of our arrangement.

That we may have sex, but we don't sleep together.

That we shouldn't blur the lines any more than we already have.

Then her eyes soften as her lips curve up into a smile.

"Yes."

FORTY-ONE

Rowan

I shouldn't have said yes. I should have reminded Hayden of our agreement. Of the rules. Of the boundaries I've insisted we keep in place.

But when his voice lost that teasing edge and turned quiet and vulnerable, I couldn't do it. I couldn't deny him.

Or maybe I couldn't deny myself.

His mouth finds mine again as he guides me down the hallway, slow and unhurried, like he has all the time in the world. The house is quiet except for the faint hum of the heat blowing through the vents and the soft brush of our feet against the hardwood floor.

We cross the threshold into his bedroom, and he kicks the door closed behind us, the sound echoing around us.

He pulls back slightly, his eyes tracing over my face, slow and deliberate.

It unnerves me.

This was easier when it was reckless.

When we fucked like horny teenagers who didn't know better.

When we were just bodies colliding.

When it didn't mean anything.

But Hayden doesn't look at me like I mean nothing to him tonight.

He looks at me like I matter.

Like he loves me.

The thought petrifies me.

But not enough to leave.

Not when this man is a drug. And not the recreational kind. The slow, intoxicating kind that seeps into your bloodstream and rewires you from the inside out. Even though I know the eventual withdrawal will destroy me, I take the hit anyway.

He runs a hand along the curve of my face, his thumb settling on my lower lip. "You are so beautiful."

A shaky exhale leaves me before I can stop it. It's not just his words that undo me. It's the way he says them. Like he can't go another second without sharing this with me.

"And I'm not talking about your body," he murmurs, his lips brushing mine. "But your soul. Your spirit." He slides his hand over my collarbone until his palm rests over my scar. "And your heart. You have the most beautiful heart I've ever known."

He presses his mouth fully against mine, coaxing my lips to part.

It takes everything in me not to blurt out the truth. That the heart he admires so much once belonged to his late wife. But I can't stomach the idea of never feeling him again.

So I selfishly keep my secret to myself and let him guide me toward the bed. When the back of my legs hit the mattress, he releases me, but keeps his eyes trained on me.

He shrugs off his jacket, loosening his tie and tossing it onto the floor before slowly unbuttoning his shirt.

I've seen this man naked dozens of times. Touched every inch of him. Learned the feel of his body. The sound he makes when he can't contain his hunger.

But this feels different.

More intimate.

More dangerous.

Once he drops his shirt onto the floor, he pulls me against him and I melt into him as he touches his lips to mine.

His fingers find the hem of my sweater, and he breaks away to lift it over my head, discarding it along with his clothes. His hands roam my body, as if imprinting every inch of me to memory. When his fingers tease the waistband of my jeans, a shiver rolls through me.

I allow him to lower the zipper and push them down my legs. I kick them to the side, feeling more vulnerable than I ever have. And I'm not even naked yet.

He curves toward me, capturing my mouth in another kiss I feel in the deepest parts of my soul as he unclasps my bra, removing it. He spins me around, splaying a hand on my stomach and pressing soft kisses to my neck.

I crane my head, allowing him better access as he worships my body. When he pinches my nipple between his thumb and forefinger, I release something between a yelp and a moan, hunger curling through me.

I'm on the brink of telling him to get on with it already. To throw me on the bed and fuck me.

But I'm enjoying this. The buildup. The anticipation. The need.

He slides his hand from my breast and down my torso. My muscles tighten as he teases my hipbone before moving toward the apex of my thighs. I widen my stance slightly in invitation.

"Is this what you want?" he murmurs against my neck. "For me to touch you?"

"Yes," I whimper, my breathing increasing as his hand moves closer and closer.

"Then I need you to do something for me."

"Anything." The word rushes from me. "Whatever you want."

And in this moment, it's true. I'll give him anything if he touches me.

I'll get on my knees. I'll beg. Hell, I'll fucking crawl if that's what it takes.

But that's not what he wants.

His lips brush my neck, his unshaven jawline rough against my skin.

"I want you to watch."

I shift to look at him, confused.

He nods toward the mirror across the room, and I follow his line of sight, swallowing hard at our reflection staring back.

"I want you to watch yourself get off, Rowan." He moves a free hand to my throat, locking my head in place as his other hand continues moving toward my clit. "Want you to see what I do when I make you come."

His other hand inches further and further south, and I hold my breath, bracing for his touch. When he finally slides a finger through my folds, I release a shuddering gasp.

Hayden doesn't talk. Doesn't tell me how wet I am. Doesn't tell me how much he loves my pussy.

Instead, he keeps his stare trained on mine through the mirror as he rubs my clit, bringing my body to heights I've never experienced before.

This is intimate in a way I didn't expect, looking directly into his eyes as I watch him work my body with his expert touch. And the man has certainly become an expert over the past several weeks. He knows exactly where to touch to make me sing. Make me fly. Make me soar.

And he knows the moment I'm ready to do all three.

He tightens his grip on my throat, keeping me locked in place as I gently thrust against his hand. I'm so lost in the moment, I close my eyes.

"No, Rowan. Look at me."

I snap my eyes open once more, meeting his through the mirror.

"Look at what I do to you. What only I can give you."

I'm not sure if he says it because he's starting to sense my confusion. But it's the last thing on my mind as wave after wave of one of the most intense orgasms I've ever had crashes through me. But Hayden doesn't stop. He drags it out, keeping my body upright when it feels like the world's given out beneath me.

Moving his hand to my hip, he turns me around and slams his mouth against mine, his tongue brushing against mine as he fumbles with his pants, pushing them down.

"I will never get tired of watching that. Seeing what I do to you."

Once he kicks off his pants, he lowers me onto the mattress and brings his erection up to me.

I expect him to thrust inside.

He doesn't.

He braces himself over me, his eyes wild with hunger as he eases into me, savoring every inch. Once he's fully seated, he releases a long exhale, his mouth hovering over mine, giving me his breath.

When he starts to move, he's slow. Deliberate. He takes my hands in his, his eyes glued to mine as he circles his hips against me. I wrap my legs around his waist, attempting to urge him on.

"Faster."

"No, baby. Like this. I want you to feel me like this." He lowers his mouth back to mine.

I try to resist. Try to encourage him to pick up the pace.

But as his tantric rhythm propels me higher once more, I surrender to him completely.

My mind.

My body.

And my heart.

FORTY-TWO

Hayden

Something tickles my nose.

Soft. Warm. Faintly floral.

For half a second, I don't know why my chest feels heavier than usual. Then I look down.

Rowan is curled against me, her cheek resting over my heart, her hair spilled across my shoulder and collarbone.

She's still here.

She didn't slip out before dawn.

She didn't retreat to her own room.

A contented sigh leaves me as I slide my arm more securely around her and pull her closer.

She stirs slightly, her fingers tracing gentle circles on my chest.

"You're still here," I murmur, my voice rough with sleep.

"You asked me to stay." She cranes her head back to meet my eyes. "So I stayed."

"I'm so glad you did." I touch my mouth to hers, coaxing her lips to part. She opens for me, and I gently nudge her onto her back, settling between her legs. "Do you know the best part about waking up beside you?"

"What's that?" She chews on her bottom lip.

"That I get to do this." I slide into her, and her body eagerly accepts me.

"And I thought you were going to say because then you didn't have to walk through the house with a raging hard on."

I chuckle as I bring my lips back to hers. "That, too. But I like this, Rowan." I circle my hips against her, burying my head in the crook of her neck. "I *really* like waking up to this."

She sighs, running her fingers up and down my back.

"I really like waking up to this, too."

"He's in a mood," Margaret warns when I step inside the office later that morning.

This is the last place I want to be today. But the promise of spending the night with Rowan in my arms is enough to make even the worst day seem survivable.

"I figured," I respond, not even needing to ask who she's talking about.

I already know.

And I know why, too. Because I skipped the memorial, then ignored all of Robert's calls. I didn't want anything to ruin my time with my kids.

Not anymore.

"Wish me luck," I tell Margaret.

"You might need more than luck this time."

I laugh under my breath as I continue down the hallway, my head still held high.

When I enter my office, I'm not surprised to find Robert sitting behind my desk.

"What the hell were you thinking?" he grits out, his jaw tight with barely controlled anger.

I calmly turn around and close the door. Then I face him. "I assume this is about yesterday."

"You humiliated this family," he snaps, jumping to his feet and stalking toward me. "Do you have any idea what people were saying? Missing your wife's birthday memorial to…what? Galivant around town like it's a cause for celebration? People reported seeing you mini golfing. And at the trampoline park. And the arcade."

"I was spending the day with my kids. Celebrating Cora's life in a way that wasn't centered on her death."

"So is that it? You're just going to blow off your responsibilities now so you can spend time with that nanny of yours? What will people think?"

"I don't give a fuck what people think."

He stiffens, his eyes flashing with anger, his face becoming even redder.

"I've let you dictate how I grieve for over a year," I continue. "You can mourn however you need to. But from now on, I'm going to remember Cora the way I choose."

He leans into me, spittle forming in the corners of his mouth. "You're forgetting what's important."

"No," I say quietly, at complete odds with his demeanor. "I'm remembering."

I move past him and open the top drawer of my desk, pulling out the folded paper I've been hiding for days. I hand it to him.

"What is this?" he barks out as he hastily unfolds it. His expression immediately darkens.

"I accepted a position as Head of Emergency Medicine at St. Andrew's," I explain. "This is my two weeks' notice."

Silence floods the room, and I can physically feel his temperature rising.

I had a feeling he'd react this way. It's one of the reasons I haven't told him until now. I was offered the position earlier in the month, and they gave me a few weeks to think about it.

Even when I wrote this resignation letter, I wasn't sure if it would ever see the light of day. Thought it might sit in that top drawer for the rest of my life.

This weekend changed that.

"You can't be serious," he scoffs.

"I've never been more serious."

"What about Cora?"

"What about her?"

"This is a family medical practice. Considering you're the reason she's not here to continue the family legacy, it falls to you."

"Cora didn't want any part of this legacy either. Why do you think she never left Chicago?"

"You," he stammers. "She—"

"She would want me to be happy," I cut in. "Not chained to something that makes me miserable out of obligation."

"This is all *her* doing, isn't it?" he says coldly, his lip curling. "That nanny."

My spine stiffens protectively.

"I've heard the rumors," he continues. "The looks. The way you two hover around each other in public. So is that it? Are you screwing her?"

"It's none of your business."

"I warned you she wasn't a good choice when you hired her."

"Rowan's the best nanny I've ever met. The best *person* I've ever met. She's gotten Presley to laugh again. To smile again. And me…" I trail off, collecting my thoughts. "Well, she's helped me realize how important living in the present is. Life is short. I don't want to spend whatever time I have left miserable. And working here with you? I've never been so damn miserable. I'm done living this way. Done choosing things I think I have to. Instead, I'm choosing things that make me happy."

My words don't shake.

Don't waver.

For the first time in a long while, I feel like I'm finally on the right path.

"Now if you'll excuse me, I have patients to see."

I don't wait for him to dismiss me. I walk out of my office and do what I've always loved doing.

Take care of people.

FORTY-THREE

Rowan

The house is quiet except for the hum of the dishwasher and the soft rhythmic swish of the brush in my hand.

I've already washed this pan twice, but it gives me something to do.

Something to occupy my mind.

It doesn't help.

Today's been tougher than I thought it would be.

Every time I've replayed the way Hayden looked at me this morning like I belonged in his bed, my chest has ached in a way that has nothing to do with scar tissue.

This year was supposed to be about saying yes.

Yes to experiences.

Yes to adventure.

Yes to living instead of waiting to die.

It wasn't supposed to be about falling in love with a widower and his two children.

I should leave.

The thought has been circling me all day like a vulture. And every time I convince myself it's the right thing to do, I think of Jemmy's adorable voice calling my name first thing in the morning. Presley's quiet smile as we cook together. The way they both light up whenever they see me.

Leaving them will break their hearts.

But staying might destroy mine.

Footsteps sound on the stairs, and my pulse immediately increases.

Hayden steps into the kitchen, his hair slightly mussed in that sexy way I can't resist.

"The kids asleep?" I ask, keeping my back to him as I set the pan onto the rack.

"Jemmy was out after one book. Presley claims she's not tired. She'll be asleep in ten."

I nod, pretending to be busy cleaning the counters in the hopes he won't ask me to spend the night in his bed again.

Because I won't be able to tell him no, even though I should.

"Rowan." His voice is gentle as he touches a hand to my arm, forcing me to drop the towel. "I was hoping to talk to you about something."

My stomach drops. "Is everything okay?"

"Better than okay." His mouth curves into an almost boyish smile, making him look years younger. "I accepted a position at St. Andrew's as their Head of

Emergency Medicine. My last day working with Robert is next Friday."

For a split second, I just stare at him, shocked. Then I throw my arms around him before I can think better of it.

"I'm so happy for you," I breathe into his chest. "That's amazing."

He pulls me close, burying his face in my hair as he lets out a long, relieved sigh. "Thank you."

I allow him to hold me for a beat before pushing against him and creating space between us. "I'm guessing your schedule won't be the same."

"Actually, that's what I wanted to talk to you about."

"What do you mean?"

"I've been doing a lot of thinking." He threads his fingers through his hair, pushing out a nervous laugh. "I don't want you to be the kids' nanny anymore."

"You're...firing me?" I ask, emotions warring inside me, part relief, part confusion.

"No." He steps closer, taking my hand in his and running a reassuring thumb along my knuckles. "Not like that. I just..." He pauses, licking his lips before returning his eyes to mine. "I don't want you here because I'm paying you to be. I want you here because you *want* to be."

My throat goes dry. "What are you saying?"

"I don't want to employ you." His eyes lock on mine, unguarded and certain. "I want to date you."

The room tilts, dizziness overtaking me as I struggle to catch my breath. I pull my hand from his and use it to steady myself against the counter.

"We talked about this," I whisper.

"I know. But I'm taking risks today. I stood up to Robert and quit the job I've hated since I moved here. I figured it was a good day to go after the one other thing I've been wanting, too."

"Me?" I ask, even though I know.

"You," he says, as if it's the easiest thing in the world.

"You promised," I manage to say through the knot in my throat. "No future. Just the present."

"That's what I'm doing. Living in the moment. Like you taught me." His Adam's apple bobs up and down. "I love you, Rowan."

The air whooshes from my lungs, making it nearly impossible to breathe. "You… You can't."

"I can." He erases the last remaining space between us, pressing a steady hand to my cheek. "And I do. It doesn't have to change anything."

"But it does." My voice cracks. "It changes everything."

"How?"

"There can't be a future for us," I whisper through the heaviness in my throat, my body physically fighting what I'm about to do. "Because I don't have one."

His body stills, the silence in the room deafening as his hand drops to his side. "What are you talking about?"

My fingers drift to the scar beneath my collarbone. The one he's traced dozens of times.

"This," I whisper. "It's not from some minor surgery."

"There's no such thing as minor when it comes to the heart."

"I know." I close my eyes, steeling myself to get through this. "A little over a year ago, I collapsed at work."

He straightens, his gaze sweeping over me. I see the physician in him now. The way his attention sharpens. "What was the cause?"

"Arrhythmogenic right ventricular cardiomyopathy."

His face goes pale, his breathing becoming shallow. He may not be a heart surgeon, but based on his reaction, he knows exactly what that is.

And the prognosis.

"They tried medications. Procedures. Nothing worked. Eventually they told me my heart was too weak to keep beating on its own." My voice wobbles but I force it steady. "So I got a new one."

I don't tell him whose heart I received. He made his choice on that matter clear. I can at least honor his wish in regards to that.

"It saved my life, but it's not permanent. I have fifteen years. Twenty if I'm lucky." I swallow hard. "Maybe less."

Silence crashes between us as he stares at me, unblinking.

"I'm sorry I didn't tell you before. I just…" I glance up at the ceiling, attempting to collect my thoughts. "Everyone else who knows the truth looks at me like I'm already gone. Like I'm temporary." My voice breaks. "You didn't. You looked at me like I was… whole."

A single tear slides down his cheek. "You are whole."

"But I'm not forever."

He squeezes his eyes shut as a sob slips free. I want to go to him. Wrap him in my arms. Assure him it will be okay.

But it won't be.

Nothing I say or do can change this.

"It's why I left home. Bought a van and started traveling the country. Avoided planting roots anywhere. And then I met you."

My voice cracks, all the emotions I've kept inside since waking up with a new heart rolling through me.

"And for the first time, I wanted to stay. Wanted to belong."

His eyes soften, and I can practically hear his response. That I *can* stay. That I *do* belong here.

"And that's exactly why I need to go. You've already lost so much. Your kids have already lost so much. I won't make you go through that again."

With a shaky hand, I reach into my back pocket and pull out the folded paper, studying it for several long moments.

When I started writing it during Jemmy's nap this afternoon, I wasn't sure if I was going to give it to him. But now I know this needs to happen.

"Here." I extend the paper toward him.

He eyes it warily, but takes it anyway. "What's this?"

"My resignation."

He stares at it but doesn't unfold it. As if by refusing to do so, it would somehow make it not real.

"Hayden, I…" I trail off.

There's so much I want to tell him.

I wish I had more time.

You make me want impossible things.

I love you, too.

But it won't change the future.

Instead, I whisper, "I'm sorry."

Then I walk away.

And I don't look back.

FORTY-FOUR

Hayden

It's been three days.

Three days since Rowan stood in my kitchen and shattered everything.

Three days since I learned she's on borrowed time.

Three days since she walked away.

And I didn't stop her.

I didn't want to believe her. Wanted to tell her medicine has advanced. That transplant survival rates are improving every year. That she can be the exception to the rule.

But I'm a doctor. I know the statistics.

With a healthy donor heart, median survival is somewhere around fifteen to twenty years. After that, the risks compound. Rejection. Infection. The body growing tired of fighting.

And second transplants?

The odds shrink.

Those numbers have looped in my head every minute of every day since she left.

I've used them like armor, convinced myself I did the smart thing.

Because when she told me, when her fingers drifted to that scar and her voice trembled, I didn't see Rowan standing in front of me.

I saw Cora.

Pale against white sheets. Machines breathing for her. The flat, sterile smell of antiseptic and impending loss. The way my colleagues wouldn't quite meet my eyes when they wheeled her down the hall for the last time.

And when Rowan told me the truth, all I could think was that I cannot bury another woman I love.

That it would be easier if I let her go before I fell even harder.

After all, I've only known her a few months. Better to cut my losses now.

So I let her walk away.

Because it felt safer.

But the house doesn't feel safe.

It feels empty.

Presley barely looks at me at dinner. She pushes food around her plate and retreats to her room early. Jemmy asks for Rowan at least a dozen times a day. I'll eventually have to tell them the truth, but it's still too raw.

"Earth to Hayden."

I snap out of my thoughts and dart my eyes to my brother.

Jude sits across from me at the kitchen table, one eyebrow raised. "Did you hear a single word I just said?"

"Sorry." I take a slow sip of the beer he brought over, a fresh brew of something new he's been working on. "What did you say?"

The last thing I wanted tonight was company. But Jude showed up after the kids went to bed with a six-pack of beer and a bottle of scotch.

"I was just saying how I drew the short straw."

"Short straw?" I furrow my brows. "For what?"

"To come and talk to you." He leans closer, his concerned gaze meeting me. "What's going on? What happened with Rowan? Why did she leave?"

I stare at my bottle and push out a long sigh. "Because she's dying."

The words feel dramatic and wrong, but they're true. She *is* dying. And there's nothing anyone can do to stop it from happening.

There's nothing *I* can do to stop it from happening.

"What makes you say that?"

I take another large swallow of my beer. "Because she is."

He shakes his head, furrowing his brow. "Explain."

"She had a heart transplant. She's stable now, but a transplant is more like a twenty-year bandage than a permanent fix."

"And that's why she left?"

"She didn't want the kids to lose someone else." My jaw tightens. "Didn't want me to go through that again."

Jude studies me. "And what did you say?"

I hesitate, searching for an answer to his question

that doesn't make me look like a complete asshole. But there isn't one.

"Nothing."

"What do you mean?" Jude presses.

"Exactly that. I said fucking nothing, Jude. I just stood there as she walked away, and I didn't fight for her. I did nothing."

"Why? Why didn't you stop her? It's obvious you didn't want her to leave."

I shoot to my feet and storm toward the counter, grabbing the scotch and drinking straight from the bottle, hoping to dull the ache in my chest.

"Of course I didn't. But when she told me the truth…" I shake my head and turn to face him. "I saw Cora. Saw the machines. Heard the monitors. And being the selfish bastard I am, the only thing I thought was how I can't do that again. I can't watch someone I love fade away."

Jude stands and moves toward the island, leaning against it. "So you let her go instead."

"It felt like the right thing to do."

He brings his bottle up to his lips. "For who?"

"For my kids."

He rolls his eyes. "Don't use them as an excuse. You're better than that."

"I'm not using my kids as an excuse." I take another long swig of scotch.

"Yes, you are!" His voice thunders in the kitchen, seeming to echo around us before falling silent, the only sound that of the ticking clock.

He draws in a deep breath, then says, "Do you remember the nursery?"

"Of course."

I may not have lived here at the time, but I remember how distraught Jude was after losing his newborn daughter when she was only hours old. I didn't think he'd ever smile again.

"I kept it the same for years," he explains. "Didn't step foot in it. Wouldn't let Krista touch it. Wouldn't let her pack up anything. I told myself it was about honoring her. Keeping her memory alive."

He meets my eyes.

"But in reality I was afraid if we took it down, she'd be gone for good. So I froze. Lived in a house with a ghost. And I lost Krista because of it, too. Because she couldn't stand being in that house with a ghost."

I swallow hard, his words hitting me harder than I expected.

"You may have moved here, but you brought Cora's ghost with you."

I part my lips, struggling to come up with an argument in my defense.

"You don't need to forget her." He pushes off the island and steps toward me, touching a hand to my shoulder. "And you don't need to stop loving her. But I think it's time you finally let her go."

"I have," I protest weakly.

"Have you?" His voice sharpens, and he releases his hold on me. "Because from where I'm standing, you're still making decisions based on how to avoid losing her all over again. It wasn't Rowan that scared you. It was what loving her would cost. When you learned she might only have another twenty years, you didn't see all those hours and minutes you'd be able to make memories." He holds my gaze steady, not allowing me to avoid the truth in his words. "You saw the end."

I exhale a long breath and close my eyes.

I can't even argue. Because the second I learned the truth, all I saw was another hospital bed.

Another funeral.

Another set of small hands gripping mine while I explain why another person we love isn't coming home.

"Tomorrow isn't guaranteed for any of us," Jude says quietly. "Abbey could get hit by a car. I could drop dead of an aneurysm. That hasn't stopped us from living our lives to the fullest. From loving each other to the fullest."

"I was just trying to protect my kids."

"Or were you protecting yourself?"

That lands.

Because beneath all the rationalizations, beneath the statistics and worst-case projections, there's a simpler truth.

I was scared.

Not of her illness.

Of loving her enough that losing her would destroy me.

"Rowan isn't the problem," he finishes. "You are. You were just looking for a reason to push her away."

The kitchen is quiet except for the hum of the refrigerator and the echo of my own breathing.

I think of Rowan laughing in this kitchen. Of her

dancing with Presley as they cooked together. Of her singing and making silly faces with Jemmy.

Twenty years.

I would have given anything for twenty more years with Cora.

And I threw away the chance at twenty with Rowan because it might end someday.

"Grief doesn't get to dictate your life anymore," Jude says, placing his hand on my shoulder once more. "Only you get to do that. You just need to decide if you want twenty years of happiness, or twenty years of being an absolute bear." He flashes me a smirk. "I know which one I'm voting for."

FORTY-FIVE

Rowan

I've been driving for five days.

Five days of highways blurring into each other. Gas station coffee. Rest stops. Audiobooks I've barely paid attention to.

I thought if I just kept moving, something would call to me.

But nothing has, and I've somehow ended up back in Illinois.

The Chicago skyline rises in the distance, familiar against the gray afternoon sky. My chest tightens as I drive through the suburb I grew up in. Tree-lined streets. Tidy lawns. The same bakery my nanny always took me to after school on Fridays.

I don't remember deciding to come here.

I guess my heart did.

After making my way closer to the city, I pull up in

front of Emily's townhouse and cut the engine, not immediately moving. I haven't told her I was coming. But within seconds, the front door opens and she runs outside.

I step out of the van, and am instantly assaulted by my best friend's embrace.

"Oh, my god. You're here. I've missed you so fucking much."

I sigh, relishing in the love I always feel around her. "I've missed you, too."

"But why are you here?" She pulls back and I meet her gaze.

Her blonde hair is piled on top of her head, and she's wearing a pair of leggings and an oversized sweatshirt with Northwestern emblazoned across it.

It reminds me of Hayden's faded Northwestern t-shirt, and I have to fight back the tears.

"I promised I'd be home for your birthday." I shrug.

"My birthday isn't for another four months."

"I guess I didn't want to be late," I choke out.

"Oh, sweetie." She pulls me into her arms again, and the tears come.

And not the quiet, dignified kind. The kind that have been locked up tight for days, waiting for permission to be set free.

"It'll be okay. You'll be okay. What have I always told you?"

"I don't know."

"Yeah, you do. Now say it."

I push out a long breath. "I'm a tough bitch."

"Damn straight you are. Now come inside." She

drapes her arm around my shoulders and ushers me into the familiar living room. "I think this calls for some day drinking. In the immortal words of the great Jimmy Buffett, 'It's five o'clock somewhere.'"

I let out a wet, broken sob.

God, I've missed her.

———

An hour later, after a much-needed shower, I'm sitting at Emily's kitchen island with a half-empty glass of rosé. Sunlight filters through the blinds, a welcome sight for January. Chicago is normally gray and depressing this time of year.

Not today.

I wonder if it's the universe telling me this is where I'm supposed to be.

"So tell me," Emily begins. "What happened?"

I shake my head, unsure where to start with this story. So much has happened since I last spoke to her. Growing closer to Hayden. My breakthroughs with Presley. Our yes day. Our yes night. But that's not why I'm here.

"He told me he loves me."

She sucks in a breath, feigning aghast. "The nerve."

"Em, I'm being serious."

"So am I." She winks before she tempers her playful expression. "I assume his declaration wasn't well-received."

"What choice did I have?"

"Oh, I don't know. You could have told him you love

him, too. Because I know you do. You wouldn't be the hot mess you are right now if you didn't."

I fidget with the stem of the wine glass, averting my gaze. "You know why I couldn't do that."

"Actually, I don't."

"Because of this." I gesture to my scar. "He's already lost his wife. His kids lost their mom. I will not be the next woman they bury."

"I could die tomorrow."

"That's not the same." I scoff weakly.

"Isn't it?"

"Not even close," I respond, although my voice lacks conviction.

She studies me for a long moment, the silence unnerving me. "You know, for someone who's spent the last year preaching about living in the present, you're still letting the future dictate a lot of your decisions. Including this one."

"I'm just being realistic."

"No. You're being stubborn. There's a big difference."

"He's already lost so much," I argue once more.

I've repeated these words so many times over the past few days they sound like a broken record. But it's the only thing that's made the ache in my heart even remotely bearable.

"I can't put him through that again."

"And you don't think he's going through something similar right now?" she retorts. "You didn't even give him a choice. You made the decision for him."

"I had to."

"Why?"

"Because what if he didn't choose me?"

The question slips out before I can stop it, and the kitchen goes quiet.

"He's not like Landon," Emily soothes, her eyes soft and full of understanding.

I swallow hard, instantly transported back to that hospital bed, staring at the man whose ring I wore, his expression pale and distant after my cardiologist laid out the risks and complications of my prognosis.

I don't think I can sign up for that.

As if I was simply an insurance policy with unfavorable terms.

"You don't know that," I tell her.

"Maybe not. But based on everything you've told me, Hayden sounds like a good person."

I stare at the light pink hue of my wine, unable to come up with anything to say in response. She's right. Hayden *is* a good person. One of the best people I've met in a long time.

And it makes my heart ache even more.

"Did you tell him?" she presses after a beat.

I don't need to ask what she's talking about.

I know.

The transplant.

The fact that his wife's heart beats inside me.

"No," I respond softly. "It wouldn't have made a difference."

Her eyebrows lift. "Or it could have made all the difference."

I give her a tight smile, fighting back another wave of tears threatening to fall. "I guess we'll never know."

She sighs, covering my hand with hers. "Listen to me, Rowan. You are not temporary. You are not a tragedy waiting to happen. You deserve to be happy just like everyone else. Deserve love like everyone else. Deserve those happily ever afters we read about in our dirty books."

I laugh, but it's brittle. "Except you're forgetting one important detail."

"What's that?"

"I don't get a happily ever after."

"What makes you say that? Because you might not live to be a hundred and have tons of babies? Who the fuck cares about that? Hell, some of my favorite romances don't end with a wedding and babies. It ends with them finding happiness in each other and themselves. Being present. Being happy in the now, to hell with ever after."

I try to find comfort in her words, but it's hard when I know what my future looks like.

Or my lack thereof.

"So what's your plan?" she asks after a protracted silence, sensing I need to talk about something else.

"I have no idea. I drove for days, hoping something would feel right."

She arches a perfectly manicured brow. "And?"

"Nothing did."

She nods in understanding.

But being the good friend she is, she doesn't ask if nothing felt right because I never should have left.

"Do you want to stay with me while you figure things out?"

"Are you sure you don't mind?"

"Of course not. You're my ride or die. Whatever you need, I'm here for you. Always."

I grab her hand and squeeze, grateful to have someone like Emily in my life. Right now, she's all I have.

"Thanks, Em."

FORTY-SIX

Hayden

As much as I hate to admit it, Jude was right.

I've been living with a ghost.

I hadn't realized how much Cora's presence still haunted my life until he forced me to come to terms with it. I may have moved away from Chicago. May have even finally quit working for her father.

But her presence was still here.

So, over the past few days, I've started doing the one thing I should have done months ago.

I've started getting rid of her things. Which is why I'm currently in my home office, finally going through all the paperwork I've avoided this past year.

I work methodically. Keep what matters. Shred what doesn't.

Every so often, a notification pops up on my phone,

and I rush to it, praying it's Rowan finally replying to one of my texts.

It's not.

While I'm desperate to hear from her, I also don't want to overwhelm her. So I've been giving her space, hoping she'll eventually reach out.

As I set my phone back on the desk, I grab another stack of files and start going through them, my chest tightening when I read the label.

DONOR CORRESPONDENCE

After Cora passed, I received letters from the various recipients of her organs, facilitated by an organization to remain anonymous.

I read the letters once, then filed them away, choosing not to respond or learn who they were.

But maybe that's been part of the problem.

Maybe I need to reach out.

Maybe this is part of the closure I need.

So instead of putting the letters into the box of items to be shredded, I pick up the folder and sit behind the desk, reading the first letter from a woman in her late sixties who'd been in renal failure.

Because of your family's sacrifice, I was able to attend my granddaughter's graduation. I walked her across the stage myself.

I picture an older woman standing a little straighter. A girl gripping her arm. A future that almost didn't happen.

I set the letter aside and read the next one. This one's from a woman in her early thirties with two children around the same age as mine.

I can chase my boys in the yard again. Now when I get tired, it's because I ran, not because my body is failing.

I swallow hard through the tightness in my throat. Cora would have loved to learn this. To know she gave a mother more time with her children.

I move on to the next letter. This one's from a teenager. A liver recipient.

I get to do summer swim team this year. I didn't think I'd still be alive this summer.

My heart warms. She didn't just save older people. She saved a child, too. Gave them life.

Just like the person who donated Rowan's heart gave *her* life.

I reach for the next envelope and lift the flap, pulling out a piece of cream cardstock and unfolding it.

I've read all these letters before.

But this one hits differently.

Because it's from the woman who received Cora's heart.

Now all I can think about is Rowan. Did she write a letter like this to the family of the person who donated *her* heart? Of course she did. There's no way she wouldn't have shown her appreciation the first chance she got. I could almost picture her with her journal, toiling over what she wanted to say, worried it wouldn't properly convey her gratitude.

I smile at the picture in my head and read the letter written by the woman who now has Cora's heart.

Dear Family,

I hope you don't mind me calling you that. Because in my mind, you are my family, even if we never meet. You will always hold a very special place in my heart, and not because it belongs to someone you love.

There are not enough words in the English language to properly thank you for what you have given me.

A few months ago, I collapsed at work. One moment I was talking to my assistant. The next, I woke up in a hospital bed with doctors explaining that my heart was failing.

For months, I lived on borrowed time. Medication. Procedures. Waiting.

Waiting to see if my body would stabilize.

Waiting to see if it would give out.

Eventually, I was told the only thing that would save me was a new heart.

I hate that someone else had to die so I could live.

But someone did.

And because of them, I'm still here.

I don't know their name. I don't know what their laugh sounded like or what kind of music they loved. But I carry them with me. Literally and figuratively.

Every morning when I wake up, I press my hand to my chest and whisper thank you.

I promise I will not waste this gift.

To that end, I made a list while I was waiting. A life list. A promise to honor my new life by truly living it.

The air in the room shifts.

Life list.

Rowan had a life list, too.

Maybe it's just a coincidence.

It's not unusual for someone who's been given a second chance at life to make a list of things they want to do. I've seen it countless times with some of my patients.

This is no different.

With that reassurance, I keep reading.

This will also be my year of yes.

Yes to travel.

Yes to new experiences.

Yes to joy, even when it feels terrifying.

I bought a van and plan to drive across the country. I want to see mountains and oceans and tiny roadside attractions that make no sense.

I plan to make every moment count.

To find joy.

To live.

Because someone doesn't get to.

I hope that brings you even a sliver of comfort.

Your loved one's heart beats strong. I feel it every day. I will take care of it. I will honor it. I will build a life worthy of it.

I hope to thank you in person one day.

If not, know you will always have my endless gratitude.

Thank you for the gift of more time.

I blink, staring at the paper for several long moments. Life list. Year of yes. The van.

It's a coincidence. It has to be.

But the handwriting. I've seen this handwriting before.

I shove back from the desk so hard the chair slams into the wall. My legs don't work as fast as I want them to as I bolt upstairs into my bedroom, pulling out the resignation letter Rowan gave me earlier in the week.

With trembling hands, I lay them side by side on the bed.

The same rounded a.

The same narrow e.

The same curling t.

There's no mistaking it.

These were written by the same person.

"Oh, my god." My knees give out and I fall heavily onto the mattress, struggling to breathe.

Rowan has my wife's heart.

All the nights she lay against my chest, all the mornings I felt her heartbeat under my palm, it was Cora's heart I was feeling.

The sound of the door opening cuts through, followed by my sister's voice.

"Hayden, we're back."

I snap out of my stupor and grab the letters before hurrying downstairs.

"Woah," Dylan says when I enter the kitchen. "What's wrong?"

I slam the papers down onto the island. "Were these written by the same person?"

Dylan blinks at me in confusion. "What are you going on about?"

"Just tell me what you see."

She studies me for a protracted beat, still confused.

"Please, Dylan," I beg, my voice barely audible.

Sensing my desperation, she steps forward, her confusion giving way to focus as she examines the pages. When she notices one letter is Rowan's resignation letter and the other is from an organ recipient, she darts her eyes back to mine, sucking in a sharp breath.

"Tell me I'm not imagining it or seeing something I *want* to see."

She nods, returning her attention to the papers. She tilts her head, comparing the slant, the spacing.

But before she can answer, Presley moves closer and touches the letter from the heart recipient.

"Rowan."

The sound is fragile. Scratchy. Like a door that hasn't been opened in a long time.

Dylan and I both freeze, unsure what to do.

Presley just spoke for the first time in over a year.

We've heard a few laughs and hums over the past several weeks, although that all went away when Rowan did.

But to hear her voice again?

I drop to my knees in front of her, not wanting to make a big deal of it and scare her off from ever talking again.

"Yeah, baby," I say gently, forcing my voice steady. "I think Rowan wrote that letter."

Dylan nods behind Presley, confirming my suspicions.

"She has Mom's heart?" Her words are barely audible.

"It appears so."

Presley takes a moment to absorb this, her gaze dropping to the paper again. "Do you love her?"

My chest tightens as tears burn the back of my eyes. "I loved your mother very much."

She shakes her head. "No. Rowan. Do you love her?"

I nod slowly. "I do."

"Then why isn't she here?"

My mouth opens, but no words come.

What do I say?

That I was afraid?

That I chose statistics over love?

That I didn't want to risk losing someone again?

"I think… I think she thought she was protecting us. And I think I let her go because I was trying to protect myself."

Presley considers my response for a long moment before returning her determined gaze to mine. "Then get her back."

"I tried to reach out, but she hasn't responded. She might… She might not want to come back."

"Then try harder."

I glance up at Dylan, who simply shrugs. "The kid's got a point."

I look back at my daughter, tracing my eyes over her soft features. Her eyes are Cora's. Same shade of green. Same intensity.

But the quiet strength in her posture? The raw determination in the face of adversity?

That's all Rowan.

"Okay, Presley. I'll try harder."

"Thank you." She leans forward and wraps her arms around my neck.

I hold her tighter than I have in months, fighting back the tears welling in my eyes.

"Can I go play now?" she asks matter-of-factly.

I huff out a laugh and pull myself to my full height. "Of course."

She slips out of the kitchen like she didn't just flip my world upside down.

"She spoke." Dylan moves toward me, her eyes wide.

"I know." I shake my head in disbelief. "I thought that part of her was gone."

Dylan gives my arm a squeeze before staring into the distance, seemingly deep in thought. She could just be thinking about the fact that Rowan has Cora's heart, but I get the feeling there's something else on her mind.

Call it an older brother's intuition.

"Is everything okay?" I ask.

She sucks in a sharp breath, snapping out of her thoughts. "Oh. Of course." She forces a smile.

I step closer. "Are you sure?"

"It's nothing." She averts her gaze.

"Dylan…"

"Hayden," she retorts, mimicking my tone.

"Nice try. What's going on?"

"I told you. It's nothing." She opens and shuts her mouth several times. "Did you know Archer Ward was in town?"

Of course. I should have known this had something to do with our old neighbor. I never knew Archer that well. But I certainly know *of* Archer Ward. Any self-respecting hockey fan does.

"I don't exactly stay informed of his movements."

She nods, seeming to process this. Then she clears

her throat, returning her focus to me. "So what are you going to do about Rowan?"

I exhale a deep breath. "I don't know. She hasn't responded to my texts and didn't leave any forwarding address."

I glance at her letter once more. At the last few lines.

I hope to thank you in person one day.

A slow smile crosses my face as an idea pops into my head.

"But I think I might know another way."

FORTY-SEVEN

Rowan

"I'm not sure I can do this," I say as Emily walks into her living room, wearing a knee-length navy blue dress in a similar style to the red one I'm wearing. Halter top. Fitted through the waist before flaring out and falling to the knees.

I chose red because I thought it an appropriate color to wear to a fundraiser supporting an organ donation charity.

Now I'm second-guessing everything.

Including my decision to attend in the first place, considering Hayden will also be there and will be hoping to meet the recipient of his wife's heart.

"Yes, you can." Emily turns me away from the mirror and forces me to face her. "And you should. Isn't this the entire purpose of your year of yes? To say yes to things that scare you?"

I swallow hard. "But after today, there's no going back. He'll know the truth."

"Is that what you're scared of? Him learning the truth?" She tilts her head, studying me. "Or are you scared of seeing him again because it will remind you that you're actually in love with him?"

I shrug. "Both."

"Then you need to do this. Remember what you said when you got the phone call from The Organ Network? How you didn't think Hayden ever wanted to learn who received his wife's organs, so the fact he does is a big step for him." She squeezes my biceps. "He deserves to know the truth. Deserves closure. So do you."

Closure.

The word feels sharp and soft at the same time.

"Okay," I say, blowing out a breath.

"Year of yes," she reminds me.

"Year of yes," I echo.

The ballroom in the downtown Chicago hotel glitters like a diamond. Crystal chandeliers spill warm light over white-linen tables. A string quartet plays something soft from the stage. The air smells faintly of roses and expensive perfume.

A new wave of nerves washes over me, and I wipe my sweaty palms on my dress.

"Thanks for being here, Em," I whisper as we make

our way through the room, already keeping an eye out for a familiar face.

"Do you think I would have missed this for anything?" she asks, swiping two glasses of champagne off a passing server. "I never say no to an open bar."

She hands me a flute, and we clink glasses.

"Plus, I'm dying to meet Dr. McDreamy."

I take a sip of much-needed champagne. "Dr. McDreamy?"

She grins. "It's how I picture him. Older. Handsome. Brooding."

She's not far off. Hayden definitely gives off that Derek Shepherd vibe. Dark hair with flecks of gray. Dark eyes that look like they've seen too much and felt even more.

And God help me, I still want him.

As we continue skirting through the hundreds of people in attendance, a woman with kind eyes and a sleek navy suit approaches us.

"Rowan Montgomery?"

"Yes," I draw out.

She extends her hand toward me. "I'm Marissa from The Organ Network."

"Oh." I place my hand in hers. "Nice to finally meet you."

"I hope you don't mind me approaching you like a crazed stalker. I recognized you from the photo in my file."

"Not at all."

"I just want to say how grateful we are that you're

here. And we were so moved to hear the donor family wanted to meet in person."

"Yes," I manage. "Me, too."

I try to act excited about the prospect of meeting the donor family after over a year of waiting, but I'm worried how Hayden will react when he learns the truth.

Will it be worse than the day he found out I'd had a transplant to begin with? The look on his face when I told him I was on borrowed time still haunts me. The fear. The anger. The grief.

And now he'll learn the heart beating inside my chest, the one he's pressed his palm against, belonged to his wife.

I sway slightly, debating if it's too late to change my mind when Emily's fingers tighten around my wrist, grounding me.

"It's okay," she murmurs. "Year of yes."

I drag in a breath. "Year of yes."

"Good." She gives my arm one last squeeze.

"If you're ready, I'll make the introductions now." Marissa smiles gently.

I don't think I'll ever truly be ready for this, but I nod anyway, setting my flute down on a nearby table.

Emily stays glued to my side as Marissa leads us through the maze of tables, past laughter and clinking glasses.

And then I see him.

He's seated at a round table with his mother, Presley, and Jemmy. His suit jacket is off, his white shirt sleeves rolled to his forearms. Presley is coloring on the paper table covering. Jemmy sits in a high chair, cheeks round and pink, clutching what looks like a dinner roll.

My heart stutters so violently I wonder if everyone can hear it, especially when Hayden lifts his head and our eyes meet for the first time in weeks.

I brace myself for shock. For confusion. For the way his features might harden when he realizes the truth.

But there's none of that.

There's only peace.

Understanding.

As if he already knows.

Before I can process that, Presley looks up, her eyes brimming with excitement. She's out of her chair in an instant, racing toward me.

"I've missed you!" she cries, throwing her arms around my waist.

I suck in a startled breath, my hands hovering for a second before I wrap them around her small body as my gaze flies to Hayden, a thousand questions on the tip of my tongue, the most pressing being when Presley started talking.

He stands, lifting Jemmy from his high chair. The little boy points a chubby finger at me. "Ro-Ro! Ro-Ro!"

"She's been talking for about a month," he explains as he smiles down at his daughter. "Now I can't get her to stop."

Marissa looks between us, confused. "I'm sorry. Do you…already know each other?"

Hayden's gaze never leaves mine. "We do."

"Oh." She blinks. "Well. Then you don't really need me anymore."

He finally glances her way. "Thank you."

"Of course, Dr. Lawrence. Good to see you again."

"You, as well."

Emily clears her throat dramatically. "And I'm going to grab a drink so you two can…talk." She thrusts her hand out at Hayden. "I'm Emily, by the way."

"Hayden."

"I know." She winks before slipping away.

"Come on, Jemmy," Danielle says, reaching for the little boy in Hayden's arms. "Let's give Daddy and Ro-Ro some privacy." She squeezes my bicep, tears shining in her eyes. "It's wonderful to see you again, dear."

"You, too."

"Are you going to do crush business?" Presley asks, her voice carrying through the room.

A chuckle rumbles from Hayden's throat, and I can't help but join in.

God, I've missed these people.

"We'll see." He winks. "Go with Grandma."

"Kiss-kiss. Kiss-kiss," Jemmy says as Danielle leads them back to the table.

And then I'm alone with Hayden for the first time since I walked away.

The noise of the gala fades into a dull hum, the world narrowing to the space between us.

"Did you…" My voice shakes. "Did you know I—"

"That you have Cora's heart?" he finishes gently. "I figured it out."

Everything inside me goes still. "How?"

"I was clearing out the clutter. The past. I came across all the letters from the people who received

Cora's organs. The one from the woman who received her heart sounded eerily familiar." His lips curve faintly. "Life list. Year of yes. Buying a van." His eyes search mine. "And when I matched the handwriting, I knew." He swallows hard. "Did you know?"

"I found out the day you fired me," I admit with a strained smile. "I was vacuuming in the office and knocked over some papers on the desk. My letter was among them."

He closes his eyes, blowing out a breath.

"I'm sorry I didn't tell you," I whisper. "You didn't want to know. I figured the least I could do was honor that wish."

"I appreciate it." He returns his gaze to mine and takes my hand in his, running his thumb over my knuckles. "But I think… I think it was meant to happen this way."

"What was?"

"Us."

I pull away from him. "Hayden…"

"Rowan…" He brings a hand to my cheek, not allowing me to escape him. "Before you, I was stuck. In the past. In grief. In what-ifs." His voice roughens. "You taught me how to embrace each day. To live in the moment. To laugh again. To hope."

Tears sting my eyes, and I try to blink them back. Thank god Emily insisted I wear waterproof mascara today.

"When you told me about your heart, I was scared. All I could think about was how horrible it was to lose

Cora. I loved her." He doesn't look away. "But not like I love you."

The words hit me like a physical force, bursting through the wall I've tried to build around my heart since I drove away from Sycamore Falls.

From him.

"I love you differently. Deeper. Fiercer. And it fucking petrified me." His voice cracks on the last word. "Because loving you means risking that pain all over again. At the time, I wasn't brave enough, so I didn't fight for you like I should have. But I am now. And I'm not letting you walk away from me without putting it all out there. Without fighting for you, for me, for us, with everything I fucking have. With every last piece of me."

My vision blurs as more and more tears fall down my cheeks.

"I don't care if you might only live another fifteen or twenty years. In case you haven't noticed, I'm older than you." His lips curve up in a ghost of a smile. "Even so, we can all die tomorrow. Nothing in this world is a guarantee. So I'm asking you to live in the moment with me. No future. No past." His eyes shine. "Let me love you in the present. Right now. I'd rather have one tomorrow with you than none at all."

I part my lips, unsure what to say. What I *want* to say.

I remind myself of the reasons I left. To protect him. To protect his kids.

But also to protect myself. Because what if he woke up one day and decided he didn't want me anymore, like Landon did?

But like Emily reminded me, Hayden's not Landon.

He went through all the trouble of flying to Chicago and arranging this meeting because he knew it was the only way to talk to me.

He's willing to fight for me.

Maybe it's time I start to fight for myself, too.

I take his hand in mine and press it against my heart.

He sucks in a shaky breath at the feel of Cora's heart beating in my chest.

I close my eyes, drawing strength from the steady rhythm inside me.

"Yes," I whisper.

"Yes?"

I nod, meeting his gaze. "Yes. I love you, Hayden. And I don't want a life without you in it. However long that life is." I drape an arm over his shoulder, a smile tugging on my mouth. "Happily ever after is overrated anyway. I'd rather live happily for now."

"That's going in my gratitude journal," he growls as he crushes his lips to mine, his hand still pressed against my chest.

And for the first time since this heart started beating inside me, it doesn't feel borrowed.

Doesn't feel temporary.

It feels like mine.

Like home.

FORTY-EIGHT

Hayden

Two years ago today, I sat in a church filled with strangers.

I held my children close while people whispered about God's plan. I nodded at condolences from men who didn't know Cora's laugh. Women who'd never seen her barefoot in the kitchen, flour on her cheek.

Last year, I did the same thing.

Forced Presley and Jemmy into stiff clothes. Made them sit in a pew and remember what they'd lost.

I told myself it was respect.

It wasn't.

It was punishment.

For me.

For not insisting she get checked out sooner.

For not seeing what was happening inside her body.

For believing we had time.

I don't blame myself the way I used to.

What happened to Cora was out of my control. I know that now. I've said it enough times it finally feels true.

Do I still wish I'd done something different?

Of course.

But every time guilt creeps in, I roll over in bed and see the spot that used to be empty.

It's not empty anymore.

Rowan sleeps there. Tangled in our sheets. Hair wild. One arm flung across my chest like she's afraid I might disappear.

If it weren't for Cora, Rowan wouldn't be here.

I loved my wife.

I miss her.

But I can't imagine my life without Rowan.

This past year has been the happiest in recent memory.

Not just because I'm back in a job I love at the hospital. But because of the life Rowan's brought back to my existence. Every day is a new adventure. I've learned to appreciate the little things.

And say yes.

Which is what I'm doing today.

Saying yes.

Yes to ice cream for breakfast.

Yes to trampoline parks.

Yes to building a snowman together.

Yes to adventure.

Yes to living.

Yes to love.

"Where to next?" Rowan asks as we leave the trampoline park, Presley and Jemmy still bouncing despite having spent the past hour doing exactly that.

Presley glances my way and gives me a look.

A conspiratorial, very grown-up look.

Then she turns to Rowan.

"I think it's time for some cake pops."

She's been speaking for almost a year now. Full sentences. Opinions. Negotiations.

Some days I beg for silence.

Most days, I sit in awe of the sound.

Rowan beams. "Cake pops it is."

We all pile into the SUV, and I drive toward downtown Sycamore Falls, my pulse ticking faster with every block.

Over the past year, Rowan has said yes to a lot.

Yes to coming back here.

Yes to moving in with me.

Yes to loving my children like they're hers.

Yes to letting me love her.

But today, I plan to ask for one more.

And it's the biggest one of all.

Downtown is lit up for the holidays with garland draped across storefronts and twinkle lights strung from lamppost to lamppost. When I first moved back here, I avoided coming downtown this time of year because of how much Cora loved Christmas.

Now, I embrace the holiday season again.

Instead of focusing on everything we lost, the memories we'd never recreate again, we've made new memories together. Decorating the tree. Holding Jemmy up high so he could put the star on the top. Groucho Barx, our rescued shelter pup, constantly drinking water from the stand.

I park up the street from the coffee shop and rush to open Rowan's door for her before helping Jemmy out of his car seat.

Once Presley steps out, we walk together as a family through downtown, the butterflies in my stomach becoming more relentless.

As we near the coffee shop, Rowan reaches for the door.

"Rowan, wait."

She turns, confusion knitting her brows, especially when she sees the wide grin on Presley's face.

"I know this is technically supposed to be a yes day for the kids," I begin, my voice steadier than I feel, "but I was hoping you'd say yes to me."

"What did you have in mind?"

Throughout my career, I've faced hundreds of nerve-racking situations. Have had to make split-second decisions that could mean the difference between life and death.

I've never felt as nervous as I do right now.

But I've also never felt as certain.

"Marrying me," I respond as I drop to one knee.

She releases an audible gasp, her hand flying to her mouth.

Locals and tourists mill around us, some stopping to watch, but I don't see them.

All I see is her.

The woman who burst into my life wearing taco pajama pants and walking a dog named Bark Twain.

The woman who brought noise back into my house.

Color back into my days.

Breath back into my lungs.

Love back into my heart.

"A year ago in this very spot, a woman who's my opposite in every way lost control of her dog and bumped into me, forcing me to spill coffee all over myself. At the time, I wasn't living," I admit through the heaviness in my throat. "I was existing. I thought loving again would dishonor what I lost. I still miss Cora. I always will. But loving you doesn't erase her. Doesn't replace her. It just…proves my heart survived."

Her eyes fill with tears and she swipes at a few that have escaped.

"Knowing what I do now about strength and second chances, I still marvel at you. At your courage. At the way you choose joy even when there are no guarantees." I swallow hard at the reminder, but push through anyway.

"I know we promised to live for now. To stay in the present. Not plan too far ahead." I take a breath. "But I want to call you my wife. I want to be your husband. Not because it promises us forever. But because it promises us today. And tomorrow. And every day we're lucky enough to get."

I open the ring box.

"Marry me, Rowan. Say yes to this life. Say yes to me."

For a moment, she just stares at me.

Snow falling. Lights glowing. My kids holding their breath beside me.

Then she laughs, watery and overwhelmed. "Like I could ever say no to you."

I jump to my feet, tugging her against me as I bring the ring up to her finger. "So that's a yes?"

"That's a yes," she confirms.

I crush my lips against hers as several people clap and cheer, including Presley and Jemmy who say something about crush business.

"And not because it's a yes day," she adds once I bring our kiss to an end. "But because I couldn't imagine saying no to you. Not today. Not ever."

"Not ever," I repeat, brushing my mouth against hers.

"I guess I do get a happily ever after," she whispers, admiring the ring on her finger.

"Maybe." I curve toward her once more. "But I still prefer living happily for now."

"So do I," she exhales, her lips finding mine yet again.

As I pull her closer, I don't worry about what comes next. Don't think about what losing her might mean.

I just hold my wife-to-be in the middle of a small-town street, surrounded by my kids, savoring in the present.

All because I finally started living again.

Because I said yes.

Thank you so much for reading *Tempted by the Nanny*.

Curious to know more about Dylan and her hockey-playing former neighbor? Their story is next! Grab *Falling for my Brother's Best Friend* today!

I've had a crush on my brother's best friend for as long as I can remember. *Which is why becoming his private chef is a terrible idea.*

In the mood for a spicy holiday romance? Then check out Joshua's story in *The Trouble with Mistletoe*!

I did not come home for Christmas to fall for a younger man.
One-click here or scan the code below.

Want one last taste of Rowan and Hayden? Then sign up for my mailing list to get a bonus chapter. Just scan the code below.

Thank you so much for taking the time to read this book. If you enjoyed it, please let your friends know by leaving a review so more people can fall in love with Hayden and Rowan.

FALLING
for my
BROTHER'S
BEST FRIEND

I've had a crush on my brother's best friend for as long as I can remember.

Which is why becoming his private chef is a terrible idea.

Archer Ward was the golden boy of Sycamore Falls growing up… Older, the town's biggest star, and completely out of my league.

But there was always another side of Archer no one else saw.

The one who used to sneak into the old treehouse in my backyard when life at home got too hard.

The one who trusted me with secrets he never told anyone else.

Then a few years ago, we crossed a line we can't uncross.

One unforgettable night.
One broken heart.
And Archer disappeared from my life.

Now he's back, recently signed to the professional hockey team nearby and somehow the newest client for the private chef business my best friend and I are trying to build.

Working for him was supposed to be simple.

Cook the meals.
Keep things professional.
Ignore the way he still looks at me like he remembers every secret we ever shared.

Archer might be the hockey star the whole world sees, but I'm the girl who knew him before the fame.

Falling for my brother's best friend once was a mistake.

Falling for him again could break my heart for good.

the
TROUBLE
with
MISTLETOE

I did not come home for Christmas to fall for a younger man.

I came home because my soon-to-be-ex-husband bought diamond earrings for his assistant.

Merry Christmas to me.

I expected snow.
I expected family.
I expected awkward questions.

I did not expect Joshua.

He used to be the sweet boy next door.

My brother's best friend.

The kid who followed me around like I hung the moon.

Except he's not a kid anymore.

He's six feet, four inches of confident, flannel-wearing temptation who looks at me like I'm the only gift he wants under the tree.

He says I'm not too old.
He says I'm not broken.
He says he's not a boy anymore.

But in a town this small and with my heart this bruised, wanting him feels like trouble.

And this Christmas I'm not sure I'm strong enough to resist him.

ACKNOWLEDGMENTS

Thank you so much for reading *Tempted by the Nanny*. I hope you loved falling for Hayden and Rowan as much as I loved writing their story.

This book has been a long time coming.

The idea has been quietly simmering in the back of my mind for close to ten years. It started with a single image I came across online… A photo of an organ recipient meeting the family of their donor. And I couldn't stop thinking about it.

And then my romance writer brain kicked in.

What if one of those recipients fell in love with the husband she left behind?

The idea wouldn't let me go.

I originally tried to shape that storyline around an existing character in my T.K. Leigh universe. (This was 2017, after all. It would be more than 5 years until I'd finally launch my small town pen name.)

I wanted it to work. I outlined. I plotted. I rearranged timelines.

But it never quite fit.

As Rowan would say, the universe was telling me it wasn't the right time.

So I tucked the idea away along with the hundreds of other story ideas I've come up with over the years.

Then I decided to branch into small town romance.

And almost instantly, this story resurfaced.

It was actually the first book I plotted in this series. But I ended up writing *The Grump Who Saved Christmas* first while this one continued simmering in the background.

Because even then, I knew this was always going to be Hayden's story.

Now, after all these years, I'm so glad it's finally out in the world. And the wait was worth it because it's better than I originally imagined all those years ago.

Before I dive into what's next in Sycamore Falls, I want to take a moment to thank the incredible people who make these stories possible:

To my family, Stan and Harper Leigh. Thank you for your constant love, patience, and support. You're my anchor through every deadline and draft.

To my amazing PA, Melissa Crump. You keep me sane, organized, and on schedule, and I couldn't do this without you.

To my wonderful beta readers, Melissa, Stacy, and Sylvia. Thank you for reading early, giving thoughtful feedback, and catching all the little things that make a story shine.

To my review team. Thank you for taking the time to read and share your thoughts. Every review helps new readers discover these stories, and I appreciate you more than you know.

To my reader group. Thank you for being the heart of this community. Your enthusiasm, humor, and love for these characters make all the long writing nights worth it.

And finally, to you. Thank you for picking up this book, for trusting me with your time and your heart, and for coming along on this journey with Hayden and Rowan. Whether you've been reading my books for years or this is your first one, I'm so grateful you're here.

Until next time…

~ Tracy Leigh

ABOUT *the* AUTHOR

Tracy Leigh is the spicy small town alter ego of USA Today Bestselling author T.K. Leigh. She lives outside of Raleigh with her husband, daughter, special needs rescue dog, and three cats.

When she's not penning her next small town romance filled with heat and heart, she can be found reading, spending time with her family, or planning her next escape to Hawaii.